TWENTIETH CENTURY VIEWS

The aim of this series is to present the best in contemporary critical opinion on major authors, providing a twentieth century perspective on their changing status in an era of profound revaluation.

Maynard Mack, *Series Editor*
Yale University

ROBERT BROWNING

ROBERT BROWNING

A COLLECTION OF CRITICAL ESSAYS

Edited by

Harold Bloom and Adrienne Munich

Prentice-Hall, Inc.   A SPECTRUM BOOK   *Englewood Cliffs, N.J.*

Library of Congress Cataloging in Publication Data
MAIN ENTRY UNDER TITLE:
ROBERT BROWNING: a collection of critical essays.

(A Spectrum Book) (Twentieth century views)
Bibliography: p.
1. Browning, Robert, 1812-1889—Criticism and
interpretation—Addresses, essays, letcures.
I. Bloom, Harold.   II. Munich, Adrienne.
PR4238.R59   821'.8   78-15615
ISBN 0-13-781484-4
ISBN 0-13-781476-3 pbk.

Ac~ 3/8/80

Editorial/production supervision by Eric Newman
Cover illustration by Stanley Wyatt
Manufacturing buyer: Cathie Lenard

10   9   8   7   6   5   4   3   2   1

PRENTICE-HALL INTERNATIONAL, INC. (London)
PRENTICE-HALL OF AUSTRALIA PTY. LIMITED (Sydney)
PRENTICE-HALL OF CANADA, LTD. (Toronto)
PRENTICE-HALL OF INDIA PRIVATE LIMITED (New Delhi)
PRENTICE-HALL OF JAPAN, INC. (Tokyo)
PRENTICE-HALL OF SOUTHEAST ASIA PTE. LTD. (Singapore)
WHITEHALL BOOKS LIMITED (Wellington, New Zealand)

To the memory of William Clyde De Vane

Contents

ROBERT BROWNING

Introduction: Reading Browning

by Harold Bloom

A tower that crowns a country. But alas,
The soul now climbs it just to perish there!
For thence we have discovered ('Tis no dream—
We know this, which we had not else perceived)
That there's a world of capability
For joy, spread round about us, meant for us,
Inviting; and still the soul craves all. . . .

This is Browning's Cleon, describing what Shelley had called "thought's crowned powers," the aesthetic dilemma of an elite beyond religion. That dilemma was not Browning's own, as a man, but in some ways it was his, as a poet. Yet it is cited here as the inevitable dilemma of Browning's reader, and so as an epigraph to an introductory discussion of the difficulties of reading one of the strongest and most perplexing poets in the English language.

Of all the problematic elements in Browning's poetry, what increasingly seems the central challenge to a reader is the peculiar nature of Browning's rhetorical stance. No poet has evidenced more than Browning so intense a will-to-power over the interpretation of his own poems. The reader rides through the Browning country with the poet always bouncing along at his side compulsively overinterpreting everything, very much in the manner of his own Childe Roland, who thus usurps the reader's share. Browning as self-interpreter has to be both welcomed and resisted, and he makes the resistance very difficult. Such resistance, though, may be Browning's greatest gift to his attentive reader. The Sublime, as Longinus formulated it, exists to compel readers to forsake easy pleasures in favor of more strenuous satisfactions, and Browning, like his master Shelley, crucially extends the possibilities of a modern Sublime.

One of the greatest achievements of English or Wordsworthian Romanticism was an uneasily transitional Sublime, which retained just enough of a Miltonic aura of theophany without committing itself to biblical doctrine. This uneasy or skeptical sublimity, which Browning had learned to love by reading Shelley, was not available to Browning nor to the central poets after him, whether we take these to have been Pound and Eliot, or else Yeats and Stevens. Browning's quite nihilistic Sublime, founded upon the abyss of a figurative language always declaring its own status as figuration, became a major influence upon all four of these poets, and goes on working in contemporary poetry, though frequently in hidden ways.

To read Browning well we need to cope with his poetry's heightened rhetorical self-awareness, its constant consciousness that it *is* rhetoric, a personal system of tropes, as well as a persuasive rhetoric, an art that must play at transcendence. Browning is read very badly when that apparent and deeply moving transcendence is too easily accepted, as Browning in his social or public self tended to accept it. But Browning teaches his more strenuous readers not only the Sublime necessities of defense against his poems' self-interpretations, but also a healthy suspicion that poet and reader alike are rhetorical systems of many selves, rather than any single or separate self. Here I think is the true center in reading Browning. The problems of rhetoric—of our being incapable of knowing what is literal and what figurative where all, in a sense, is figurative—and of psychology—is there a self that is not trope or an effect of verbal persuasion?—begin to be seen as one dilemma.

If Browning did not share this dilemma with all poets and their readers, then he would not be representative or even intelligible. However, his particular strength, which insures his permanent place in the canon, is that he appropriated the dilemma for his time with a singular possessiveness. An informed reader, brooding upon the rhetorical limits of interpretability, and upon the labyrinthine evasions of self-identity, will think very quickly of Browning when these problematic matters rise in the context of English poetic tradition. Browning's strength, like Milton's or Wordsworth's, is finally a strength of usurpation, in which a vast literary space is made to vacate its prior occupancy so as to permit a new formulation of the unresolvable dilemmas that themselves constitute poetry.

A number of the traditional issues that vex Browning criticism can be reoriented if we see them as burdens of rhetorical stance, when that stance itself determines Browning's psychopoetics. The dramatic monologue is revealed to be neither dramatic nor a monologue but rather a barely disguised High Romantic crisis lyric, in which antithetical voices contend for an illusory because only momentary mastery. The frequently grotesque diction appears a reaction formation away from Shelleyan verbal harmony, which means that the grotesquerie becomes a pure irony, a bitter digression away from meaning itself. The violent thematicism of Browning, including his exuberance in declaring a highly personalized evangelical belief in Christ, becomes something dangerously close to a thematics of violence, in which fervor of declaration far surpasses in importance the supposed spiritual content of the declaration. The notorious optimism begins to look rather acosmic and atemporal, so that the hope celebrated is much less Pauline than it is Gnostic. The faith demystifies as a Gnostic elitist knowledge of Browning's own divine spark, which turns out to be prior to and higher than the natural creation. Most bewilderingly, the love that Browning exalts becomes suspect, not because of its manifest Oedipal intensity, but because something in it is very close to a solipsistic transport, to a wholly self-delighting joy. He is a great lover—but primarily of himself, or rather of his multitude of antithetical selves.

The Browning I describe is hardly recognizable from much if not most of the criticism devoted to him, but few other poets have inspired so much inadequate criticism. Only Whitman and Dickinson among the major nineteenth-century poets seem to me as badly misrepresented as Browning has been. The prime fault of course is Browning's own, and so I return to his will-to-power over the interpretation of his own texts.

Hans Jonas remarks of the Gnostics that they delighted in "the intoxication of unprecedentedness," a poetic intoxication in which Browning, Whitman, and Dickinson share. Borges, with Gnostic irony, has pointed to Browning as one of the precursors of Kafka, an insight worthy of exploration. Against the Bible and Plato, the Gnostics refused the dialectics of sublimation and substitution, the Christian and Classical wisdom of the Second Chance. Like the Gnostics, Browning is interested in evasion rather than substitution, and does not wish to learn even the Wordsworthian version of the wisdom of the Second Chance. The "sober coloring" of a belated vision had no deep appeal to Browning, though he exemplifies it beautifully in the character and section of *The Ring and the Book* called "The Pope." The fire celebrated in the "Prologue" to his final volume, *Asolando: Fancies and Facts,* is the Gnostic fire of the First Chance, now "lost from the naked world." Browning appeals to "the purged ear," and a Voice rather clearly his own, at its most stentorian, proclaims: "God is it who transcends." "God" here is an hyperbole for poetic strength, which is Browning's violent and obsessive subject, whether in the overtly Shelleyan long poems that began his career or in the ostensibly dramatic romances, monologues, and lyrics of his more profoundly Shelleyan maturity.

Browning praised Shelley above all for

> his simultaneous perception of Power and Love in the absolute, and of Beauty and Good in the concrete, while he throws, from his poet's station between both, swifter, subtler, and more numerous films for the connection of each with each, than have been thrown by any modern artificer. ...

Perhaps Browning's truest swerve away from this strong interpretation of Shelley, was an uncanny refusal to distinguish between Power and Love in the absolute, since for Browning both were forms of his own poetic self-recognition. What is Bishop Blougram but the strong poet taunting the weak critic?

> If I'm a Shakespeare, let the well alone;
> Why should I try to be what now I am?
> If I'm no Shakespeare, as too probable,—
> His power and consciousness and self-delight
> And all we want in common...
>   ...
> We want the same things, Shakespeare and myself,
> And what I want, I have: he, gifted more,
> Could fancy he too had them when he liked. ...

The reader who believes that the bishop means chair and wine by "what I want" is indeed another silent Mr. Gigadibs, who believes he sees "two points in Hamlet's soul / Unseized by the Germans yet." Sometimes Browning simply drops the mask and declares his precise agon:

> For—see your cellarage!
>   There are four big butts of Milton's brew.
> How comes it you make old drips and drops
> Do duty, and there devotion stops?
> Leave such an abyss of malt and hops
>   Embellied in butts which bungs still glue?
> You hate your bard! A fig for your rage!
> Free him from cellarage!
>
> 'Tis said I brew stiff drink,
>   But the deuce a flavour of grape is there.
> Hardly a May-go-down, 'tis just
> A sort of a gruff Go-down-it-must—
> No Merry-go-down, no gracious gust
>   Commingles the racy with Springtide's rare!
> 'What wonder,' say you 'that we cough, and blink
> At Autumn's heady drink?'

The strength of Browning's poetry is thus professedly an intoxication of belatedness, "Autumn's heady drink," and the weak reader's rage against both Milton and Browning is due to a weak head that doubts its own capacity. Browning's splendidly outrageous aggressivity is not so much latent as it is concealed in his more characteristic poems. Even in the charming and good-natured self-idealization of *Fra Lippo Lippi*, where

Browning loves his monologist as himself, the appetite for a
literal immortality is unabated. Poetic divination, in Browning,
returns to its primal function, to keep the poet always alive:
"Oh, oh, It makes me mad to see what men shall do / And we
in our graves!" One of the Browning-selves evidently means
Cleon to show how hopeless the Arnoldian or post-Christian
aesthetic dilemma is, but a stronger Browning-self gets to work,
and expresses a yet more poignant dilemma:

> Say rather that my fate is deadlier still,
> In this, that every day my sense of joy
> Grows more acute, my soul (intensified
> By power and insight) more enlarged, more keen;
> While every day my hairs fall more and more,
> My hand shakes, and the heavy years increase—
> The horror quickening still from year to year,
> The consummation coming past escape
> When I shall know most, and yet least enjoy—
> When all my works wherein I prove my worth,
> Being present still to mock me in men's mouths,
> Alive still, in the praise of such as thou,   ·
> I, I the feeling, thinking, acting man,
> The man who loved his life so over-much,
> Sleep in my urn. It is so horrible. ...

The rhetorical consciousness here characteristically makes us
doubt the self-persuasiveness of this superb passage, since
Cleon-Browning's death-in-life is livelier still than his life-in-
death. His fate may be deadly, but the tropes are madly vigor-
ous, even the "horror" *quickening,* and the "consummation"
carrying its full range of significations, as it must, for what
poet can fail to love his own life "so over-much"? The separate
selves dance in the exuberant Browning when the reader juxta-
poses to *Cleon* the now underpraised *Rabbi Ben Ezra,* where
another poet, not imaginary, proclaims the life-affirming force
of his supposedly normative Judaism:

> Thoughts hardly to be packed
> Into a narrow act,
> Fancies that broke through language and escaped
> All I could never be,
> All, men ignored in me,
> This, I was worth to God, whose wheel the pitcher shaped.

> Ay, note that Potter's wheel,
> That metaphor! and feel
> Why time spins fast, why passive lies our clay,—
> Thou, to whom fools propound,
> When the wine makes its round,
>
> 'Since life fleets, all is change; the Past gone, seize to-day!'
> Fool! All that is, at all,
> Lasts ever, past recall;
> Earth changes, but thy soul and God stand sure:
> What entered into thee,
> *That* was, is, and shall be:
> Time's wheel runs back or stops: Potter and clay endure.

"That metaphor" is normative and prophetic, but the poem's burden is Gnostic rather than Pharasaic. The "figured flame which blends, transcends" all the stars is one with the Gnostic *pneuma* or "spark" that preceded nature. Browning's vision, and hardly the historical Ibn Ezra's, sees man as "a god though in the germ." What Browning "shall know, being old" is what he always knew, his own "*That* was, is, and shall be." Not the Old Adam nor Christ as the New Adam is the paradigm, but what we might call the Old Browning, the Gnostic primal Anthropos or preexistent Adam.

Yeats remarked that he had feared always Browning's influence upon him. In a deep sense, Yeats was right, not only because of the shared Shelleyan ancestry, but because of the shared Gnosticism, though the esoteric religion was quite overt in Yeats. Browning does all he can to evade what Yeats (following Nietzsche) named as the *antithetical* quest in Shelley, the drive beyond nature to a nihilistic annihilation that is the poetic will's ultimate revenge against time's "it was." But the evasion was only half-hearted:

> For I intend to get to God,
> For 'tis to God I speed so fast,
> For in God's breast, my own abode,
> Those shoals of dazzling glory, passed,
> I lay my spirit down at last.
> I lie where I have always lain,
> God smiles as he has always smiled. . . .

True that this is Johannes Agricola the Antinomian, chant-
ing in his madhouse cell, but no reader would dispute such
exuberance if he substituted the Gnostic alien god, the Abyss,
for the "God" of these lines. Make the substitution and
Johannes Agricola may be permitted to speak for another
Browning-self or soul-side, and for the entire *antithetical*
tradition.

Much of Tennyson's astonishing power was due to the
Laureate's not knowing what it was that his daemon or antithetical self was writing about, but Browning was so daemonic that
something in him always did know. Naming that something
becomes the quest of Browning's capable reader, a quest un-
fulfillable in the Browning country where every self is a picnic
of selves, every text a tropological entrapment. Browning's
St John, in *A Death in the Desert,* gives us two passages whose
juxtaposition helps us define his reader's quest for meaning:

> Therefore, I say, to test man, the proofs shift,
> Nor may he grasp that fact like other fact,
> And straightway in his life acknowledge it,
> As, say, the inevitable bliss of fire.
> Sigh ye, 'It had been easier once than now'?
> To give you answer I am left alive;
> Look at me who was present from the first!
> …
> Is this indeed a burthen for late days,
> and may I help to bear it with you all,
> Using my weakness which becomes your strength?

Browning's visionary is arguing against Cerinthus and other
early Gnostics, but the argument is more Gnostic than Christian (which may have been Browning's shrewd unconscious
reading of the Fourth Gospel). To be present from the first,
at the origins, is to have priority over nature and history,
and involves denying one's own belatedness, which is thus
equated with weakness, while a return to earliness is strength.
To do the deed and judge it at the same time is to impose interpretation, one's will-to-power over both text and the text of
life. Browning is most uncanny as a poet when two or more of

his selves contend within a poem to interpret that poem, a struggle that brings forth his greatest yet most problematic achievements, including *A Toccata of Galuppi's, By the Fireside, Master Hugues of Saxe-Gotha, Love Among the Ruins, The Heretic's Tragedy, Andrea del Sarto, Abt Vogler, Caliban Upon Setebos, Numpholeptos, Pan and Luna, Flute-Music, with an Accompaniment,* and *"Childe Roland to the Dark Tower Came."* These dozen poems alone would establish Browning's permanent importance, but I have space here only to glance briefly again at *Childe Roland,* which is a text that never lets go of a reader once it has found you. The poem may well be the definitive proof-text for the modern Sublime, more uncanny than Kafka, stronger than Yeats at his most uncompromising.

Browning's Roland descends ultimately from the Marlovian-Shakespearean hero-villain, by way of Milton's Satan and the High Romantic metamorphoses of Satan. Tennyson's Ulysses has something of the same complex ancestry, but he is less Jacobean than Roland, who like Webster's Lodovico in *The White Devil* could say he had limned his own night-piece, and it was his best. Roland is a savagely reductive interpreter whom the wary reader must resist, until at its close the poem so opens out that the reader suddenly wants Roland to interpret more, only to discover that the Childe is done with interpretation. The reader is left with the uncanny, which means with the self in Browning that finds both his aim and his origin in the Sublime, unlike the remorselessly reductive self that has spoken most of the poem.

The ogreless Dark Tower, where the quester must confront himself and his dead precursors, to "fail" at least as heroically as they have failed before him, is a composite trope for poetry if not for the Sublime poem itself. Indeed, the figuration is so suggestive that the Dark Tower can be read as the mental dilemma or *aporia* that Browning's reader faces in the poem. The Dark Tower is the black hole in the Browning cosmos, where Power and Love become one only through a supremely negative moment, in which loss of the self and loss of the fulness of the present pay the high price of achieved vision:

What in the midst lay but the Tower itself?
   The round squat turret, blind as the fool's heart,
   Built of brown stone, without a counterpart
In the whole world. The tempest's mocking elf
Points to the shipman thus the unseen shelf
   He strikes on, only when the timbers start.

Not see? because of night perhaps? — why day
   Came back for that! before it left
   The dying sunset kindled through a cleft:
The hills, like giants at a hunting, lay,
Chin upon hand, to see the game at bay, —
   'Now stab and end the creature — to the heft!'

Not hear? when noise was everywhere! it tolled
   Increasing like a bell. Names in my ears
   Of all the lost adventurers my peers, —
How such a one was strong, and such was bold,
And such was fortunate, yet each of old
   Lost, lost! one moment knelled the woe of years.

After a life spent training for the vision of the Dark Tower, you do not see it until burningly it comes on you all at once. How do we interpret the shock of "This was the place!" when we have learned to resist every one of Roland's earlier interpretations? Is it that we, like Roland, have overprepared the event, in Pound's fine phrasing? Roland is overtrained, which means that he suffers an acute consciousness of belatedness. We are overanxious not to be gulled by his reductiveness, which means that we suffer an acute consciousness that we have selves of our own to defend. In the Sublime agon between Roland and the reader, Browning stands aside, even at the very end, not because he is an "objective" as opposed to antithetical poet, but because he respects the *aporia* of the Dark Tower. Poetry is part of what the Gnostics called the Kenoma or cosmic and temporal emptiness, and not part of the Pleroma, the fullness of presence that is acosmic and atemporal. The Pleroma is always absent, for it inheres in the Abyss, the true, alien God who is cut off from nature and history.

   The name of that alien God in Roland's country is Shelley's trumpet of a prophecy, which enters by way of another precursor, the boy-poet Chatterton, whose poetry provides the slug-horn that is sounded:

> There they stood, ranged along the hillside, met
> To view the last of me, a living frame
> For one more picture! in a sheet of flame
> I saw them and I knew them all. And yet
> Dauntless the slug-horn to my lips I set,
> And blew. 'Childe Roland to the Dark Tower came.'

The picture is Browning's, the frame or context is given by the living but contradictory presence, where there can be no presence, of the precursors: Shelley, Chatterton, Keats, Tasso, who lived and died in Yeats's Condition of Fire, Roland's "sheet of flame." Browning as man and poet died old, but his anxiety seems to have been that his poethood *could* have died young, when he forswore the atheist Shelley in order to win back the approving love of his evangelical mother. Roland's equivocal triumph achieves the Sublime, and helps guarantee Browning's poetic survival.

Roland sees and knows, like Keats's intelligences which are at once atoms of perception and God. What he sees and knows are the heroic precursors who are met to see *him,* but who cannot know him, as presumably his readers can. Roland's knowledge ought to daunt him, and yet against it he sets the trumpet of his prophecy. His will is thus set in revenge against time's: "It was," but we do not know the content of his prophecy. After a full stop, and not a colon, comes the poem's final statement, which is at once its Shakespearean title and epigraph. Either the entire poem begins again, in a closed cycle like Blake's *The Mental Traveller,* or else Roland proclaims his story's inevitable lack of closure. What seems clear is that Roland is not performing his own poem, in direct contrast to Shelley at the close of the *Ode to the West Wind,* where the words to be scattered among mankind are the text of the *Ode.*

It is after all the many-selved Browning who is undaunted by belatedness, by the dilemmas of poetic language, and by his own struggle for authority as against both precursors and readers. Poetic self-confidence delights us when we are persuaded that it can sustain itself, that it has usurped imaginative space and has forced its way into the canon. Again we are in the Sublime of Longinus, as the reader becomes one with the power he apprehends. The danger of sublimity is that the pit of the bathetic suddenly can open anywhere, and Browning (who wrote much too much) sometimes pulls us down with him. This hardly matters, where we are given so large a company of splendid self-deceivers and even more splendid deceivers of others, of all but the wariest readers. Browning, more than Yeats or Stevens, more than his disciple Pound or his secret student Eliot, is the last of the old High line, as in the audacious rhetorical gesture that concludes his magnificent, unread *Pan and Luna:*

>   ...The myth
> Explain who may! Let all else go, I keep
> — As of a ruin just a monolith —
> Thus much, one verse of five words, each a boon:
> Arcadia, night, a cloud, Pan, and the moon.

Four Modes in the Poetry
of Robert Browning

by George M. Ridenour

I will tell
My state as though 'twere none of mine.
BROWNING, *Pauline,* lines 585-86.

I build on contrasts to discover, above those contrasts, the
harmony of the whole.
Hugo von Hofmannsthal to Richard
Strauss, June 15, 1911.[1]

Browning was always fiercely Protestant, even when he
was not especially Christian. He grew up largely by himself,
finding companions in his family, in pets, and in the great
number of books he read from his father's large library. His
contacts with school were brief and not very satisfactory, and
his formal education came largely from private tutors and,
perhaps, his father. A try at university life, in the newly established University of London, was soon abandoned, and Browning continued to live with his parents, supported by his father,
until his marriage in 1846.

The circumstances of his bringing up were certainly in-

From *Selected Poetry of Robert Browning,* edited by George M. Ridenour.
Copyright © 1966 by George M. Ridenour. Reprinted by arrangement with
The New American Library, Inc., New York, N.Y.

[1] *A Working Friendship: The Correspondence between Richard Strauss
and Hugo von Hofmannsthal,* Trans. Hanns Hammelmann and Ewald Osers
(New York: William Collins Sons & Co., Ltd., 1961), p. 90.

strumental in developing that "clear consciousness / Of self, distinct from all its qualities" that the young man—with perplexity, pride, and dismay—recognized as central to his character. His problem was what to make of so energetic an ego.

In his poem *Pauline* (published 1833), where he first defined the problem as he understood it, Browning goes on to consider two further "elements" of his character that served as checks on his consuming selfhood. The first is his power of imagination and the second his yearning after God. His imagination is an "angel" to him that sustains "a soul with such desire / Confined to clay." ("Clay" is an obsessive word with Byron, and its use here reminds us that Browning's early poems—destroyed by their author—were supposed to be in the manner of Byron, whom Browning is recalling, along with Shelley, in *Pauline*. There is strong influence of Byron's "Dream.") It enables him to master his "dark past." But the imagination itself poses problems of direction and control which are solved by the premise of a divine Love which presents itself to him as goal and as surrounding presence. The forces united for the boy in the myths of ancient Greece, which enabled his ego to exercise itself healthfully in imaginings of godlike life, and these early experiences of integration remain to some extent normative for him. It is experience of this sort he wants to regain as he addresses himself in *Pauline* to more radical representatives of imagination and religion—Shelley and Christ. It is this he seeks also from the woman Pauline, with her all-encompassing love, who is also the muse of the poem. (It was something very like this that he found in his love for his wife, a woman of deep piety and a poet.)

A similar view is presented sequentially in the speech of the dying Paracelsus, in Browning's drama of that name, defining a progression from the most primitive form of being to man, and from man to God. Two traditions have been traced by scholars here. There is that of man as the culmination of all lower forms, moving steadily toward God, and taking the whole creation with him into the divine life, which Browning might have been more likely to know in an occult version, though it is found in orthodoxy. And there is the more nar-

rowly eighteenth-century tradition of plenitude and the chain
of being that may, I suggest, have some obligation to James
Thomson, author of *The Seasons.*

> By swift degrees the love of nature works,
> And warms the bosom; till at last, sublimed
> To rapture and enthusiastic heat,
> We feel the present Deity, and take
> The joy of God to see a happy world.
> (*Spring,* lines 899-903)

> God is ever present, ever felt,
> In the void waste as in the city full,
> And where he vital spreads there must be joy.
> ("Hymn to the Seasons," lines 105-7)[2]

The two traditions unite in *Paracelsus* V, 641-47, where the
hero claims to have known

> what God is, what we are,
> What life is—how God tastes an infinite joy
> In infinite ways—one everlasting bliss,
> From whom all being emanates, all power
> Proceeds; in whom is life for evermore,
> Yet whom existence in its lowest form
> Includes; where dwells enjoyment there is he.

Browning's combination of the two traditions presents a
view that is in effect anticipatory of Teilhard de Chardin's
vision of an unbroken progression from the geological to the
biological to the mental, and on to the divine, each stage once
manifest revealing its implicit presence in all preceding stages.

The vision of Paracelsus does not in itself, however, provide
means for its implementation in other kinds of poem. It was
only after years of attempts at writing a successful play for the
stage that Browning fully developed the form of the dramatic
monologue, brought to its maturity in the two volumes of *Men
and Women* of 1855. Through this succession of self-preoc-
cupied egoists, engaged in existential defense of the being each

---

[2]Browning remembers the last line of the "Hymn" in a letter to Kegan Paul,
July 15, 1881.

has made for himself, Browning, as J. Hillis Miller has pointed out, is able both to exercise his own ego and "get out of himself" by objectifying his drive to egoistic self-assertion in the creation of fictional characters. When we have noticed that in the course of their self-revelation they further reveal in their personal situation, directly or indirectly, the intensely Protestant version of the Incarnation that was Browning's governing myth, we can see how the monologues meet the demands of the earlier poems.

Browning's speakers in the monologues are apt to be persons of extremes in extreme situations. Even so winning a character as Lippo Lippi has something grotesque about him and displays an element of the pathologically self-dramatizing, in excess of what might be ascribed to the demands of the form. But like Dostoyevsky or the early Wordsworth, Browning uses his strange or abnormal types to dramatize what he regards as centrally human, which can be seen in these cases with especial clarity. In the following lines, for example, in which Fra Lippo lists the subjects of his first attempts as painter, he reveals not only his own personal situation but that of all men as Browning sees it:

> First, every sort of monk, the black and white,
> I drew them, fat and lean; then, folk at church,
> From good old gossips waiting to confess
> Their cribs of barrel-droppings, candle-ends—
> To the breathless fellow at the altar-foot,
> Fresh from his murder, safe and sitting there
> With the little children round him in a row
> Of admiration, half for his beard and half
> For that white anger of his victim's son
> Shaking a fist at him with one fierce arm,
> Signing himself with the other because of Christ
> (Whose sad face on the cross sees only this
> After the passion of a thousand years)
> Till some poor girl, her apron o'er her head,
> (Which the intense eyes looked through) came at eve
> On tiptoe, said a word, dropped in a loaf,
> Her pair of earrings and a bunch of flowers
> (The brute took growling), prayed, and so was gone.
>   (lines 145-62)

Here he elaborates the pictorial qualities implicit in the scene of the breathless murderer, the admiring children, the frustrated vindictiveness of the victim's son, and the girl's thankless devotion to the criminal—passions that arrange themselves by their inherent forces of attraction and repulsion into a satisfying composition. The picture is "placed" against another genre, that of the Man of Sorrows on the Cross. It is the world of the painting that Lippo is presented as gaining for art, but he himself sees it as under the judgment of the second, more traditional and more static mode. The exhibition of non-moral human energies, however fine, asks the complement of the image of the dying God. The assimilation of the world of the painting into art has the effect of censuring it as life, but also, since the censor gains much of his authority by his presence to us in art, of encouraging us to enjoy the beauty produced by intense experience of any kind.

It must be confessed, however, that our main impression from the passage is less one of harmony than of competing claims that are hard to choose between, and the feeling grows that Browning's aim as a poet in the Romantic tradition is to devise forms in which the elements of reality as he experiences it may be comtemplated as unified. (There seems to be at least a shift in emphasis in the development of Browning's poetry from problems of internal integration to those of perceiving reality itself as an integrated whole.) The list of attempted unions is imposing: power and love, love and knowledge, knowledge and power, imagination and reason, self and not-self, conscious and unconscious, spirit and matter, natural and supernatural, lyric and discursive, verse and prose. His attempts may usefully be broken down into at least four major types: the personal, the typical, the mythic, and the analytic. We may take "Fra Lippo Lippi" as representing the first, the vision of the dramatic monologues, where divisions are overcome in living, or which point toward harmony ironically through the dissonances of the speaker's life. The typical, mythic, and analytic modes, while not inherently more valuable, are in some ways harder to grasp, and it may be helpful to pay special attention to them. The modes will be examined by means of comment on poems drawn, like "Fra Lippo Lippi," from the great work of Browning's middle period, the *Men and Women* of 1855.

What I have called the typical mode may be seen most clearly in "Childe Roland to the Dark Tower Came." It is this typicality that causes our uneasiness in either calling the poem an allegory or in refraining from doing so. The knightly quest lends itself easily to allegorical treatment, because we are all of us looking for something all the time, in all our acts. The formality of the poem also encourages us to think of it as allegorical, even though it is not clear at once what it is allegorical of. This is especially striking since the allegorical mode invites simple and mechanical equation between the contents of the work and the world of values outside it. (This is true of even so refined a work as *The Faerie Queene,* as in the head-verses to the separate cantos. Though the poem is not limited to these crude equations, they influence our understanding of the dense and irreducible materials of the poem proper.) The allegory of "Childe Roland," in other words, is strangely self-contained, turning back on itself, so that the "allegoricalness" of the poem calls attention to itself as part of the meaning.

To shift the terms, allegory is apt to be strikingly rational and subrational, presenting a moral and conceptual organizing of the materials of fantasy; the moral will enters into close union with fierce unconscious drives. In Browning's poem the relations between the two elements are uncommonly problematic. This also tends to turn our attention into the poem in a manner unexpected in allegory, while we are still expecting the poem to fulfil its implied promise to be allegorical of something. One might be tempted to say, then that the poem is an allegory of allegorizing (with Hawthorne's *Scarlet Letter* as partial analogy). But this would be too narrow, since the allegorical element is a metaphor of our attempts at directing our acts and at understanding them as purposive. It serves to represent the element of moral will in our acts and our understanding of those acts as directed by the moral will. It corresponds to our attempts, that is, at acting humanly for human goals — as "knights." The poem understood in this way becomes an allegory of what is involved in apparently purposeful human acts. It is "typical" of them.

Since the *geste* of Browning's knight is largely a trial by landscape, it may be useful to examine the handling of landscape in another poem, published in the same volume but apparently written later. In "Two in the Campagna" a woman speaks of her inability to love completely and constantly the man she addresses. She loves him only so much and for only so long. Her confession is placed against the reaches of the Roman Campagna, on a May morning.

> The champaign with its endless fleece
>   Of feathery grasses everywhere!
> Silence and passion, joy and peace,
>   An everlasting wash of air—
> Rome's ghost since her decease.
>
> Such life here, through such lengths of hours,
>   Such miracles performed in play,
> Such primal naked forms of flowers,
>   Such letting nature have her way
> While heaven looks from its towers.
>   (lines 21-30)

The setting suggests, through its vast extent, vast ranges of possibility, and the impression is reinforced by the burgeoning life of early spring. At the same time, however, it suggests immedicable solitude and a tendency in the nature of things for life to squander itself, dispersedly, to no effect:

> Must I go
> Still like the thistle-ball, no bar,
>   Onward, whenever light winds blow,
> Fixed by no friendly star?
>   (lines 52-55)

Man's state and nature's correspond in their interplay of possibility and restriction, freedom and slavery: "Nor yours nor mine, nor slave nor free!" But the emphasis is on defeat.

These passages should recall the landscape of "Childe Roland":

> For mark! no sooner was I fairly found
>   Pledged to the plain, after a pace or two,
>   Than, pausing to throw backward a last view
> O'er the safe road, 'twas gone; gray plain all round;

Nothing but plain to the horizon's bound.
I might go on; naught else remained to do.
(lines 49-54)

Here the extent of plain works similarly, with important differences. The possibilities are as great, the limitations more
oppressive, and we get a feeling of stuffiness in a wide expanse.
This reflects the mingled purposefulness and purposelessness,
will and compulsion in the mind of the knight. But the effect is
different from that of the landscape in "Two in the Campagna."
The vast and monotonous spaces, as well as their painful contents, diminish, to be sure, the single human being who acts in
them, but also "enlarge" him, extend his range, ennoble him.
The impression is rather that of Burke's "sublime," with its
vision of infinite possibility rising from experience of pain and
monotony.[3] "Childe Roland" would seem, then, to celebrate
the value of man's acts as he blunders doggedly toward goals
which are both commonplace and unique:

> The round squat turret, blind as the fool's heart,
> Built of brown stone, without a counterpart
> In the whole world.   (lines 182-84)

The mythic mode is in some ways similar to what I have
called the typical, but the differences are important enough to
make distinction worthwhile. The main difference is that the
mythic mode attaches its action not merely to a central and
recurring form of human experience, but to such a form as
shaped and celebrated by the imagination of the race. A version
of this is found in "The Heretic's Tragedy," which is presented
as "a glimpse from the burning of Jacques du Bourg-Molay, at
Paris, A. D. 1314; as distorted by the refraction from Flemish
brain to brain, during the course of a couple of centuries."
Jacques du Bourg-Molay had been grand master of the Order
of the Knights Templar and was burned at the stake for reasons

---

[3]The use of landscape in these poems looks back to Shelley's in "Julian and
Maddalo" and forward to Swinburne's in "On the Downs." (Geoffrey Hart-
mann, in his *Wordsworth's Poetry, 1787-1814* [New Haven: Yale University
Press, 1964] , pp. 118-25, discusses the landscape of *Salisbury Plain* in similar
terms. The influence of Burke—or of the tradition he represents—is surely
present in Wordsworth's poem.)

apparently more secular than religious. But he had been formally convicted of crimes against the faith, and was burned as a heretic.

The first thing to be noticed is Browning's emphasis on the fact that the event dealt with in the poem has been *distorted* as the account of it has passed down orally over a long period of time. It has been distorted by the un-Christian hatred of the pious Christians who cherished the tradition and handed it on, constantly sharpening in their account the hateful elements in it. By the time represented by the composition of the poem, the impiety of the victim has been made so grotesque as to be incredible. We respect Jacques du Bourg-Molay because he is hated so violently by persons of so little moral perception.

But the effect of this malice is not merely to discredit the speakers and to honor the victim. The distortion is also clarifying. The corrosive hatred of the generations of faithful has burned away the accidents of the situation, leaving only an archetype which condemns them still more radically. What one sees in the situation of the master of the Temple, as simplified by hate, suggests typically the state of charity, burning in the flames of love (cf. John of the Cross's *Burning Flame of Love*), and mythically the suffering Master on the cross, exalted by the hatred of his executioners. The imagination will tell the truth, it seems, whatever the intent of the imaginer, even as the imaginations of Lippo Lippi, Childe Roland, and the singers of "The Heretic's Tragedy" reveal not merely themselves but permanent forms of truth as the imagination knows them.

The analytic mode, as its name suggest, breaks down experience into its separate elements and examines possibilities of interrelationship. All of the poems so far examined have done this to some extent, but there are poems that set about doing just this. The classical analytic work, in this sense, would be Cervantes' *Don Quixote,* read from a perspectivist viewpoint (i.e., as acting out relationships between the opposed but complementary world views expressed in the figures of Don Quixote and Sancho Panza). Closer to Browning in some ways would be Euripides, his favorite Greek dramatist, who gives many examples of "scenes where a situation is realized first in

its lyric, then in its iambic aspect—that is to say, first emotion-
ally, then in its reasoned form."[4] There is a good example in
the *Alcestis,* which Browning himself translated, in which
Alcestis, dying, celebrates her death and its meaning in song,
and then argues it out argumentatively. Euripides "has simply
juxtaposed these two aspects of Alcestis' parting from life,
rather than leave either incomplete."[5] And though Browning,
as A. M. Dale points out, tries to ground the argument psycho-
logically in his rendering of the scene, the comparison is still
useful.

There is a still closer resemblance, however, to works by the
modern German poet and dramatist Hugo von Hofmannsthal,
especially in texts for operas by Richard Strauss. This is especially striking in *Ariadne auf Naxos,* in which the oppositions
of kinds of love and views of life—generally, tragic (in Ariadne)
and comic (in Zerbinetta)—are united both ironically (as Hofmannsthal partly understood) and actually (as he apparently
did not grasp) through qualities inherent in all love, and
through the "harmony" of Strauss's score. The two points of
view expose their weaknesses and strengths, their kinds of opposition and union, within the reconciling medium of music.[6]

It is this last, the use of music to define oppositions which
are at the same time harmonized, that reminds one most vividly
of Browning, whose poems on music attempt something very
similar. If you are worried, as Browning often was, about the
relation between fact and value, mind and heart, reason and
imagination—summed up generally as an opposition between
fact and fancy—music can be very helpful. A musical statement can be more abstract than anything in language and still
more sensuous than language can ever be. This may give it a

---

[4]A. M. Dale, in the commentary to her edition of Euripides' *Alcestis* (New
York: Oxford University Press, 1954), p. 74.

[5]Dale, pp. 74-75.

[6]Browning's drama *Colombe's Birthday* suggests a Hofmannsthal libretto
in the manner of *Rosenkavalier,* anticipating some of Hofmannsthal's favorite
themes. The opposition of moods or types of personality is found also in the
Eusebius-Florestan contrast in Schumann, e.g., the "Papillons" (as also in
Handel's setting of Milton's "L'Allegro-Il Penserose"). It appears in another
form, based on Jean Paul's *Flegel-jahre,* in Schumann's "Carnival," which
Browning cites in *Fifine at the Fair,* one of his virtuoso works in the analytic
mode.

unique closeness to reality and at the same time a quality of remoteness, spirituality, fancifulness. Furthermore, it helps us see the two terms as interchangeable: the abstract pole may suggest both reason and unreality, the sensuous both concrete fact and imaginative sentiment. In more formal terms, either pole may suggest comedy or tragedy, poetry or prose.

Browning's finest achievement in this mode is probably "A Toccata of Galuppi's." Among the oppositions to be worked with here is that between eighteenth-century Italy and nineteenth-century England, as well as that between the "scientist" who speaks and the composer who answers. But it is the scientist who is inclined to put stress on value and the composer whose view is cold and analytic, chilling to the inhabitant of a century that is more humane and less elegant. The scientist's union of fancy and fact is unstable, and Galuppi has denied fancy in the name of fact, though his analysis is carried on in a mode that is itself an expression of fancy—i.e., through art. The main agent of union is the composer's clavichord piece, which both includes and is included by the speech of the scientist.

Within the culture that produced the musical form there are grave differences of caste and point of view, brought out by the relations between Galuppi and his audience. They are aristocrats and he a superior servant; their preoccupation with sexual conquest is the object of his rationalistic contempt. But both rationalism and sensuality are part of the period style, as formalized in its music, and the aristocratic audience is not wholly deceived in enjoying it. Furthermore, they find in Galuppi's art a compassion and solace the composer surely did not intend, but which is built into the formal qualities of the music, since it is in support of human purposes that all art inherently subsists.[7] The music, accordingly, in its expression of the central qualities of its period, is not limited by the points of view of artist or audience. The style at the same time separates and unites within its own period as well as between periods. It is in doing the first that it is able to do the second.

The identification of mode is largely on the basis of relative emphasis. It is useful to notice that a particular poem is en-

---

[7]See my account of "Flute Music: With an Accompaniment" in "Browning's Music Poems: Fancy and Fact, *PMLA,* LXXVIII (1963), 369-377, pp. 372-73.

gaged in a certain kind of activity with special concentration,
but that does not mean that it is not doing other things too.
"Fra Lippo Lippi" is primarily an expression of a personal
state; both problems and ways of handling them are developed
in terms of a vividly realized individual personality. But there
are strong elements of other modes. The poem is analytic in its
reduction of the problem to a competition between opposed
areas of value, typical in that the state is seen as that of all
men. In the same way, "Childe Roland" has a strong mythic
side, as well as displaying analytic and personal aspects, and
"The Heretic's Tragedy" reveals an important typical strain,
as was noted in the analysis of the poem. "Galuppi" alone
of the poems examined seems to be overwhelmingly in one
mode, though even here there are elements of the personal
and perhaps the typical.

None of this lessens the value of noticing, however, that all
of these strains are united with especial force and clarity in
Browning's longest and most ambitious work. *The Ring and
the Book* is in this as in other ways the climax of Browning's
career. *The Ring and the Book* makes a great point of the claim
that it is true, and it is largely in terms of the modes I have
defined that this claim is substantiated. (From the point of view
of literary history, there are two main traditions of works that
claim to be true and build this claim into themselves as part of
their meaning.[8] There is the analytic tradition of which *Don
Quixote* is exemplary, as we have seen. Works in this tradition
often claim to be "true to nature." The other tradition is the
mythic, represented by *Paradise Lost*, which claims to be true
because the myth it enacts is true. These traditions meet in *The
Ring and the Book*.)

In exploring possible relationships between the antitheses
it includes, a work in the analytic mode might discover that
the opposed elements fit without reduction into mythic form.
This is what happens in *The Ring and the Book*, which attempts a sweeping transformation of brutal fact into ideal

[8]This is to leave out of account such relatively simple forms as the philo-
sophic-didactic and satiric modes, the usually less problematic modes of
reportorial realism and of "sincerity," as well as the complex but more limited
"epistemological" mode, in which an act of knowing is enacted in such a way
as to be, presumably, self-verifying (e.g., Shelley's "Mont Blane").

fancy. In terms of the four modes, *The Ring and the Book* is typical both ironically and unironically. Ironically, it is a typical story of intrigue, adultery, revenge, enacting a recurrent pattern in human affairs. But the irony stems from the fact that it is unironically typical in very different terms, as a type of the action of divine love. Mythically, it reenacts the scandal of a manifestation of the divine in the sordid story of a Jewish wife who bore a child not conceived by her husband, as told by Luke. Analytically, it sees in the unlikely materials of the murder story both a clear opposition between the competing claims of fancy and fact and possibilities of overcoming the division. And both oppositions and possibilities of union are developed in terms of real human beings we are made to care about.

The general outlines of the story are clear enough, and I give it in Browning's own normative account, in the first book, since all of the other accounts given in the course of the poem are to be understood as modulations of this:

> Count Guido Franceschini the Aretine,
> Descended of an ancient house, though poor,
> A beak-nosed bushy-bearded black-haired lord,
> Lean, pallid, low of stature yet robust,
> Fifty years old—having four years ago
> Married Pompilia Comparini, young,
> Good, beautiful, at Rome, where she was born,
> And brought her to Arezzo, where they lived
> Unhappy lives, whatéver curse the cause—
> This husband, taking four accomplices,
> Followed this wife to Rome, where she was fled
> From their Arezzo to find peace again,
> In convoy, eight months earlier, of a priest,
> Aretine also, of still nobler birth,
> Giuseppe Caponsacchi—caught her there
> Quiet in a villa on a Christmas night,
> With only Pietro and Violante by,
> Both her putative parents;[9] killed the three,
> Aged, they, seventy each, and she, seventeen
> And, two weeks since, the mother of his babe
> Firstborn and heir to what the style was worth

---

[9]The parents are described as "putative" because Violante claimed that she had bought the child from a prostitute, unknown to Pietro.

O' the Guido who determined, dared and did
This deed just as he purposed point by point.

In this first account, Browning is careful to label Pompilia
explicitly as good and to make it pretty clear that for reasons
as yet not understood, she was right in what she did and that
Guido was wrong. He points up the pathos of the ages of the
victims and of the fact that Pompilia was a mother of two
weeks. It is less that he is unsure of the self-validating nature of
truth or of his own ability to present it adequately than that he
does not trust us to read correctly without help. He is conscious
of the experimental nature of his poem, and he is not sure that
we will be able to keep our bearings. The story of the murder
will be told again and again, from different points of view.
Some of these, such as the speeches of the "three halves" of
Rome, of the lawyers, and of Guido, are exercises in dramatic
irony, in which the speaker betrays himself and his own weaknesses, and in doing so makes clear the sense in which, in his
version, the truth is being distorted. This is to help us see what
then the truth is. In the case of Caponsacchi and, especially,
Pompilia, deductions for personal limitations are minimal.
What distortion there is tends to be a reflection of their own
goodness. And the Pope, it is clear, is presented as entirely
authoritative. It is in his vision, Browning would have it, that
the truth revealed in the other accounts is contemplated as
such, is defined and judged. For "the joke" is that the per-
plexed circumstances and multiple accounts do not, as we
might expect, lead to relativism and an inability to make clear
moral judgments, but to a polarizing of the issues into choices
between radical good and radical evil, clearly recognizable as
such.

It is in the speech of the Pope that all of the modes defined in
this introduction manifest themselves with special clarity:
typical in the enactment of the archetype of moral judgment;
analytic in the understanding of the relation between unlikely
fact and fanciful actuality; mythic in its integration of the life
and death of Pompilia into that of Christ; personal in its de-
piction of a rich human being to whom we respond, and in
whose personality, as we experience it, the problems raised by
the work are persuasively resolved. And it is finally on the

personal level, no doubt, that the poem justifies itself, in the vitality of the human beings whose lives raise the issues and offer ways of dealing with them.

It may also be at this level that it is most vulnerable. There is a cold-blooded ferocity in the handling of Guido, for example, by both Caponsacchi and the Pope that has some of the effect of the hatred of the singers of "The Heretic's Tragedy," without, in this case, the excuse of intentional irony. We are to take it all at the speaker's evaluation, and admire the speaker all the more for it. For many readers this may be hard to do. The tone is that of Browning himself at his most viciously self-righteous. It reflects a failing rather common in Browning, who had great faith in the poetic value of his own sentiments.

This weakness is increasingly evident in the volumes that follow *The Ring and the Book,* which tend to impress one as exercises in perversity or as lazy thinking in casual verse. There is nothing comparable to the rich harmonies attained by works of the middle period. Only rarely, as in "La Saisiaz," is he able to integrate argument into an imagined whole, and his success here is precarious. There are brilliant individual pieces in these later books, such as the stunning "Thamuris Marching," or some lyrics of surprising sharpness, but they must be sought out. This makes the success of his final volume, *Asolando,* all the more remarkable and gratifying. While it does not suggest the mellow old age of a Titian or Verdi—it is too thin for that—it is charming and in its way impressive. Browning takes up again his lifetime's preoccupation with "Fancies and Facts" (the subtitle of the volume), and announces his choice in the Prologue of "The naked very thing." But a world so seen is more magical, and not less, in that it points to a transcendent reality beyond itself (in the last lines of the Prologue) and that as our vision of fact becomes clearer, the more clearly we see it encompass the values of fancy (in "Flute Music," or "Development"). The tone of the book is one of delighted acceptance, the manner engagingly playful. It is a fitting *vivace*-finale to Browning's life's work.

Browning's Anxious Gaze

by Ann Wordsworth

In *On Heroes, Hero-worship and the Heroic in History,* Carlyle writes "Poetic creation—what is this too but *seeing* the thing sufficiently—the Word that will describe the thing follows of itself from such clear intense sight of the thing. The seeing eye—it is this that discloses the inner harmony of things. To the poet, as to every other, we say, first of all, *see.*" Browning agrees, for he writes to Joseph Milsand about his volume *Men and Women:* "I am writing...lyrics with more music and painting in them than before so as to get people to hear and see."

And yet, this act of seeing which Carlyle acclaimed so confidently, how uncannily it manifests itself if one rejects an idealist account of its nature in favour of a psychoanalytical one: how quickly then "the inner harmony of things" dissolves, once the matchings of a reflexive consciousness are no longer assumed. For what Carlyle's directive takes for granted are two notions which psychoanalytical theory rejects: the presence of a unified consciousness and the primacy of representation. And this in itself might make one want to reconsider the critical commonplaces that take too easily this matter of making people see.

Browning's work so hauntingly calls for a more subtle reading than falls to his lot as purveyor of experience—and yet could the dramatic monologues be discussed at all without assuming "a literature of empiricism"? Is it possible to account for their success and the pleasure they provide without the expected appeal to empathy and identification? More precisely,

"Browning's Anxious Gaze" by Ann Wordsworth. This article appears for the first time in this volume.

is it possible to draw in a psycho-aesthetics, Lacan's account of "the pacifying Apollonian effect of painting," and coordinate it with Harold Bloom's theory of poetry, the relation of influence and the revisionary processes—that is, to use two accounts of creative effects that take scant heed of the categories of perception and experience?

According to Bloom, the hardest thing in reading Browning is to distinguish the literal from the figurative and vice versa.[1] So it is obvious that this matter of getting people to see turns on more than a heightened sense of vision and a tapping of experiential wisdom. How fortunate then that one of Lacan's most interesting seminars, *Of the Gaze as Objet Petit a*,[2] should be on the scopic drive and that this should show how the gaze, the relation of desire, structures the visual field beyond the organizations of the conscious system.

It is the factitiousness of the analytic experience that Lacan's work centres on, its indifference to relations of truth and appearance. "In our relation to things, insofar as this relation is constituted by the way of vision and ordered in figures of representation, something slips, passes, is transmitted from stage to stage and is always to some degree eluded in it—that is what we call the gaze" (ibid., p. 73). This drift is not accounted for in theories of geometral vision; for they do no more than map space, and contain so little of the scopic itself that, as Diderot proves, this mapping can be reconstructed without loss for the touch of a blind man. Anamorphosis, the disarrangement of geometral space by a skewed perspective, shows more of what is missed by the reflexive consciousness; hence the power of the anamorphic object in Holbein's painting *The Ambassadors*, where the viewer is shown his own eclipse as he turns back to see the enigmatic shape as a human skull. However, it is not the presence of symbols which organizes the field of the visible, but the gaze itself, which does not only look but also *shows*—that is, forms as desire like the dream (itself a gratuitous showing), and situates the perceiver where he

[1] Harold Bloom, *Poetry and Repression* (New Haven, 1976), 175.

[2] Jacques Lacan, *The Four Fundamental Concepts of Psychoanalysis*, trans. Alan Sheridan (London, 1977), 67.

cannot any longer say "After all, I am the consciousness of this. ...."

There is another dislocation; unconscious desire is not humanized. Lacan makes this clear when he is questioned at the end of a seminar, "When you relate psychoanalysis to Freud's desire and to the desire of the hysteric, might you not be accused of psychologism?" Lacan's answer is that there is no original subjectivity at stake: desire is an object in the unconscious functioning, and not to be confused with events and relationships in biographical life (ibid., p. 13). So it is never a matter of relating creative processes to psychobiographical details—unless perhaps to show a blurring of the process by unmanageable biographical material, as, say, in *The Professor* or *Oliver Twist*.

So, art and the spectator, art and artists, are bounded neither by the empirical relations of geometral space nor by shared subjectivities, but, according to Lacan, by the field of the scopic drive—a field orientated by the eye, whose appetite the painting feeds, and which is satisfied not by representations but by what Lacan calls the *trompe-l'oeil* and the *dompte-regard*, the lure and the taming of the gaze. The first, which in poetry might be the lure of *its* representations (in Browning, "Men and Women"), satisfies and attracts, not because of its fidelity to experience, but because through the pretence of representation we glimpse our relation to the unconscious. When Plato protests against the deception of art, his contention is not that painting gives an illusory equivalence to the object. "The painting does not compete with appearance, it competes with what Plato designates for us beyond appearance as being the Idea" (ibid., p. 112). What solicits us in painting is shown quite boldly in the pleasure given by a technical *trompe-l'oeil* —that moment of shifted focus when the illusion does not move with the eye, when it vanishes as what it feigned and emerges as something else not subject to appearance, in Lacanian terms, the "objet petit a," the unrepresentable object of desire. And this relation between *trompe-l'oeil* and *objet a* could also be the unconscious structuration beyond the slide of literal and figurative in Browning's poetry, the troping movement which Bloom shifts across the formal divisions of grammar and rhetoric into the revisionary processes, the interplay of rhetorical, psychological and imagistic moves which constitutes poetic energy. If the lure of art, its allure, is this glimpsing, then it accompanies the intra-poetic relations that Bloom describes by the uncanny dissolution of precursor-poet into *objet a:* unconscious and formal processes merge under the auspices of a seeing eye, though not indeed as Carlyle intended.

The other move that Lacan describes, the *dompte-regard,* the taming of the gaze, is the *showing* that gratifies the appetite of the eye; yet this also has no reference to representation, for it is not an optical pleasure that is described. As it functions in relation to the unconscious, the eye is voracious, possessed by *invidia,* the envy exemplified by St. Augustine as he gazed on his brother at his mother's breast: "the envy that makes the subject pale before the image of a completeness closed upon itself, before the idea that the *petit a,* the separated *a* from which he is hanging, may be for another the possession that gives satisfaction" (ibid., p. 116). The pacifying effect of art is that it permits the laying down of this gaze by its recognition of the eye's desire. As if the painter said—how different his tone from Carlyle's—"You want to see. Well, take a look at this. ..." And this effect, which Lacan calls "the taming, civilizing and fascinating power of the function of the picture," is what has never been well described before, the Freudian sublimation. Might it not be found also in the assuagement of the voracious unrest which marks creative anxiety, in the poet's power to acknowledge desire and lack in the formulations of poet-and-precursor?

There is one more move in this seminar *Of the Gaze* which can be drawn in. Critics insist on Browning's power to think himself into character and events—indeed this virtuosity is seen as his main achievement ("one's normal processes of judgment are well nigh suspended and one emerges from the experiences of the poem dazzled by the illusion of having actually penetrated an alien being and a remote period of history," as J. W. Harper puts it). To settle the question of how the subject places himself within the scopic field, Lacan uses the analogy of mimicry. This is not simply a matter of adaptation— that is, behaviour as bound up with survival means—but a series of functions manifesting themselves outside any biologistic explanation. Travesty, camouflage, intimidation, all have structural and psychic implications. "All reveal something in so far as it is distinct from what might be called an *itself* that is behind" (ibid., p. 99): camouflage, the production of the background; travesty, the breaking up of being between itself and its semblance; intimidation, the extension of being by overvaluation. All the moves suggest that imitation is not a faithful representation, but rather the subject's involuntary insertion within an unconscious function. The parallel between mimicry and art is taken for granted by Roger Caillois, whose work Lacan quotes; it is used with more reserve by Lacan himself. But here too there are implications for Browning criticism. If mimicry (travesty, camouflage, intimidation) were embodied in the representations of the dramatic monologues, Browning would be screened from the full play of influence anxiety while still inscribing the poet-precursor relation within the poems. Character and events would no longer be transcriptions of experience but signs of a defensive energy—a creative play that slips, passes and eludes capture altogether as representation.

The difficulty by now, of course, is obvious enough: the factitiousness of Lacanian description could hardly be further from the robust pleasures of recognition that Browning's readers expect. Instead of the assurance of a heightened vision, there is only a glimpse of processes so obscure that consciousness has no sense of them. But there are advantages in such a reading. The narrative ingenuities that are so admired soon pall and yet critics are still ready to accept tacitly Oscar Wilde's verdict: "Yes, Browning was great. And as what will he be remembered? As a poet? Ah, not as a poet. He will be remembered as a writer of fiction, as the most supreme writer of fiction, it may be, that we have ever had."[3] No matter, it seems, that Wilde's assumptions about fiction ("men and women that live") go unquestioned, and that this in its turn presupposes a neglect of Browning's early poetry and a simplistic account of his poetic development (an overall movement from the confessional Shelleyan monodramas to the achieved objectivity of the later poems after a radical break in 1842). In place of this, it is surely possible to suggest the presence of creative processes

[3]*The Artist as Critic*, ed. Richard Ellmann (New York, 1968), 345.

which form around the obsessive preoccupations of the belated poet and which gain power from the transindividual linking of art and unconscious functioning. And this would mean questioning idealist accounts of poetic language (its unique power to match human consciousness),[4] although substantiating its indifferent and inexhaustible energies. If the monologues are not as Wilde describes them, supreme fictions, but rather fictive substitutions, *trompe-l'oeil* displacements of creative lack and desire, then reading them would involve a slide away from representations and a recognition of a mimicry whose relation is with the envy of the scopic drive, with the *objet a* reformed as the precursor. This process centres formally in the play between literal and figurative; its material is not just the historic figure, the event but the use of these representations as displacements—richly dramatised effects behind whose *trompe l'oeil* are glimpsed the figurations of desire and lack condensed as the relation to the precursor.

How is this shown? All the monologues at first reading seem like anecdotes, held together by solid figures, animated by a plot with ironic undertones and psychological nuances. *My Last Duchess:* the subject seems so clearly and movingly apparent, disturbing only in the ambivalence the reader feels through his own admiration of the Duke's style. Surely then, it is just a matter of seeing how the dramatic irony works out, of making a choice such as is offered, say, in *The Browning Critics*—a choice between Browning's witless Duke and Browning's shrewd Duke?[5]

If one no longer centres on the referents, the characters, but tries to reconstitute the other scene, then a very different movement emerges—a beautifully complex play on the obsessive

[4]Movingly described by Geoffrey Hartman in his account of the paradox of the human imagination ("that it cannot at the same time be true to nature and true to itself"): "If poetry, then, is a way of expressing statements of identity, we may not think that the value of simile, metaphor, and poetic symbols in general stands in proportion to 'points of likeness.' ... Neither effect nor value come from each relation taken separately; they both exist as a function of an immediately perceived identity, and this identity reposes upon the mind's capacity for non-relational and simultaneous apprehension" (Geoffrey Hartman, *The Unmediated Vision* [New Haven, 1954] , 45).

[5]*The Browning Critics,* ed. Boyd Litzinger and K. L. Knickerbocker (Lexington, Ky., 1967), 329.

themes that haunt the creative mind, chiefly *invidia,* the fear, anger and avenges of influence anxiety. Ostensibly, the clash in the poem is between life and art — the warmth and carnal beauty of the woman and her subjection to the Duke's murderous fantasy. But behind this lies the relation of poet and precursor, doubly disguised insomuch as the precariousness of the belated poet is masked as a helpless subjection to critical misjudgements; in effect, J. S. Mill's critical misreading of *Pauline* stands in as a cover for Browning's misprision of *Alastor.* At the narrative level the poem can seize a triumph over the tyrannies that master it. The Duke intends the listening envoy to judge his last Duchess as he does, but her erotic charm escapes his description and we see her not as the mute victim of his fantasies but in her own involuntary triumph over them. Nevertheless anxiety is in the poem too. The figurations are entirely unstable and shift from level to level as literal narrative, compensatory fantasy, representations of psychic processes. Though the Duchess is obliterated, her presence hauntingly survives, figuring indifferently as poetic victory over detractors, or as precursor, negated but still active. The poem plays on the aporia between literal and figurative, in a nonrelational movement whose enigmatic activity is beautifully idealised by who but Shelley in *The Defence of Poetry:*

> The mind in creation is a fading coal which some invisible influence like an inconstant wind awakens to transitory brightness; this power arises from within, like the colours of a flower which fades and changes as it is developed, and the conscious portions of our nature are unprophetic either of its approach or of its departure.

The Duke unintentionally allows a presence to revive; whereas all he meant to do was draw back a curtain, show a picture, lift a shroud. And amidst the poem Shelley's fading coal is ablaze again — indifferently, as the presence of the precursor, as the *objet a,* whatever it is that tames and allures in the pulsations of literal and figurative, that is, in poetry.

In the monodramas, direct dramatizations of creative experience, this play is not made; but it is in the two poems *Porphyria's Lover* and *Johannes Agricola in Meditation,* first printed in Fox's *Monthly Repository,* January 1836, six years before the supposed break. In *Porphyria's Lover,* the play of substitutions moves from the narrative surface of character and macabre action to another secret act of violence. By murder the lover transforms his wayward mistress into his puppet-doll—so too would the poet reduce his precursor. But barbarous action is only one part of the poem, the surface logic of a jealous panic, casting its power over the defiant resistancies of sexuality and of the master poem. Under this is the mimicking—a blackly comic play of the creative mind, shuffling and redealing the cards of our mortality time, change, age, infidelity, death. When played straight, as in Rossetti's *House of Life,* "a hundred sonnets on the theme of one lover's fight against time," the mind is given its victory in visionary claims like those of Tennyson in section XCV of *In Memoriam.* Time and change are abolished; the erotic moment sustains itself against all mortal erosions, suspends laws, defies death, creates its own space and time. But in *Porphyria's Lover,* in the redealing of the substitutions, the erotic and creative triumph is got through murder not vision. Death is the trump card. Inconstancy and belatedness are overcome by dealing death to the mistress— and to the precursor—controlling them forever. Both the lover who knows time and change are destroying his erotic bliss, and the poet who knows his poems are too late, achieve their desire by an act of violence—a victory as false as it is vain. The poem turns back against vision and against all experiential wisdoms, against the acceptance of sexual loss, against the solaces of the compensatory imagination. It is derisive and uncanny and has great sustaining energy, for if the dramatic monologues are indeed fictions about influence anxiety and the struggle of the poet to gain priority, then any poem which plays and works this theme, however indirectly, wins the poet some power over his creative anxieties and readies him for his open triumph over them.

This is not the standard description of the monologues. As *Johannes Agricola* was printed as a companion poem in the 1845 volume, it might be interesting to take a more orthodox look at this second of the pair. In such terms it is a typical dramatic monologue, and so in studying it we shall be dealing with

what Robert Langbaum in *The Poetry of Experience* calls
"empiricism in literature." "We might even say," he writes,
"that the dramatic monologue takes as its material the literary
equivalent of the scientific attitude—the equivalent being,
when men and women are the subject of investigation, the
historicizing and psychologizing of judgment." Hence Langbaum adds Johannes Agricola to Tennyson's St Simeon Stylites
as another example of "religious buccaneering," and shows
that "though Browning intends us to disapprove of Johannes'
Antinomianism, he complicates the issue by showing the lofty
passion that can proceed from the immoral doctrine." This
brings the reader to the characteristic tension between sympathy and moral judgment which draws him into the dilemma
of the monologue, loosening him from his customary moral
certainties and offering him the new insights of an empiricist
and relativist age. Thus we learn to read from within the material itself, no longer dependent on our own external standards of judgment. It is a logical development of romantic
inwardness and is uniquely achieved as an effect of the
form, "that extra quantity," Langbaum explains, "which makes
the difference in artistic discourse between content and
meaning."

Clearly the orthodox reading is very different from Bloom's,
for whom "every poem...begins as an encounter *between
poems*," for whom "acts, persons and places...must themselves be treated as though they were already poems, or part
of poems. Contact, in a poem, means contact with another
poem, even if that poem is called a deed, person, place or
thing".[6] Whether it is with the precursor, or the unconscious,
or with both, this encounter engenders poetry, and to recall it
restores the sense of Browning's uncanny energy, which the
standard description reduces to lessons in nineteenth-century
humanism.

In *Johannes Agricola* there is the same shift from literal to
figurative as in *Porphyria's Lover*, and the same shuffling of
effects, though this time they belong to religious and not erotic
experience. Again the subject is not the imaginative triumph

[6]Harold Bloom, *A Map of Misreading* (Oxford, 1975), 70.

unmediated, but rather the triumph deliberately askewed. Johannes is God's child:

> For as I lie, smiled-on, full-fed
>   By inexhaustible power to bless,
> I gaze below on hell's fierce bed
>   And those its waves of flame oppress
>   Swarming in ghastly wretchedness:
>   Whose life on earth aspired to be
> One altar smoke, so pure—to win
>   If not love like God's love for me,
> At least to keep his anger in.

Do we really hestitate here between sympathy and judgment? Are we not rather drawn in by the recognition of desire to watch the speaker's impermissible bliss as he lies "smiled-on, full-fed," our envy pacified by the poet's acknowledgement? And through the displacement do we not glimpse the poet's desire for such a creative gratification that no rival can threaten him?

> Priest, doctor, hermit, monk grown white
>   With prayer, the broken hearted nun,
> The martyr, the wan acolyte,
>   The incense-swinging child—undone
> Before God fashioned star or sun!

And after all, isn't the poem really a brazen mimicry of Shelley's *Ode to the West Wind?*[7]

The mysterious moment that Bloom places between 1840 and 1842 marks, not a change from solipsism to humanistic concerns, but a displacement of the dramas of creative life on to fictive substitutes. The movement is therefore not from a pastiche of Romanticism to an authentic Victorian voice, but from a poetry too dangerously open to desire and death to a deflection, screening, mimicking of the same themes—a movement towards the polymorphic, towards processes which play and re-play the original themes through parallels and equivalences at a narrative level. It is not an ironisation of the early poems,

---

[7]In Lacanian terms, "mimicry" is not, of course, a synonym for the literary term *parody*. See above.

a progress from delusion to insight. Sordello, like Alastor and Hyperion, dies, not as a punishment but as a gratification of desire. The pattern is a dangerously repetitious one—both a vicious circle and a dead-end—and if poetry were only the release of our primordial narcissisms, it would perhaps always involve a surreptitious privileging of beautiful and enigmatic deaths. But great poems are not just narcissistic reveries, and Bloom's theory of revisionism is a powerful attempt at defining a creative process which is as necessary and constitutive to the writing of poetry as the Freudian dream-work is to the encounter with the unconscious. Hence the triumph of *Childe Roland* over both *Sordello* and the monologues.

Sooner or later, Browning realized the creative cost of the early poems. He never devalued *Sordello* as a poem, and his fellow poets Swinburne and Rossetti read it deeply, but after it he realigned his material, displacing it onto all the substitutes, imitations, travesties of vatic intensities which flicker in and out of ordinary life—erotic and religious fantasies, deathbed reveries, self-projections, narcissisms. Browning shifts ground, not because he is too multifaceted and red-blooded to stay with Shelleyan idealism, but because poems like *Sordello*—unless achieved through the full processes of revisionism—can end only in submission to the deathwish. The shift produces a near-inexhaustible defensive play over the now latent theme, the same old one: the desire of the creative mind for priority. And if this is not Browning's greatest poetry, it is only because it is a play which brings him closer and closer to the moment in which the full revisionary process can be achieved.

Back to the First of All: "By the Fire-side" and Browning's Romantic Origins

by Leslie Brisman

Because "By the Fire-side" puts in question the boundary between objective, dramatic monologue and subjective, autobiographical narrative, the poem offers a special "top of speculation" from which to view some of Browning's most habitual concerns. The line between art and life necessarily draws our attention when we are reading the work of what Browning called a subjective poet. To a lesser extent the objective poet arouses our curiosity about the relationship between the life and the work, but Browning's status as an objective poet is nowhere more in question than in this poem which appears to present in a thinly transmuted form the central event of his life as he viewed it: winning Elizabeth Barrett. When the speaker of "By the Fire-side," looking back to the moment when friendship turned into declared love, announces that he is "named and known by that moment's feat," we are tempted to read the feat of that literary moment as a dream condensation of the Brownings' courtship.

Beyond that biographical referent, however, the poem invites inquiry about the abstract idea of the "infinite moment," and by extension about the impersonality of all the great revelatory moments in the dramatic monologues. More broadly, we might question to what extent the poet of *Men and Women* is writing about characters rather than his own character. Coleridge said of Shakespeare's characters that they are exag-

"Back to the First of All: 'By the Fire-side' and Browning's Romantic Origins" by Leslie Brisman. This article appears for the first time in this volume.

gerations of essential, rather than eccentric, aspects of human nature—of Shakespeare's own human nature. Is Browning, as he said of Shakespeare, an "objective poet," or a reviser of the techniques by which a Romantic explores his own subjectivity? How involved in literary history, and how local, is the poet's subjectivity?

Both Robert Browning, in his essay on Shelley (1851), and Elizabeth, in a letter to Robert (January 15, 1845) refer to the terms *objective* and *subjective* as familiar in their day. Elizabeth praises Robert for his combination of talents: "You are both subjective and objective in the habits of your mind. You can deal with abstract thought and with human passion in the most passionate sense." For Robert, *objective* refers to the "manifested action of the human heart and brain," and thus to the passions—one's own or others'—in their past and present state of development; *subjective* refers to the abstract, Shelleyan thought of human perfectability, and thus to the portion of the soul that stands apart and above the experiencing self and aspires beyond present fulfillment or engagement of the mind and the affections. In "One Word More," the coda to *Men and Women,* Browning submits that by entering each and all of his monologuists, he has half revealed himself—the side of himself "finished" and available for public inspection. But there is another, unfinished, and still aspiring self, and this is the basis of intimacy: "God be thanked, the meanest of his creatures / Boasts two soul-sides, one to face the world with, / One to show a woman when he loves her." Browning does not pause to consider whether he really means one out of two of God's creatures in any possible relationship, and whether it is more often a man who is a moon to his beloved's earth, above and beyond her and revealing to her alone a dark side of himself. Part of the charm of "One Word More" is that the poem drops its generalization at this point and reverts to the central image of Elizabeth as moon, shining above—though not hopelessly above—Robert. In a passage all the more endearing for its entanglement in spatial metaphor, Robert describes his privileged access to his wife's dark soul-side:

> This to you—yourself my moon of poets!
> Ah, but that's the world's side, there's the wonder,

> Thus they see you, praise you, think they know you!
> There, in turn I stand with them and praise you—
> Out of my own self, I dare to phrase it.
> But the best is when I glide from out them,
> Cross a step or two of dubious twilight,
> Come out on the other side, the novel
> Silent silver lights and darks undreamed of,
> Where I hush and bless myself with silence.
>
> (ll. 188-97)

Most aspiring while most fancifully extending the reach of metaphor, the passage appears to give the reading public as good a view as it could wish of the poet's intimate side— whether that means his domestication of sublime ambition (confining and pestering an immortal free spirit in a pinfold here) or his transmutation of domestic situation into metaphors for the sublime.

Which is it? Browning had years before been wounded by the public reception of *Pauline* and *Sordello,* and he had repeatedly expressed reluctance to have Elizabeth read *Pauline.* Though he finds ways to mythologize his courtship in "By the Fire-side" and his marriage of true minds in "One Word More," he invites us, by his very notice of the difference between the dark side and world side, to regard the domestication of visionary aspiration in "One Word More" as yet another public guise. I would like to argue that Browning's development as a poet meant a development of the mechanisms of defense by which he safeguarded his own dark side, the side which must remain the focus of critical inquiry beyond *Pauline, Paracelsus,* and *Sordello.* Even in "One Word More," which returns overtly to the relationship between Browning's aspirations in love and poetry, he playfully evades self-revelation when he turns from section XVII to XVIII, from the soul-side "to show a woman when he loves her" to the soul-side the poetess shows this man when he persists in his love for her. Representing Elizabeth as the visionary ideal toward which he faces and climbs, Browning defends himself against the sorrow of subjective idealism which decrees the incommensurability and incompatibility of dark soul-sides.

On his dark side Browning is, like Shelley, one who goes on

till he is stopped and never is—not even by the image of fulfillment he makes of his wife. The aspiring poet seeks the dark
side of his ideal predecessor, but finds that he is shown the
public side, for his predecessor's dark side is likewise turned
upward. The ladder of aspiration admits only one per rung,
and one's reach for the rung above necessarily exceeds one's
grasp. As students of poetry we hold the faith that finished
poems can be analyzed to reveal more of the poet than ostensibly meets the eye—the way Browning thought the whole
of Shelley, all his ambition and awareness of limitation, available from the poems without any knowledge of his letters or
life; but the poet, in his dark self, seeks always to know more
than he can reveal in any finite articulation, and so pursues the
infinite course of the soul that beacons from above.

If in aspiring above any actuality the dark soul-side shows
itself asocial, then love between persons must be in fact an arrangement of convenience between two souls' world-sides, or a
mystification predicated on one lover's extravagant projection
of a beloved from a rung below to a rung above. "One Word
More" plots the second alternative, while suggesting that the
former may be the case. But "By the Fire-side" attempts wholly
to transform or arrest the soul's dark visionary metaphysics
and to posit a shared darkness by two souls standing side by
side on the same rung, as it were, of the ladder that would reach
to the moon. *Side* is an important word in "By the Fire-side,"
and proleptic nostalgia for the romance of sitting by the side of
another replaces the sidereal aspirations of the Romantic
selfhood. Yet "replaces" is too easy a word, and before exploring how temporal anxieties and those related to the vertical
ladder of love are transmuted into a myth of horizontal landscape in "By the Fire-side," we need to linger over the vertical
imagery of the soul's quest in the early poems.

In *Sordello* (I.466-567) Browning distinguishes two classes
of poets on the basis of how they conceive of the relationship
between soul and outer forms. Poets of the first class, denying
or repressing selfhood, "would belong / To what they worship." Poets of the second class, denying or repressing awareness of the objectivity of the outside world, refer every external
"revealment" to their own souls. The passage reaches its climax

as Browning apostrophizes the subjective poet who soars "to heaven's complexest essence" and establishes for all who would follow the trajectory of desire:

> In truth? Thou hast
> Life, then—wilt challenge life for us: our race
> Is vindicated so, obtains its place
> In thy ascent, the first of us; whom we
> May follow, to the meanest, finally,
> With our more bounded wills?

"Our race" can mean our pursuit of transcendence, though its primary meaning is mankind or that elect portion of mankind who are drawn heavenward by the example of the subjective poet the way Christians are "vindicated" of original sin and drawn heavenward by Christ. Even objective poets, like angels in heaven, cast off "their borrowed crowns / Before a coming glory," recognizing in such a poet "a touch divine." Wordsworth praised Milton for the line "Far off his coming shone," where the Messiah himself is almost lost in the indefinite abstraction, "his coming." Such "coming" serves as synecdoche for the apocalyptic abstraction of the Shelleyan or subjective poet, though if the poet, like Christ, must "task his nature for mankind's good," he works for mankind's good more by his example of energetic soaring towards the divine than by his actual immersion in the politics of his time. So Browning describes Shelley "drawing out, lifting up, and assimilating his ideal of a future man, thus descried as possible, to the present reality of the poet's soul already arrived at the higher state of development, and still aspirant to elevate and extend itself in conformity with its still-improving perception of, no longer the eventual human, but the actual Divine."

At the end of *Sordello* Browning envisions his own spirit soaring along the vertical axis established by the subjective poet:

> Suns waxed and waned,
> And still my spirit held an upward flight,
> Spiral on spiral, gyres of life and light
> More and more gorgeous.   (VI. 802-5)

Presumably Shelley beacons to Browning the way Eglamor,
Sordello's precursor, is imagined to beacon from above. The
passage closes with the abstracted image of "that upturned
fervid face and hair put back," but leaves uncertain whether
that face is Eglamor's, Shelley's, or Browning's.[1] Such is the
spiral of poetic life and light that whoever pursues its "exclusive track" lifts his own fervid face in search of the upturned
face to model in the golden courts above. There remains the
hope that vision will be mediated by love, that a precursor will,
in an act of divine grace, cause his countenance to shine upon
one; but the track, at least as it is known by the poet aspiring
on this earth, is the track of those who aspire, though they cannot attain, to see their maker face to face.

In *Pauline,* Browning explores the possibility that the necessarily unfulfilled aspirations of the poet can find restitution in
the thought of a perfect love, Pauline, "by his side" (1. 906).
Actually, the thought of Pauline by his side is a side effect to
the poem's scheme, which is the re-presentation of the vertical
axis of imagination as though it were brought into being
through a fall. Once, before he became an aspirer, the poet had
sat beside Pauline, and he would have been spared a fall, he
tells us, if he could have stayed by her side for ever.[2] Though
now fallen and lost, the poet remembers a time of perfect presence when he stood not only with Pauline, but with his personal ideal Shelley (1. 163), before he understood that poet to
be "as a star to men" and beyond the need and possibility of
being personally canonized by him. The awareness of Shelley's
popularity makes the poet believe he is, like everyone else,
facing Shelley's world-side; this recognition he counters with
the myth that he once faced the dark side the way souls are
sometimes imagined to have walked with God before falling
into earthly life. In the era of the poetic soul's preexistence
there was no up and down; and since the whole past is a fiction
of the present poet's dark side, he can imagine it to have been

[1]The best reading of this passage is by Herbert F. Tucker in *Time's Revenges in Browning* (Yale Univ. Diss., 1977).

[2]"The *Pauline* speaker wants the permanent security of his old place in
God's cave and his literal protection in Pauline's arms." Eleanor Cook,
Browning's Lyrics: An Exploration (Toronto: Univ. of Toronto Press, 1974),
p. 209. Cook relates these enclosures to the imagery of "By the Fire-side."

a time when, like Adam in the garden before the Fall, he en-
joyed the visitations of both his visionary Pauline and the
slightly later incarnation of Presence, Shelley.

In recollecting that gravity-free space, the imagination yet
appears

> a very angel, coming not
> In fitful visions but beside me ever
> And never failing me.   (11. 285-87)

As the poet grows, however, he becomes increasingly aware of
his isolation, of the fact that only a projection of his own consciousness could stand *beside* him. He feels how low he is compared to Shelley, and he becomes "a watcher whose eyes have
grown dim / With looking for some star which breaks on him"
(11. 227-28). The price he pays for apprehending "the orb / Of
[Shelley's] conceptions" is realizing how far out of the orb of
Shelley he is. He imagines himself a satanic "dark spirit" to
whom troops of shadows do homage, but only to confirm his
sense that if they will worship him, his heart must worship too
and keep forever in mind the height from which he must have
fallen.[3] Very much a Browningesque rather than a Miltonic
Satan he finds that the imaginative gain associated with this
new state is the "delight of the contented lowness / With
which I gaze on him I keep for ever / Above me" (11. 555-
57). Like the poet in Shelley's cave of the witch Poesy, the poet
of *Pauline* knows himself the keeper of his visions, but he
knows also that imaginative power depends on resisting the
folly of trying to forget the Power above one. Discovering that
the soul will "rest beneath / Some better essence than itself,
in weakness" (11. 818-19), the *Pauline* poet prepares himself
both for Christianity and for the return to the dream of a loving
Pauline bending over him. He prepares himself also for what
seems like an even more extravagant thought than a perfect
beloved or a personal God hovering in a way that makes of
the ladder of ·vision an umbrella of love. The closing line of

---

[3] A parallelism between "Only God is gone / And some dark spirit sitteth
in his seat" (*Pauline*, 471-72) and "I see a mighty darkness / Filling the seat
of power (*Prometheus Unbound*, II. iv. 2-3) is cited by Frederick A. Pottle,
Shelley and Browning: A Myth and Some Facts (1923; reprint: Hamden,
Conn.: Archon Books, 1965), p. 51.

Pauline requests that Shelley himself shed his mild influence
and turn the visionary's solitary quest into sweet society: "Love
me and wish me well."

If we approach "By the Fire-side" from the perspective of
Pauline, we may regard the Leonor of the love poem as in some
measure a spirit like Pauline who is projected out from and
above the aspiring poet, bending over him with compassionate
care. The speaker of "By the Fire-side," like the poet of *Pauline,*
can be imagined as one who re-presents to himself a form of
maternal Presence presiding over the youth or preexistence of
his matured poetic soul:

> But, doubting nothing, had been led by thee,
> Thro' youth, and saved, as one at length awakened
> Who has slept through a peril.   (*Pauline,* 11. 36-38)

The peril of youth and the danger of sleeping beyond it become much more explicitly a subject of "By the Fire-side."
Yet remembering Pauline as a soul-projection, a fiction of
benevolent Presence that fades before the greater dream of a
visionary master leading and loving the poet, we may wonder if
"By the Fire-side" is not troubled by the thought of Leonor as a
projection that must ultimately give way to the poet's un-
diminished visionary aspiration after Shelley. In the concluding verse paragraph of *Pauline* the poet imagines himself
"dying, as one going in the dark / To fight a giant." If we
think of the dark side of the subjective poet always engaged in
fighting a giant, we may regard the turn from *Pauline* to "By
the Fire-side" not as a turn from a projected to a "real" ad-
dressee but as a turn from a youthful to a more sophisticated
mechanism of defense against exposure of the dark side of the
soul. If we see "By the Fire-side" triumphing as a love poem,
we may wish to explore how it aborts the process by which a
fiction like the presence of Pauline dissolves before the wished-
for presence of Shelley.

Accustomed to the world's view of socialization and marriage, we often tend to dismiss the visionary aspiration of
Sordello, Paracelsus, and the *Pauline* poet as adolescent or
immature; approaching the situation of falling in love as it is
represented in "By the Fire-side" from the perspective of the

early poems, we may regard the picture of two spirits standing side by side as a re-presentation of a time of heavenly innocence before the imagination recapitulated the satanic fall into the essential verticality of desire. The delicate arrest of time before the moment of choice of love in "By the Fire-side" gathers into a moment the wide-ranging dream of an arrested, prelapsarian peace. In "Notes toward a Supreme Fiction" Wallace Stevens images "a stop to watch / A definition growing certain and / A wait within that certainty." Such a pause is made by the lovers before they are so defined in "By the Fire-side":

> We two stood there with never a third,
>   But each by each, as each knew well:
> The sights we saw and the sounds we heard,
>   The lights and the shades made up a spell
> Till the trouble grew and stirred.
>   (11. 186-190)

We may conceive of this trouble as the potential interference of a shadowy third, a giant like the one put out of thought by Stevens at the beginning of the section quoted, or a giant like the one stalking the dark side of the Pauline-poet's imagination. Were Spenser rather than Browning describing this moment the giant might assume the form of Orgoglio, sexual pride, and the trouble could take on the contours of a specifically sexual excitement. This is, as Browning goes on to describe it, the moment at which the crossing between friends and lovers takes place—or rather (since it is a moment of falling in love, not a moment of falling to sex) the moment of romantic origin given to the crossing between friendship and love. The romance of the origin for Browning the man comes from the fact that he has transposed the events of Wimpole Street to an Italian setting imagined or actually shared with his wife several years later; the transposition turns a real or historical origin into a romantic or far away one. For Browning the poet and his readers, the romance of the origin involves a transposition from particular to mythic space and time.

The scene I wish to consider that lies far away for the poet of "By the Fire-side" (but no farther than the memory impressed on the dark side of his soul) is the great model of awakened love in the Indian Caucasus of Shelley's *Prometheus Unbound*.

Because it is a drama, and a drama in which Asia as well as
Prometheus speaks, Shelley's greatest work may be said to ob-
jectify the passions; at the same time, *Prometheus Unbound* is
about ideal rather than actual love, and hence lays open to our
view the internal drama of the subjective poet's mind. Act II
of *Prometheus Unbound* is one of the most extended and
profound accounts of the awakening to love—to that "abstract
thought" of love (to borrow again Elizabeth's phrase) so intimately blended in Shelley's and Browning's consciousnesses
with the thought of the perfectability of human kindness and
thus human kind. In its initial scene, and indeed in the whole
succession of its scenes, Act II reveals the relationship between
the visionary and the sexual aspects of the giant troubling the
innocence reimagined at the dawn of love.

Recalling his resistance to love, the poet of "By the Fire-
side" explains, "For my heart had a touch of the woodland-
time, / Wanting to sleep now over its best" (ll. 201-2). *Prometheus* Act II opens with Asia's anxiety about two things that
half prefigure and half figure the awakening of love: the arrival of spring and the arrival of her sister Panthea, the belated sleeper. Panthea describes her habitual posture in sleep
and the late disturbance of her rest in a way that makes her
experience a prefigurative miniature of what is about to be
actualized in her encounter with Asia: the turn from a time of
innocence to awakened love:

> Erewhile I slept
> Under the glaucous caverns of old Ocean
> Within dim bowers of green and purple moss,
> Our young Ione's soft and milky arms
> Locked then, as now, behind my dark, moist hair,
> While my shut eyes and cheek were pressed within
> The folded depth of her life-breathing bosom:
> But not as now, since I am made the wind
> Which fails beneath the music that I bear
> Of thy most wordless converse; since dissolved
> Into the sense with which love talks, my rest
> Was troubled and yet sweet; my waking hours
> Too full of care and pain.   (II. i. 43-55)

The embrace of Panthea and Ione offers a picture of sensuous innocence not to be attempted again.[4] The poet of "By the Fire-side" imagines himself sitting by the side of his beloved Leonor in old age, and he recaptures a memory of having stood by the side of the lady at the moment when friendship opened into love. Lying, sitting, or standing, these side-by-side positions represent a time of innocence when visionary ambition is laid aside or yet to be assumed. Panthea herself describes the new sensation of being made "the wind / Which fails beneath the music that I bear." As a form of love Panthea is indeed "beneath" Asia, and in moving from the thought of Panthea and Ione as equal sisters side by side to Panthea and Asia as lower and higher love-bearing souls, we move to the subjective poet's sense of a fallen world and his visionary aspiration to transcend it.

In the essay on Shelley, Browning describes the subjective poet as one who "does not paint pictures and hang them on the walls, but rather carries them on the retina of his own eyes: we must look deep into his human eyes, to see those pictures on them." Though Shelley's Panthea is herself only embryonically a figure of the subjective poet, she holds the mirror up to Asia's dark subjectivity, and allows Asia to discover in Panthea's eyes the reflection of Asia's own form of desire. "Lift up thine eyes," Asia asks Panthea, "And let me read thy dream." Unequal to Asia's visionary hope, Panthea asks the question that could reduce the subjective poet to a dreamy solipsist: "What canst

[4]On Browning's transposition of sensuous (and sensual) matter into landscape description in "By the Fire-side," see Isobel Armstrong, "Browning and Victorian Poetry of Sexual Love," in *Writers and Their Background: Robert Browning*, ed. Isobel Armstrong (London: G. Bell and Sons, 1974), pp. 269-70. Jean Stirling Lindsay argues that the autobiographical significance of "By the Fire-side" centers about a moment several years after the Brownings' marriage, and she uses as one piece of evidence a detail of the poem that suggests marriage, rather than a premarital courtship (or sibling relationship like that between Panthea and Ione): "One suspects that the poet would be averse to representing his relationship with Elizabeth Barrett, even in metaphor, by the figures in the lonely gorge, 'arm in arm and cheek to cheek.' Neither of them was indifferent to the requirements of Victorian decorum." "The Central Episode of Browning's 'By the Fire-Side'," *SP* 39 (1942), 572.

thou see / But thine own fairest shadow imaged there?" What
Asia can see is the form of Prometheus, and the form of Prometheus is at once the form of this subjective poet's idealized
love and the object of her visionary hope for mankind. No
sooner is the shape of Prometheus beheld, however, then the
spectre of Panthea's other dream rears its head. In "By the
Fire-side" Browning muses how "If two lives join there is oft
a scar, / They are one and one, with a shadowy third" (ll. 228-
29). Though Browning insists on a wondrously unshadowed
meeting of minds, we can better understand the spectre he
banishes or refigures if we attend to Panthea's second dream,
the "shadowy third" between Asia and her envisioned
Prometheus.

The second dream is personified and envoiced to speak just
two words, "Follow! Follow!"—but that is enough to suggest
both the nature of the action in the remainder of *Prometheus*
II and the nature of the sentiment and the narrative of "By the
Fire-side." Three kinds of "following" are important in "By
the Fire-side": following the lady placed before the speaker
where he can look up to her; following the lead of nature, to
whose agency the transformation of consciousness is attributed;
and following transformed from a temporal to a spatial act,
that is, following down the backwards path that slopes from age
and experience to youth and a moment of romantic origin.

The first of these modes of "following" we have already encountered in *Pauline* and the conclusion of "One Word More."
Whatever the depth of Robert Browning's admiration for his
wife's work, there is no evidence that he was ever, as a poet,
significantly influenced by a line of hers.[5] But the letters be-
speak his need to look up to her, and in a way the less we believe

---

[5]See his appreciation of her "Vision of Poets": "Shelley's 'white ideal all
statue-blind'—is—perfect,—how can I coin words?" (letter postmarked August 4, 1845). What more *could* he say about her poem or her understanding of
Shelley?

On the other hand, Sonnet XXII of *Sonnets From the Portuguese,* which
begins "When our two souls stand up erect and strong, / Face to face, silent
…" and turns on the injunction, "Think," may be profitably juxtaposed to
the stanza in "By the Fire-side" beginning "Think, when our one soul understands / The great Word which makes all things new." What is particularly
interesting is Barrett's attribution of aspiration to the angels rather than the
lovers. Her sonnet concludes strongly with "A place to stand and love in for a

in the reasonableness of his admiration the better our chance of seeing the literary re-presentation of infatuation as an act of imagination, and a significant act of the subjective imagination at that:

> Oh I must feel your brain prompt mine,
>   Your heart anticipate my heart,
> You must be just before, in fine,
>   See and make me see, for your part,
> New depths of the divine!   (ll. 136-40)

"The most sublime act is to set another before you," Blake wrote in *The Marriage of Heaven and Hell,* and we can best approach the significance of the assumed secondariness in "By the Fire-side" if we take seriously Blake's term "sublime." Since the hierarchy of persons is established by imaginative fiat rather than careful weighing of objective facts, it can represent the subjective poet's ambition rather than his accommodation to the external world and his awareness of limitation.

"By the Fire-side" posits a second subservience, and that is to nature. Like Asia, who both feels Panthea's brain prompt hers and awakens to the external spring before an internal one, the poet of "By the Fire-side" is both prompted by Leonor and respondent to what he takes to be nature's lead:

> Shake the whole tree in the summer-prime,
>   But bring to the last leaf no such test!
> 'Hold the last fast!' runs the rhyme.
>
> For a chance to make your little much,
>   'To gain a lover and lose a friend,
> Venture the tree and a myriad such,
>   When nothing you mar but the year can mend:
> But a last leaf—fear to touch!
>
> Yet should it unfasten itself and fall
>   Eddying down till it find your face
> At some slight wind—best chance of all!
>   Be your heart henceforth its dwelling-place
> You trembled to forestall!

---

day, / With darkness and the death-hour rounding it." The enclosure, taking on prophetic, Miltonic resonance in Barrett's sonnet and determining the landscape as well as the framing devices of "By the Fire-side," was one ideal, or one metaphoric transposition of an ideal, that the two poets shared.

Browning's "slight wind" is a masterful and characteristic turn
on the familiar Shelleyan trope of the apocalyptic wind. In
Prometheus Unbound (II. i. 135) Panthea remembers the wind
in her second dream blowing the blossoms of an almond tree —
itself an emblem of apocalyptic haste. The almond blossoms
early, but Browning transposes Shelley's earliness into a figure of his own belatedness, and remembers a wind belonging
not to April but November. By refiguring Shelleyan urgency
in the form of his own ability to stand and wait, Browning sets
Shelley before him and makes passive attending on the slight
wind a figure for the subjective soul's attending on the pre-
venient spirit who has become one with nature. For the prophet
Jeremiah the almond tree represented not simply the apocalyptic threat of the wind-god YHVH but His moral attentive-
ness to His people's history, His *watchfulness* — a world that
bears the same root (SKD) as the *almond.* The extraordinary
fiction of "By the Fire-side" that "The forest had done it," not
the incipient lovers, makes of the poet's watchfulness an approximation of divine both prophetic urgency and divine
reconciliation to the slow workings of human history — the history of a developing relationship.

The third transmutation in Browning of the injunction "Follow! Follow!" concerns the double nature of the landscape
progress. "I follow wherever I am led," the fireside poet announces, and where he is led is not simply to Italy but to
"youth, by green degrees." Were the subjectivity of the soul
reducible to present discontent and apocalyptic hope, we could
not long hold on to the distinction between a personal and a
world side. But the element of ambition is complexly inter-
twined with romantic origins, and even if our biographical
histories become public, nothing remains more personal than
the way we reimagine our origins. "Come back with me to the
first of all!" the fireside poet invites Leonor. His "first of all"
is his romantic origin in the sense that he sees himself recreated
at the moment when the very woods seemed to whisper, "Let
there be love!" "Come back with me to the first of all" could
also be the cry of Panthea's second dream, where "first of all"
is the romantic origin of the fallen universe as we know it.
Asia follows, and the path she takes brings her to Demogorgon.
And beyond. For Act II of *Prometheus Unbound* closes not

with the vision of the origin of speech, thought, and the repression of love; the scene with Demogorgon continues and leads to an extraordinary exchange between Asia and a "Voice in the Air" in which "the first of all" means a romantic origin in two senses of *romantic:* the place far away from present reality, and the place of love. Guided by the voice from above, Asia's boat of desire sails to "Realms where the air we breathe is love." If this is the place towards which the subjective soul aspires, it is also the place from which the subjective soul imagines it has come. Panthea tells us that the birth of Asia was attended with a universal sunburst of love:

> Love, like the atmosphere
> Of the sun's fire filling the living world,
> Burst from thee, and illumined earth and heaven
> And the deep ocean and the sunless caves
> And all that dwells within them.   (II. v. 26-30)

Though the light of Asia has since been eclipsed, Asia's love-inspired journey returns her to the place where love and light are one. It is an upstream journey—against the temporal flow of experience—passing "Age's icy caves, / And Manhood's dark and tossing waves, / And Youth's smooth ocean, smiling to betray." In "By the Fire-side" the river journey is likewise a backwards path, a path accessible to lovers but closed to those who know only "the obvious human bliss"—sex, society, even the institution of marriage, but not the "safe hem" of love.

With Leonor beside him, the poet of "By the Fire-side" can pursue the path back and linger over the crossing from friendship to love because, having lingered and found each other, they made the path safe for retrospection. The path of memory is itself represented as the riverside path the incipient lovers once followed to a stagnant pool crossed by a bridge on the other side of which stands a deserted chapel. Since the bridge must be crossed and recrossed if the travelers are to take in the chapel on their walk, the bridge and the "stopped" river water of the pool become landscape emblems of their willingness then and now to "wait" (l. 180)—to linger over the crossing. What about the chapel itself?

> Stoop and kneel on the settle under,
> Look through the window's grated square:

Nothing to see! For fear of plunder,
    The cross is down and the altar bare,
As if thieves don't fear thunder.
                        (ll. 171-75)

Retrospectively the lovers can make of the empty church a
figure for their freedom from a shadowy third. Kneeling *outside* the church, before no God or emblem of His Presence,
they discover, as Demogorgon tells Asia, that "the deep truth
is imageless." They share at this point something like the
subjective poet's discovery that "of such truths / Each to itself must be the oracle (*P. U.* II. iv. 122-23). What they take
with them is not an architectural fact (like "the dead builder's
date") but a sense of the weightiness of the moment, a sense that
the time is now. So Demogorgon answered Asia: "These are
the immortal Hours, / Of whom thou didst demand. One
waits for thee." In "By the Fire-side" this becomes the "moment,
one and infinite," the arrested moment of choice.

What happens when those who have negotiated the crossing
between youth and maturity without waiting for love, without
having created for themselves a romantic origin for their adult
consciousness, attain the age where there is more experience
behind than ahead of them? Looking backward to a period of
crossing is something such "grey heads abhor," and while they
dare not look back to an actual past they scorn the idea of a
path back to a reimagined transition to love and marriage. The
path back

    leads to a crag's sheer edge with them;
    Youth, flowery all the way, there stops—
    Not they; age threatens and they contemn,
    Till they reach the gulf wherein youth drops,
    One inch from life's safe hem!

I find it hard to believe that any detail about the Piedmont or
Abennine mountains (the two literal settings critics have
proposed) will ever resolve the difficulty of this stanza.[6] It

---

[6]Eleanor Cook (p. 223) assumes that "Grey heads abhor' the path toward
age and death," but she offers no explanation for the extension of flowery
youth to the gulf of death at the end of old age. For arguments about the
Italian setting, see Jean Stirling Lindsay (op. cit.), and William Clyde De-
Vane, *A Browning Handbook,* 2nd ed. (New York: Appleton-Century-

makes little sense to identify the crag's sheer edge with the "straight up rock" (l. 46) bounding the narrow path on the other side of which is the drop down to the river bed. Despite the "till," which suggests further progress along a walk, I think the craggy edge must be the edge of the gulf separating the innocent and wandering path of youthful desire from the severer grade of maturity and commitment. It, and not, for example, the abyss of death, is the only experiential chasm about which Browning is concerned. At the infinite moment of redemption for Shelley's Asia, a "young spirit" guiding a chariot of love replaces "a spirit with dreadful countenance [who] / Checks its dark chariot by the craggy gulf" (II. iv. 142-43). Neither Browning's lovers nor his grey heads find a chariot waiting for them, but perhaps one has only to keep in mind that the first chariot to come along the craggy gulf in *Prometheus Unbound* is for Demogorgon in order to see what Browning's would-be lovers gain by waiting. For grey heads who crossed precipitously there is always the scar tissue (stanza XLVI) reminding them of sloppy surgery—of having joined life to life without romance; the "shadowy third" is the spectre of that failure forever haunting them. But the apocalyptic patience of the poet and Leonor turned them from actors into spectators and followers of nature's lead. Having waited for the last leaf to "unfasten itself and fall," the friends-that-were set the form of love above them, and freed themselves not only to regard love and vision as one, but to return, in memory, to the revivifying scene of that union. Like Asia, the poet of "By the Fire-side" has heard the song of the spirits, the "powers at play":

> We have bound thee, we guide thee; Down, down!
> With the bright form beside thee;
> Resist not the weakness,
> Such strength is in meekness
> That the Eternal, the Immortal,
> Must unloose through life's portal
> The snake-like Doom coiled underneath his throne
>   By that alone.   (II. iii. 90-98)

Crofts, 1955), pp. 221-22. Jacob Korg argues for the poem's setting as essentially imaginary in "Browning's Art and 'By the Fire-Side,'" *Victorian Poetry* 15 (1977), 147-58.

The concept of strength in weakness, so much at the heart of Browning, may be said to be an extension of these spirits' directive. The two souls who stand each by each "till the trouble grew and stirred" discover their power to unbind their fate from Demogorgon and bring about "a diviner day."

At the end of *Prometheus Unbound* Act II, Asia's progress through song, like the lovers' progress through memory in "By the Fire-side," is backwards in time laid out, as it were, on a visionary plane. What Shelley envisions as the path "through Death and Birth, to a diviner day," Browning represents as the death of the old self, the woodland youth, and the rebirth when "nature obtained her best of me— / One born to love you, sweet!"[7] Whatever the world records as one's date of birth, majority, or marriage, the dates that matter are the priviledged moments of time inscribed on the dark side of the soul—and they are inscribed less by experience than by the hand of the poet recreating an event from the events and thoughts of the personal and literary past. Because of the "diviner days" thus half recreated and half recaptured, one lover can say to another, "Grow old along with me / The best is yet to be." The simple verticality of the visionary aspiration, ever soaring away from the present and the past, is challenged by the thought of a redemptive crossing that has already been negotiated:

> My own, confirm me! If I tread
> This path back, is it not in pride
> To think how little I dreamed it led
> To an age so blest that, by its side,
> Youth seems the waste instead?
> (ll. 121-25)

[7]Shelley's "diviner day" is also—and characteristically— a dawn image, while "By the Fire-side" is a poem of grey evening—the day's, like life's, November. Like the infinite moment of "By the Fire-side," the great moments of revelation in *Sordello* and "Childe Roland to the Dark Tower Came" take place at sunset. The temporal setting of all three poems may have more to do with *Julian and Maddalo* (a text of special importance to Browning) than with a mellowing of the apocalyptic dawn of *Prometheus.* Cf. *Julian and Maddalo,* ll. 120-140. That poem's bell tower beheld in sunset may have been no less important to "By the Fire-side" than to "Childe Roland."

"By its side" means, primarily, "in comparison with it"; but the phrase captures too the remarkable geography of the soul in a poem which maps both the copresence of past and future and the copresence, side by side, of lovers forever denying from each other the sorry solipsism of exclusive visionary ambition.

Since there are no definitive verbal echoes of *Prometheus Unbound* in "By the Fire-side," no objective evidence internal or external to connect the two poems, the supposition that Shelley's poem is Browning's precursor text must rest on our sense that the awakening of love, the politics of visionary power, and the transposition into a visionary landscape of the concepts before and after, higher and lower, are central concerns which could have directed Browning back to Shelley's magnificent example. Even the remarkable urbanity of "By the Fire-side" (the studied casualness of lines like "And the whole is well worth thinking o'er / When autumn comes") Browning could have learned from *Prometheus Unbound.* It is not a text he met in his first encounter with Shelley (the 1826 edition of the lyrics), but he undoubtedly procured the text shortly thereafter and was involved with it by the time of *Pauline,* first published in 1833.

We must, however, be careful not to turn Shelley's poem into a source or quarry for the later poet seeking to load every rift of his own ore with the gold of the past. Though Shelley's influence on Browning is indisputable, the concentration on *Prometheus* Act II in this essay must ultimately be termed heuristic rather than inevitable. This is not to say that there are any number of poems which could serve equally well, but rather that the confluence of visionary concerns in *Prometheus Unbound* is fortuitous, whether for Browning or for us, and that if Browning had not or did not find such a text he would have had to invent one, compounding his precursor from elements of the subjective, ambitious style he found in the Romantic tradition generally and Shelley in particular. Whether or not we can point a finger at a single poem and say, "This, this surely is the text in antithetical relation to which our poet came into his own," the figures (both poetic egos and particular figures of speech) with which a poet counters the figures that seem to hover over him are chosen, not inevitable. When Asia sings that the Voice in the Air "doth like an angel sit / Beside a helm," conducting the enchanted boat of her own soul, or when the *Pauline* poet imagines "a very angel, coming not / In fitful vision but beside me ever," they invent more than they conjure the rhetorical figures that allow for the fiction of company on a level with them. In "By the Fire-side" Browning may even have turned specifically against *Alastor* and "Hymn to Intellectual Beauty" in rejecting fitful vision and insisting on the lingering presence of a Form of Love by his side; but it is *Browning's* turn against what he himself chose to regard as the given: the Shelleyan fitful vision, beautiful but evanescent. Perhaps the choice of a specific precursor text not only cannot be a matter of objective fact but must not be so lest the poet's attempt to extend the dark side of his soul and our attempt to track him there prove no acts of imagination but what Coleridge termed fancy: playing with fixities and definites.

If the reach of the subjective poet exceeds his grasp of the visionary form above him, then criticism must follow with similar ambition. It may be that there never is such a thing as a precursor text, that the subjective poet and the critic who would follow him always project figures that may bear some resemblance to this or that poet, but who must remain reimagined or composite rather than real. Though the choice of a specific precursor text may prove somewhat arbitrary, there is nothing arbitrary about privileging a quarrel with a precursor as the repressed but ever-pressing business of the subjective poet. We can best approach his dark side by seeking to discern the nature of the conflict with the giant he is forever "going in the dark / To fight."

The Inside of Time: An Essay on the Dramatic Monologue

by Loy D. Martin

Victorian poets employ far more non-stative verbs than Romantic poets do.[1] Such small semantic and syntactic regularities characteristic of a writer's culture can bear an important relation to spectacular discontinuities in literary history like the invention of new genres or the radical revision of old ones.[2] In the following discussion, I want to show how the interaction between language and literary form can be traced in a particular case: Browning's dramatic monologue. Rather than proposing a complete definition of the monologue, I shall largely confine my discussion to the ways in which Browning's language and his poems locate literary discourse within spatial and temporal continuities. These techniques imply important epistemological and moral functions for both text and spoken discourse.

To begin with the historically rather simple matter of verb stativity, the following can provide an explanation of how to tell the difference between stative and non-stative verbs:

> With a state, unless something happens to change that state, then the state will continue: this applies equally to standing and

"The Inside of Time: An Essay on the Dramatic Monologue" by Loy D. Martin. This article appears for the first time in this volume.

[1] About 55% more in four thousand word samples taken from the poems of Wordsworth, Byron, Shelley, Browning and Tennyson.
[2] I have tried to explain this theoretical statement in "Literary Invention: The Illusion of the Individual Talent," forthcoming in *Critical Inquiry*.

to knowing. With a dynamic situation, on the other hand, the situation will only continue if it is continually subject to a new input of energy.[3]

A poet or speaker who is chiefly interested in using speech to articulate temporal change might tend to favor non-stative verbs over stative verbs. A syntax rich in non-stative predication is, in a sense, already dramatic in structure, marking continual shifts in the "input" and maintenance of energies in dynamic situations. But this already begins to be a dangerous kind of statement. It seems to be saying that a preference for non-stative verbs has direct implications at the level of complex discourse or even literary genre. This would be inappropriately metaphoric reasoning, since the relative frequency of non-stative verbs might potentially be explained in terms of several different syntactic norms, and these different norms would, in turn, place different constraints on the organization of discursive or literary conventions. In other words, a single stylistic trait might lead us along many different syntactic "networks" toward many different discursive types. This means that a method of inquiry in which one merely collects an assortment of such traits and assigns them common conceptual implications can be misleading as an attempt to find the linguistic constituents of a literary type. In order to describe the linguistic constraints on a writer's shaping of genres, we need to develop a logic whereby traits at lower levels of complexity limit or interact with particular modes of organization at *successively* higher levels until sentence structures and rhetorical structures combine to give discourses of recognizable types.

The procedure here will be first to investigate which kinds of syntactic norms are associated with non-stative clauses in Browning's idiom. This will involve a look at verb aspect and methods of adverbial modification which are related to aspectual distinctions. At that point, a few preliminary connections with the dramatic monologue will be possible, and these will be expanded in a discussion of deixis. As the stylistic net widens to include characteristic strategies of syntactic elabora-

[3]Bernard Comrie, *Aspect* (Cambridge, England, 1976), p. 49.

tion in Browning's sentences, I shall examine one poem at length and try to show how understanding the linguistic basis of the genre can affect interpretation.[4]

The first thing we can say about non-stative predicates in Browning is that they often express what linguists call "proximity time relations."[5] As we shall see, this can be done in several ways, but one of the most important, and the most subtle, is through progressive aspect in the verb. When a non-stative verb is made progressive (*be* + *verb* + *ing*) its action is not a whole; it is incomplete, and it is viewed from inside the time sequence in which it occurs. A sentence like "Robert was writing a poem" tells us that, at a particular time, an action was in process, but it implies a temporal extension beyond the verb's "moment" in which the beginning and the ending of the act presumably take place. By contrast, for a verb with "perfective" aspect ("Robert wrote a poem"), the moment of the verb and the moment of the action are identical and refer to no condition of temporal proximity.

Progressive forms of verbs can create the effect of proximity time relations in positions other than that of the main verb. The most common example is the participial adverb, as in the following passage from Browning's "How It Strikes a Contemporary":

> He walked and tapped the pavement with his cane,
> Scenting the world, looking it full in face,

Though the two main verbs, "walked" and "tapped," carry perfective aspect, the modifying adverbial phrases are transformations of two sentences containing verbs of progressive aspect: "He was scenting the world" and "He was looking it full in face." These embedded progressives modify the main verbs precisely by placing them within a dynamic situation of unbounded continuous duration and thus function in the same

---

[4]To a degree, starting with the non-stative verb is arbitrary. Other relatively high frequency elements, such as definite determiners, might serve equally well as initial access to the same syntactic "track." Neither does this study claim to be exhaustive; any number of other sets of features may also contribute to the monologue's characteristic shape.

[5]Marmo Soemarmo, "The Semantics of Proximity Time Relations," *Foundations of Language*, 14 (1976); 359.

way as temporal adverbs which signify proximity time relations directly:

> But do not let us quarrel *any more*.

The progressive, as Bernard Comrie suggests, "looks at the situation from inside, and as such is crucially concerned with the internal structure of the situation, since it can both look backwards towards the start of the situation, and look forwards to the end of the situation. ..."[6] Andrea del Sarto, as he begins his monologue, is inside the situation, he looks backward to a time when quarreling began, and he pleads for a future time when the process will end; the situation's "internal structure" is his entire concern. And yet the verb, taken by itself, is perfective in aspect. From this and similar examples, I conclude that we need to recognize as related a number of predicate forms which signify *indefinitely bounded dynamic processes viewed from within.*[7]

I shall be discussing the three which seem to me the most frequent and the least ambiguous in Victorian poetic language:

1. adverbial phrases signifying temporal proximity
2. present participles of non-stative verbs used as adverbs
3. verbs of progressive aspect

To speak of frequency is to invoke statistics, and this essay is not the occasion for detailed statistical analysis. Still, it is worth mentioning that, in counts of the total devices in the three listed categories, Victorian poets were found to employ these predicate forms from two to four times more frequently than the Romantic poets I examined. This result held true not only for samples of poetic language but for samples taken from the poets' correspondence as well, suggesting that a period shift in linguistic habit has occurred rather than an accommodation of normal speech patterns to specialized poetic needs.

What then do these regularities imply in terms of poetic style? By way of showing their relation to more familiar aspects of Browning's verbal strategy, I should like to call attention to the opening passages of "Fra Lippo Lippi." The initial relation-

---

[6]Comrie, *Aspect,* pp. 3-4.
[7]See J. J. Katz, *Semantic Theory* (New York, 1972), ch. 7.

ship between Lippo and the magistrate who apprehends him in the street is based on the executive power of the latter. Lippo is in trouble, and his immediate need is to interrupt the exercise of the magistrate's power. This he does by invoking a social context in which the asymmetry is reversed:

> Aha, you know your betters! Then, you'll take
> Your hand away that's fiddling on my throat,
> And please to know me likewise. Who am I?
> Why, one, sir, who is lodging with a friend
> Three streets off—he's a certain...how d'ye call?
> Master—a...Cosimo of the Medici.

Instead of only one power relationship (officer/miscreant), there is now also a second, inverted relationship (patron's favorite/public servant) which exists simultaneously and functions to prevent temporarily the consequences of the magistrate's initial advantage. Lippo accomplishes this correction of the power imbalance by placing himself and his captor syntactically in parallel: the noun phrases, *your hand* (metonymically representing the magistrate) and *one* (pronominally representing Lippo) are modified by relative clauses of similar structure. The similarity of these clauses derives chiefly from the fact that both verbs are non-stative and carry progressive aspect *(is fiddling/is lodging).* Linguistically, Lippo characterizes both himself and his captors according to the "internal structure" of an open-ended situation. For Lippo, the doubtful sequel of the unfinished action could be disastrous, and he wishes to influence that outcome by suggesting that the sequel might as easily be disastrous for the magistrate. The present moment for both antagonists is, in other words, rendered fragmentary and uncertain by verb phrases which adopt an interior, or progressive, perspective on incomplete action.

Lippo's stratagem works, but he knows his victory is only temporary. Freeing himself from that "gullet's gripe" is not the same as exonerating himself or avoiding the consequences of arrest. He must do more than instill a prudent caution in his captors; he must gain their sympathy. Hence, he attempts to transform the two offsetting power asymmetries into a single symmetrical solidarity relationship (comrade/comrade):

Tell you, I liked your looks at very first.
Let's sit and set things straight now, hip to haunch.
Here's spring come, and the nights one makes up bands
To roam the town and sing out carnival,
And I've been three weeks shut within my mew,
A-painting for the great man, saints and saints
And saints again. I could not paint all night—

Lippo's invitation to the magistrate to share vicariously in his
experience depends on several of the syntactic features that
relate to progressive aspect in their interiorizing effect. In the
first two lines quoted, for example, the temporal adverbials,
at very first and *now,* connect the present with a specific beginning in terms of the comradely feeling that Lippo wishes to
instill in his listener. Lippo would pretend that the discontinuity between a relationship based on power and one based
on solidarity has been misleading, that he has entertained
"solidarity feelings" for the magistrate throughout the duration of their acquaintance. The second two lines establish a
public temporal context—night time in the spring—within
which the magistrate can sympathize with a monk's dilemma.
Moreover, what the magistrate is invited to feel vicariously is
tedium, the passage of three weeks with only the repeated
painting of "saints and saints / And saints again" for occupa-
tion. Here again, the projection of an interior temporal con-
tour into Lippo's experience is achieved through the adverbials, *three weeks* and *all night,* along with the crucial
phrase, "A-painting for the great man, saints and saints / And
saints again." The importance of this phrase is both semantic
and syntactic. First, Lippo has transformed "the great man,"
his patron, from an ally in the power relationship to a mild
adversary viewed from within the new solidarity relationship.
And the rhetorical basis for this shift is his implicit request
that the magistrate identify with him in his private trials. This
means imagining what it would be like to sit in a room painting
for three weeks with no apparent end of the situation in sight.
This is, of course, the approach to non-stative "situation"
characteristic of syntactic progressivity, and the participial
phrase which identifies painting as Lippo's activity is accordingly a transformation of the sentence, "I *have been paint-*

ing saints and saints and saints again." To put the matter succinctly, the rhetorical shift from the expression of two public power relationships to the expression of one private solidarity relationship is marked, syntactically, by the replacement of two parallel progressive time sequences with one such sequence which is imaginatively shared by the poem's speaker and implied listener.

There is one more important point to be made about these two passages. My entire analysis implicitly suggests a distinction between conscious rhetorical artifice, responding to the demands of the immediate fictional moment, and linguistic habits, re-enactments of patterns found throughout Browning's writing. Thus, the *parallelism* of the two clauses, *that's fiddling* and *who is lodging,* serves a local rhetorical purpose; but the constitution of the two clauses, the fact that both of their verbs have taken progressive aspect, is part of a wider-ranging pattern of phrase structures and cannot be explained as a response to an individual situation. It is possible, however, to make this distinction too sharply. The syntactic manners that create the poem's time scheme as an open-ended process do, in fact, cluster; they are to some degree responsive to situation. But they are responsibe to many situations in these poems, so many that it becomes extremely doubtful whether the situation requires the expression or the expression has selected what kinds of situation the form can treat.

This question, then, raises directly the question of how linguistic habit can be related to literary genre. The dramatic monologue, in one of its principal functions, creates a poetic moment of a certain duration which is viewed internally and which is contiguous with an implied extra-textural past and future of indefinite extent. The "present" of the dramatic monologue is thus implicitly one open-ended fragment in a succession of fragments which do not, even projectively, add up to a bounded whole. To adopt an immediately relevant linguistic analogy, Browning, by inventing the dramatic monologue, discovered an inclusive form for the manifestation of imperfectivity. It is not just a few verbs but whole poems which we may assign something like "progressive aspect."

When we speak of a poem as a "fragment," we are largely making an inference from the way it either begins or ends, or both. Thus, it is not surprising that, when we examine the opening lines of several of the monologues in *Men and Women,* we find characteristic modes of verb modification, along with other syntactic traits, signifying an immediately contiguous past of which the poem's moment grows. The first two lines of "Andrea del Sarto" supply an apt example:

> But do not let us quarrel any more,
> No, my Lucrezia; bear with me for once.

The two temporal adverbials, "any more" and "for once," refer to a situation preceding the moment of utterance. Moreover, the relation between that relevant past and the linguistic present is one of unbroken continuity. Quarreling is an ongoing process, albeit non-stative since it requires continuous new inputs of energy. Browning indicates this *experiential* continuity by implying a *linguistic* continuity: a first clause preceding the poem and linked to it by the coordinating conjunction, "But." This reference back to an actual line of discourse is just one method Browning uses to begin monologues in the midst of an unbroken time stream, but even this limited technique takes several forms. The speaker of "A Light Woman" reveals a story already in progress when he begins *"So far as our story approaches the end,* / Which do you pity the most of us three?" In another variation, the speaker may begin by referring to someone else's discourse in the third person: "My first thought was, he lied in every word. ..." In this example, from "Childe Roland to the Dark Tower Came," the contradiction between the initiatory boundary of the poem and the absence of a coinciding boundary to the ostensible experience has been focused in the adjective, "first." Roland's "first" thought is indeed the first of the poem, but syntagmatically, the sentence seems to be an incomplete portion of the pattern, "My first thought after he said X and Y," where X has been omitted or deferred in the text of the poem itself.

Reference to an immediate linguistic past is not the only way Browning's initiatory devices create their characteristic effects. When Fra Lippo Lippi exclaims, "You need not clap your torches to my face," he refers to an action which has presumably already taken place. Other speakers refer to extratextual knowledge, using temporal adverbs to locate that knowledge in time relative to the utterance: "I said—Then, dearest, since 'tis so, / Since *now* at length my fate I know..." ("The Last Ride Together"). Bishop Blougram's well-known "No more wine?" questions an interlocutor about a decision already expressed and also, in an important corollary to the typical pattern, looks forward with uncertainty to the immediate future. Many of these devices function this way, raising questions as much about possible succeeding events as about past ones. Thus, "In Three Days" begins with the coordinating conjunction, which suggests unbroken discourse prior to the poem's present, but it rapidly shifts to the future tense for the verb, which is, as usual, modified by a temporal adverbial phrase:

So, I shall see her *in three days...*"

Browning has many incidental ways of indicating a relevant continuous past as well as a relevant future. But somehow these local devices, however they differ, seem to be built out of remarkably regular habits of verb modification:

> Said Abner, "*At last* thou art come! *Ere* I tell, *ere* thou speak, Kill my cheek, wish me well!"
>
> ("Saul")

> They give thy letter to me, *even now:*
> I read and seem as if I heard thee speak.
> The master of thy galley *still* unlades
> Gift after gift; they block my court *at last*
> And pile themselves along its portico
>
> ("Cleon")

> Stand still, true poet that you are!
> I know you; let me try and draw you.
> *Some night* you'll fail us. ...
>
> ("Popularity")

> I wonder do you feel *to-day*
> As I have felt. ...
>
> ("Two in the Campagna")

Let us *begin* and carry up this corpse,
   Singing together.
   ("A Grammarian's Funeral")

Stop playing, poet! May a brother speak?
("Transcendentalism: A Poem in Twelve Books")

These passages illustrate very clearly how the dramatic monologue's meaning, its very quality of being "dramatic," depends
in case after case on syntactic structures which approximate
non-stative imperfectivity of aspect. Nevertheless, even syntactically, the entire burden of generating indefinitely extensive temporal continuities is not carried by verbs and their
modifiers. In the example from "A Grammarian's Funeral,"
I have emphasized "begin." If true monologues present a poetic
beginning which is not an experiential beginning, a poem that
"begins" with the clause "Let us begin" would seem to fall outside the genre. But this is not the case with "A Grammarian's
Funeral." Its beginning is, in fact, a continuation, and we know
this because the object of the verb "carry" is "this corpse."
Though the act of carrying may be only about to commence, a
situation predates it in which a corpse—*some* corpse—exists.

   Here we must take a hard look at deixis and at definite determiners as they appear in Browning's idiom. The accepted
classification of determiners has been usefully summarized by
Elizabeth Traugott as follows:

> *The* and *a* are usually called the "definite" and the "indefinite"
> article, respectively. Their prime function is to signal what as-
> sumptions the speaker is making about what knowledge is com-
> mon to him and the [listener].... *The* assumes the noun has
> been referred to before, or is what is loosely called "given,
> known material."[8]

The definite article, in other words, implies a time previous to
the utterance which is epistemologically shared by the sender
and the receiver of the linguistic message. Deictics such as
"this" function in part to give a spatial dimension to a "world"
which is experientially prior to the utterance and continuous

[8]Elizabeth Closs Traugott, *A History of English Syntax* (New York, 1972),
pp. 40-41.

with it temporally. Thus, when we read "Let us begin and carry up *this* corpse," we immediately wonder "what corpse?" And the effect is fundamentally different from that of a discourse which commences "Let us begin and offer up *a* prayer."

Not all definite determiners imply a shared past knowledge or experience; or, if they do, the sharing is so general that no specific time sequence is designated. Examples are "The Weather is nice here" or "The moon is full," in which no corresponding indefinite forms ("a weather" or "a moon") exist. In such cases as these, the quality of "before mentionedness" is missing; the determiners do not have what linguists call "anaphoric" function. Anaphora is repetition, but in the poetry of writers like Browning and Tennyson, the linguistic sense of *implied* repetition is most often the appropriate one. When we speak of actual repetition, we are speaking of what Paul Ricoeur calls the "self-referential feature of language" in a special way.[9] For a word or a phrase to be recognized as a "repetition," it must bear a special relation to a previous word or phrase; it must "refer backwards" in the semiotic chain. Some syntactic devices, like anaphoric determiners, have the *force* of repetitional self-reference in the absence of actual repetition: the inevitable question, "What corpse?" is a phonomenological marker of this kind of arrest; it is a search for the repetition. Once we have seen that implied repetition and implied reference can be equated, it is easy to extend the analysis of linguistic self-reference to what Ricoeur calls "ostensive reference," reference to a non-linguistic "world" shared by a speaker and his implied listener. Reference to a previous word and reference to a pre-existing object in the material world are, formally speaking, identical acts of diachronic "arrest," and this is why anaphoric determiners and deictics need to be classified together, along with several other syntactic markers of reference.

In several places the implications of this kind of reference through deictics and determiners are especially important for Browning's style. Here, for example, is Cleon:

[9] See Paul Ricoeur, "The Model of the Text: Meaningful Action Considered as a Text," *New Literary History*, 5 (1973): 91-120; or "Metaphor and the Main Problem of Hermeneutics," *NLH*, 6 (1974); 95-110.

It is as thou hast heard: in one short life
I, Cleon, have effected all *those* things
Thou wonderingly dost enumerate.
That epos on thy hundred plates of gold
Is mine,—and also mine *the* little chant,
So sure to rise from every fishing-bark
When lights at prow, the seamen haul their net.
The image of the sun-god on *the* phare,
Men turn from the sun's self to see, is mine;
The Poecile, o'er-storied its whole length,
As thou didst hear, with painting, is mine too.

The reason this poem makes the diachronic element of Browning's mode of reference so clear is that Cleon is openly responding to a pre-existing text, Protus's letter, and the rumors that it, in turn, apparently refers to. The phrases, "as thou hast heard" and "As thou didst hear" frame a catalogue in which the deictic "That epos...") and the definite article ("the little chant") are interchangeable. Both refer in the same way to that which has been previously mentioned or previously known by both communicants. This effect also serves to explain in part a feature of Browning's style which has always fascinated his readers, the use of extraordinarily arcane diction, especially in the category of nouns. The questions, "What is a phare?" or "What is a Poecile?" are similar to "What corpse?" They imply a context of reference or earlier discourse shared by the sender and receiver of the message but not necessarily by the eavesdropper (reader). Thus, again, Browning implies a particular time sequence, previously in progress, which the speaker of the monologue experiences and expresses from within.

Readers often experience this aspect of style as a kind of familiarity with physical surroundings shared by a speaker and his implied interlocutor. Andrea del Sarto's musings to his wife provide a typical example:

My youth, my hope, my art, being all toned down
To *yonder* sober pleasant Fiesole.
There's *the* bell clinking from *the* chapel-top;

That length of convent-wall across *the* way
Holds *the* trees safer, huddled more inside;
The last monk leaves *the* garden. . . .

The passage is one of gesture toward an ostensive world, a world which has long been the context for the quarreling between Andrea and Lucrezia. Even this somewhat static scenery makes its contribution to the implied repetitions of Andrea's life. The time is evening, and this evening is like others with its clinking chapel bell and the monks leaving the garden at their regular time. These are not surprising observations, but what so often eludes us is the fragility of the syntactic patterns on which they depend. Merely change the determiners, say, "There's *a* bell clinking from *a* chapel-top," and all of the prior familiarity with the surroundings which the painter and his wife share is lost. The line as it stands in the poem entails in its syntax a relevant past; the altered version presents a new moment, an independent observation, a surprise.

So far, I have concentrated on regularities of clause and phrase structure, regularities which lie still at a distance from the complexities of whole discourses. In this final section, I shall argue that, in complex sentence strategies, the dramatic monologue typically makes use of an equally distinct mode of relating clauses to one another. In doing so, I intend to fill in a chain of logic which links stylistic features at successive levels of organization, the final stage being that of discourse itself. Since we classify discourse in literary genres, my aim is to show that classes of discourse imply classes of lower-order features in a poet's language. Let us proceed then by observing how the habits I have already described introduce the general poetic strategy of a classic dramatic monologue, "My Last Duchess."

The larger movement of "My Last Duchess" is a sequential and fragmentary revelation of character. In the first twenty lines, Browning offers information concerning the Duke, his interlocutor, Fra Pandolf and the Duchess' portrait in an alternating pattern of suggestive but incomplete references:

That's my last Duchess painted on the wall,
Looking as if she were alive. I call

That piece a wonder, now: Fra Pandolf's hands
Worked busily a day, and there she stands.
Will't please you sit and look at her? I said
"Fra Pandolf" by design, for never read
Strangers like you that pictured countenance,
The depth and passion of its earnest glance,
But to myself they turned (since none puts by
The curtain I have drawn for you, but I)
And seemed as they would ask me, if they durst,
How such a glance came there; so, not the first
Are you to turn and ask thus. Sir, 'twas not
Her husband's presence only, called that spot
Of joy into the Duchess' cheek: perhaps
Fra Pandolf chanced to say "Her mantle laps
Over my lady's wrist too much," or "Paint
Must never hope to reproduce the faint
Half-flush that dies along her throat": such stuff
Was courtesy, she thought, and cause enough
For calling up that spot of joy.

The first two and a half lines concentrate some of the devices
typically used by Browning to initiate monologues. The definite article and the two deictics ("that") create at the outset the
illusion of a conversation already in progress. This implication of an immediate "dramatic" past relevant to the poem's
moment is joined by reference to a more distant "narrative"
past. This second past appears through the adjective, *last,* and
is confirmed in the phrase, "looking as if she were alive,"
which implies that, though the Duchess was once alive, she is
not now. Finally, by using the temporal advert, *now,* the Duke
suggests a past time, *then,* at which he did not esteem the painting (or the Duchess) so highly. The sentence structure of the
opening lines gestures, then, toward the past, but it tells us very
little about that past. From an affective point of view, one important result of the formal features which characterize so many
of Browning's beginnings is to raise questions: "What corpse?"
"What cripple?" "What Duchess?"

The technique of provoking unanswered questions, delaying
the useful information that answers them as long as possible
and then, while supplying that information, raising new questions to start the process all over again, constitutes one of the

central rhetorical strategies of the dramatic monologue. The Duchess' portrait is said to be successful because it captures her passion—this we learn in line 8. Not until lines 14-15 does the Duke specify that passion as "joy," and finally, in lines 20-21, we discover that he considers her joy indiscriminate and too easily stimulated. In similar fashion, the Duke's visitor is told in lines 3-4 that Fra Pandolf painted the Duchess' portrait in a day, creating a vague suggestion of haste and carelessness. Despite the assertion that Fra Pandolf was mentioned "by design," however, it is not until lines 20-21 that the issue of the painter's superficiality is taken up again to explain that he has been the Duchess' flatterer. Thus, at all times, the poem offers an incomplete account of situation and character, along with the expectation of subsequent filling in.

This poetic strategy of delay is created and explored in part through the conscious arrangement of content and in part through sentence structure. The first four sentences of "My Last Duchess" consist mostly of simple free clauses establishing the initial series of unanswered questions about the past. As soon as the Duke begins explaining himself, however, simple sentences are abandoned in favor of a complex structure which J. McH. Sinclair calls "arrest." This is a term that "indicate[s] a sentence in which the onset of a predictable a (free clause) is delayed or in which its progress is interrupted."[10] Delays appear within delays, and this is why, by the time Browning's speaker has answered one of the questions he has raised, he has already raised new ones in profusion. We finally discover that the Duke counts Fra Pandolf among the Duchess' flatterers, but not until he has ambiguously referred to other visitors like the present one, hinted at his obsession with his own domestic power and suggested that the appropriate attitude for others within his household is one of intimidated deference. Finally, he renews the question of the Duchess' passions and responses, prolonging the reader's curiosity about his own fixation on that "spot of joy." Once again, this is a strategy identifiable with the diachronic structure of the poem—it creates a suspense relevant to the later revelations of murder and the Duke's

[10]"Taking a Poem to Pieces," in *Linguistics and Literary Style*, ed. Donald C. Freedman (New York, 1970), pp. 129-42.

intention to remarry—but, as in the case of the various initiating devices, the vehicle is a syntactic habit which is not specific to poetry. If this point remains in doubt, we need only consult the prose of Browning's letters:

> If I had felt, as you pleased to feel yesterday, that it had been "only one hour" which my coming gained—I should richly deserve to find out to-day, as I do fully, what the precise value of such an hour is.[11]

This is the beginning of a letter to Elizabeth Barrett. The sentence contains only a single free clause ("I should richly deserve..."). That clause is embedded in and completed by a virtual shower of bound clauses, and both the initial bound clause and the main free clause are arrested by secondary bound clauses ("as you pleased to feel yesterday" and "as I do fully"). Moreover, the letter begins with an unprepared reference to the past through temporal adverbs, *yesterday* and *today*. Thus, in the modes of both initiating and perpetuating discourse, Browning's non-poetic language corresponds closely to the language of his poetry. Through the same syntactic habits, he implies in both instances that the linguistic present is incomplete, part of a chain of signification that is always in touch with its past and always determining the shape that its future must take.

I have said that "My Last Duchess" instantiates a temporal fragment, but, to this point, I have only stressed the poem's connection with an implied past. Just as the opening lines stimulated questions about the past, however, the closing passages project our attention into the immediate future beyond the termination of the poem itself:

> Will't please you rise? We'll meet
> The company below, then. I repeat,
> The Count your master's known munificence
> Is ample warrant that no just pretence
> Of mine for dowry will be disallowed;
> Though his fair daughter's self, as I avowed
> At starting, is my object.

[11] *The Letters of Robert Browning and Elizabeth Barrett Browning, 1845-1846*, ed. Elvan Kintner (Cambridge, Mass., 1969), p. 932.

This is the first we know of the company below, the Count, his daughter, and the Duke's intention to remarry. All of these elements are new pieces of the past, but they are pieces of the future as well. Only here do we perceive what a small and unboundaried moment this "present" encounter has been. Twice the Duke refers to statements he has made in a past beyond the limits of the poem ("I repeat" and "as I avowed / At starting"). And both statements concern an arrangement which is just beginning and which is fraught with sinister uncertainty. Browning, then, exploits language as a temporal medium in two ways. First, he heightens our awareness that character can be known only as process and, therefore, only incompletely at any given time. And, secondly, he implies that the present is a function of both the past and the future, having no completeness or coherence independent of its place in an unfolding continuity. To return to our earlier metaphor, if a whole poem could be said to have the force of progressive aspect, "My Last Duchess" is that poem.

I think it is worth asking what bearing this view of the poem has on the traditional problems critics have encountered in interpreting it. Let us look for a moment at the last four lines. The movement away from the gallery has begun when the Duke makes a last gesture toward his collection and, almost incidentally, toward the past:

> Nay, we'll go
> Together down, sir. Notice Neptune, though,
> Taming a sea-horse, thought a rarity,
> Which Claus of Innsbruck cast in bronze for me!

This is the second work of art mentioned in the poem, the first being the Duchess' portrait. Both are objects, standing unchanged amid the flurry of life around them. Indeed, by their nature, they are incapable of embodying process. Time is the condition of their creation—Fra Pandolf "worked busily a day" to produce his picture—but the painter knows that his finished work will be a dead and static thing:

> Paint
> Must never hope to reproduce the faint
> Half-flush that dies along her throat:

The color of living flesh, to Fra Pandolf's eye, is a function of movement, but, just as Claŭs of Innsbruck cannot reproduce the interiorly experienced process implicit in the progressive clause, "[who *is*] *taming* a sea-horse," paint cannot take on life. The same is not entirely true for art which is composed in language. Language offers devices like progressive aspect *(is taming)* and temporal adverbs (worked busily *a day;* avowed *at starting*) which recall to mind the reality of temporal displacement. Poetry, for Browning, strives to manifest, however incompletely, the flux of life, a principle overtly recognized as early as the preface to *Paracelsus.* There he tells his readers that

> instead of having recourse to an external machinery of incidents to create and evolve the crisis I desire to produce, I have ventured to display somewhat minutely the mood itself *in its rise and progress.* ....[12] [Emphasis mine]

This distinction, between a verbal art which can "display" life in its "rise and progress" and a plastic art which cannot "catch" that flux, is crucial, I think, to the ironic strategy of "My Last Duchess."

Whereas Browning perceives an antithesis between plastic art and life itself, the Duke of Ferrara projects an analogy. He considers works of art as discrete static objects to be owned and controlled, and, as many readers have noticed, he thinks of persons in precisely the same way. In the opening lines of the poem, no distinction is made between the Duchess and her portrait; "she" stands before the visitor, looking to the Duke as alive as she ever looked. And when he hints that his appraisal has undergone change, "that piece" could as easily refer to the Duchess herself as to her picture. Finally, the fact that he understands people as objects becomes explicit when he amends his concern for the size of his next wife's dowry:

> Though his fair daughter's self, as I avowed
> At starting, is my object.

People, of course, will never be very satisfactory as objects as long as they remain alive; they will embody all the flux and the

[12]*The Complete Works of Robert Browning,* vol. 1, ed. Roma A. King et al. (Athens, Ohio, 1969), p. 65.

inconsistencies which characterized life in time as Browning understands it. Hence, the traits which "disgust" the Duke are summarized by a verb of process, "This grew," and his remedy is murder, the stilling of the vital instability of casual, social existence:

> I gave commands
> Then all smiles stopped together. There she stands
> As if alive.

Here the force of repetition illuminates in retrospect the opening lines. The Duchess stands as if alive, not in Browning's sense of life, but as the Duke would have human life exist in an art gallery of a world owned and controlled by himself. Fra Pandolf knows that this attitude demeans the living. To him, even dying is a living process, one which the Duke falsifies and turns into crime with his peremptory "commands."

Many critics, even those who disagree with one another, have argued that no moral judgment inheres in the structure of the poem itself. William Cadbury believes the Duke to be an ogre and contends that Browning created him "to prove a point of his own which we learn by applying the standards of an external morality."[13] Others, like Robert Langbaum, dissent, maintaining "that moral judgment does not figure importantly in our response to the duke, that we even identify ourselves with him."[14] In either case, "judgment" is something which exists only outside the poem, and the decision to apply it or not to apply it tends to be a matter of choice for the reader. But the structure of the poem seems to me to entail a serious judgment of character while simultaneously requiring our partial "sympathy" with the Duke as a ratification of that judgment. For we are allowed to see the Duke as he is incapable of seeing his fellow creatures: not as an embodiment of a changeless abstraction (his "nine-hundred-year-old name") but as a living, changing, hesitating human being who is finally knowable only in process and only in a fragmentary way. His fixed vision of his Duchesses, past and future, belies the reality of his own existence, so that the final irony of the poem consists in the fact

[13] "Lyric and Anti-Lyric Forms: A Method For Judging Browning," in *Browning's Mind and Art*, ed. Clarence Tracy (London, 1968), p. 41.

[14] Robert Langbaum, *The Poetry of Experience* (New York, 1957), p. 82.

that his misconception of those around him implies a misconception of the very self he worships. And the triumph of
Browning's poem lies in the way it prevents its reader from
repeating the Duke's error. Both we and the Duke find a vision
of life in a work of art; we as easily as he might say "there *he*
stands as if alive." But the meaning would be different. Browning has "made us see," as he was fond of saying the poet can do,
and what we "see" is life process, while the Duke in his gallery
can see only the motionless dead.

Perhaps more than any other literary type, the dramatic
monologue presents speech as action. But to be accurate, we
must distinguish between action and act. The monologue is
never a speech *act,* whole and complete. It is a fragment of the
kind of movement in human time that Walter Pater describes
so well in "Conclusion" to *The Renaissance.* "That clear,
perpetual outline of face and limb," he says, "is but an image
of ours...a design in a web, the actual threads of which pass
out beyond it."[15] The dramatic monologue, while presenting
a "clear...image," continually attempts to suggest the presence of those "actual threads" as they extend out beyond the
image in both time and space. To become a poet is to adopt
norms of poetry—conventions and genres—from past writers
whose language is that of cultural eras different from one's
own. The result is often an inappropriate matching of linguistic patterns, which the poet has little freedom to change,
and poetic or discursive patterns which he is much freer to
revise. The resolution of this basic tension is what we generally
call innovation or poetic invention. The dramatic monologue
is surely such an invention. If we accept the premise that the
syntactic patterns I have described represent a level of organization beyond conscious choice and manipulation, I think
we cannot avoid the conclusion that the literary form Browning
developed is an adequation of the aims of poetry to the demands first of language and finally, through language, of the
Victorian community itself.

---

[15]Walter Pater, *The Renaissance,* library ed. (London, 1914), p. 234.

Browning's "Modernity":
The Ring and The Book, and Relativism

by John Killham

Nowadays one comes across from time to time the suggestion that the reason Browning composed *The Ring and the Book* in the way he did, as an immense babble of voices endlessly discussing and pleading the rights and wrongs of a husband's killing his wife, is that he was bent on showing us that judgments of motives are hard to come at because the truth is never a simple thing. In this respect, it is said, he is at one with the leading novelists of our own time, who almost all accept in part the idea exemplified in the work of Henry James and Joseph Conrad, not to speak of Flaubert, that the reader of fiction should, in Pater's words, enjoy not "the fruit of experience," the author's express meaning, but "experience itself," leaving him to make his own construction of the facts and views put before him.

It is an attractive idea, if only because it makes it seem that the ambiguities of modern literature have anticipations in an eminent Victorian, and that the breach between his age and ours is not so wide as has been thought. To find that Browning may have been inclined to express the complex problems of behaviour in the modern world by elaborate poetical experiment akin to that seen in the twentieth century, does him good

"Browning's 'Modernity': *The Ring and the Book,* and Relativism" by John Killham from *The Major Victorian Poets: Reconsiderations,* edited by Isobel Armstrong and published by Routledge & Kegan Paul Ltd, London, 1969. © 1969 and reprinted here by permission of the publisher and the author.

and comforts us. We can believe that he yielded up the search for absolute truth, and invited us to see things as they are. His modernity lay in exposing men and women as weak and gullible, acting out the brutal farce of a life for which there can be no simple formula of right and wong. His end was to enable us to enter sympathetically into the human condition, to make us see and feel what it is like to look at things from a standpoint which the world at large is content to judge by imputation. Not only in *The Ring and the Book* but in many celebrated dramatic monologues, Browning suspends moral judgment in implying that circumstances alter cases. In a word, he is a relativist.

This idea, that *The Ring and the Book* and other poems show Browning to entertain a sort of relativism, can appeal not merely because it provides reason for viewing him as "modern": it may seem to put him in the forefront of those whose influence was to alter the intellectual climate of the nineteenth century. In 1866, when Browning was proudly telling his friends of the progress he had made in composing *The Ring and the Book*, Walter Pater, demonstrating Coleridge's by now old-fashioned struggle to apprehend the absolute, was defining the character of the time in terms of relativism.

> Modern thought is distinguished from ancient by its cultivation of the "relative" spirit in place of the "absolute." Ancient philosophy sought to arrest every object in an eternal outline, to fix thought in a necessary formula, and types of life in a classification by "kinds" or *genera*. To the modern spirit nothing is, or can be rightly known except relatively under conditions. An ancient philosopher indeed started a philosophy of the relative, but only as an enigma. So the germs of almost all philosophical ideas were enfolded in the mind of antiquity, and fecundated one by one in after ages by the external influences of art, religion, culture in the natural sciences, belonging to a particular generation, which suddenly becomes preoccupied by a formula or theory, not so much new as penetrated by a new meaning and expressiveness. So the idea of "the relative" has been fecundated in modern times by the influences of the sciences of observation. These sciences reveal types of life evanescing into each other by inexpressible refinements of change. Things pass into their opposites by accumulation of

undefinable quantities. The growth of those sciences consists in a continual analysis of facts of rough and general observation into groups of facts more precise and minute. A faculty for truth is a power of distinguishing and fixing delicate and fugitive details. The moral world is ever in contact with the physical; the relative spirit has invaded moral philosophy from the ground of the inductive science. There it has started a new analysis of the relations of body and mind, good and evil, freedom and necessity.[1]

Of course, the relative spirit has been abroad at all times, as Pater implies: that "Man is the measure of all things" is not a difficult idea for an independent mind to arrive at. Yet Wordsworth was far more typical of western thought when he wrote that poetry had as its object "truth, not individual and local, but general and operative; not standing upon external testimony, but carried alive into the heart by passion; truth which is its own testimony, which gives competence and confidence to the tribunal to which it appeals and receives them from the same tribunal." This utterance reflects in its very style the grandeur of the humanist claim for the spiritual unity of mankind. It is the culmination of a tradition reaching back through the Renaissance to the foundations of our civilization; it is closely associated with the so-called Romantic, but truly neo-Platonic, doctrine that the heart, or the innermost self, is at one with Nature's central law. That this confidence in the accessibility of absolute truth, embodied in the Christian religion, was undermined in the Victorian period by scientific discovery and German higher criticism is familiar to everyone. But *laissex faire* economic theory and industrialisation were perhaps even more immediately persuasive: the sharp divergence between rich and poor led to clear signs that men could be shaped by different and yet contiguous "cultures" into beings who might as well have been members of different species. Shelley's comment that the ultimate cause of this was "the unmitigated exercise of the calculating faculty" only expresses in psychological jargon the old recognition of the schismatic nature of man, virtuous heart pitted against cunning

[1]"Coleridge's Writings," in *English Critical Writings (Nineteenth Century)*, ed. Edmund D. Jones (1916), p. 493.

head. But Shelley saw clearly that in his lifetime the traditional arena in which "calculation" fought for its advantages,
namely in politics, was rapidly extending beyond politics to
cover the whole social life of the country as the old ties were
replaced by the cash nexus in a country undergoing rapid
industrialisation. Large numbers of people, herded in towns
and cities, were to be forced to become isolated, divorced from
community. The early Victorian intellectual thus had before
his eyes as a model to which all his speculations had to conform
the image of *all* men as in fact isolated, a conception that
Arnold movingly considers in his poems.

It is this that makes the difference between Wordsworth's and
Carlyle's estimate of the poet's role. Carlyle resembles Wordsworth in seeing poets able, through their innermost selves, to
perceive the secret operations of Nature, but the emphasis is
now more upon historical change than upon absolutes. Poets
have shown their genius in their sincerity, but this criterion is
a tacit admission that their beliefs are superseded. Dante and
Shakespeare express in their different ways the beliefs of the
middle ages, and for Carlyle these are not true, only valuable
insofar as they provide an outlet for religious feeling necessary for human fulfilment. It seems that Nature's operations
in time (history, that is) are inconstant, that change is the only
law. Indeed, Nature will destroy those who hold on to out-
moded beliefs; but Carlyle is not always clear over what he
takes Nature to be. Sometimes he resembles Wordsworth in
thinking of it as God: but he is also tempted by the Romantic
heresy, and is capable of writing that "The world of Nature,
for every man, is the Fantasy of himself: this world is the multi-
plex image of his own Dream."

Carlyle's case shows that a relativistic spirit was abroad in
nineteenth-century England some years before Pater wrote his
essay on Coleridge and Browning his vast poem. But it also
shows that relativism is not a simple conception. Carlyle, like
Mill, was indebted to Comte's theory of historical epochs, and
this carried with it the inescapable conclusion that history
caused institutions (and the beliefs on which they rested) to
suffer change, not regularly, but in a kind of systole and dia-
stole of the social organism. A similar idea underlies Matthew

Arnold's view of the post-Revolutionary period as an age of expansion, characterized by a renewal of social arrangements in the light of fresh thought. The relativism which grows out of this acceptance of historical change is of a social kind, that is, it is not primarily concerned with individual men and women in their personal distinctiveness but rather with the beliefs and attitudes which give society its form. Carlyle, Mill and Arnold are all possessed of a sense of this social relativism, a recognition that human institutions must be adapted to changing circumstances. It sees a sort of struggle on the part of human nature to adapt itself to a changed environment while preserving its sources of spiritual nourishment for the needs all men share.

This sort of relativism is not the same as the relativism announced by Pater as characteristic of modern thought. It is clear from what he wrote that his has its basis in science, not history, and in all likelihood owes much to Darwin. This relativism is not concerned with changing beliefs, attitudes and the like, issuing in *social* arrangements, but relates rather to the individual's personal apprehension of the world he inhabits.[2] It is intensely materialistic at bottom, and also tends to set the individual above, or in opposition to, society, which no longer appears to have so obvious a claim to the loyalty of beings whose lives are constituted out of experiences peculiar to them. The right of society to make laws and to judge and condemn in accordance with them may seem questionable. This sort of moral relativism stands in relation to social relativism as Anarchy to Culture and it clearly looks forward to many features of our own century and its literature. (The trial of Meursault in Camus's *L'Étranger* springs to mind.)

Mention of the effect of moral relativism on an individual's attitude to social rules and laws brings us back to Browning's poem about a trial. The question we are faced with in reading

[2]Edward Alexander, in his *Matthew Arnold and John Stuart Mill* (1965), p. 64, implies that Walter E. Houghton, in his pages (14-15) on relativism in *The Victorian Frame of Mind 1830-1870* (1957) did not take account of the fact that the "idea of cultural and intellectual relativism" pervades the writing of Arnold and Mill. But Houghton is concerned with moral relativism in Pater and carefully and justly distinguishes the important respects in which it differs from Arnold's views.

The Ring and the Book is whether Browning, as Dowden observed, "came more and more to throw himself into prolonged intellectual sympathy with characters towards whom his moral sense stood in ardent antagonism,"[3] or whether we in fact see, to use Pater's words, that in the poem "Hard and abstract moralities are yielding to a more exact estimate of the subtlety and complexity of our life." Is each speaker sincere according to his lights, and thus author of his own brand of truth? And must we in consequence see Browning, not wholly consciously, perhaps, subverting the belief that men may regard themselves as entitled to judge and condemn from a sense of a law written in all men's hearts, originating from the God who governs the world?

E. D. H. Johnson has answered the last of these questions in an interesting essay on the similarity he detects between the radical empiricism of William James and *The Ring and the Book*.[4] The poem, he claims, "most comprehensively exhibits Browning's pluralism" in that each of the speakers in the poem bears witness to the facts "sure that he is rendering them veraciously." The celebrated image of the gold ring symbolises the "plasticity of factual reality" and the "multiform nature of all truth." Ten of the books, Johnson observes, "present in chronological sequence the testimony of nine witnesses," who all vary from one another: yet somehow they between them reveal an ultimate unity, a universe grown out of a multiverse. That each human being *engenders* the truth upon the world is the common ground occupied by Browning and William James.

Mr. Johnson's comparison of Browning and William James is illuminating. Both do certainly accept the conditions of human life as an intelligible challenge to the individual man and woman. Moreover James's belief that on some matters we have to choose one way or the other, and that the existence of God is one such, is shared by Browning; so perhaps is the alarming corollary that if sufficient evidence to decide this and other such vital questions is lacking, then the profitability or

---

[3] Edward Dowden, "Mr. Tennyson and Mr. Browning," *Studies in Literature 1789-1877* (1892), p. 238.

[4] E. D. H. Johnson, "Robert Browning's Pluralistic Universe: A Reading of *The Ring and the Book*," *University of Toronto Quarterly*, xxxi (Oct. 1961), pp. 20-41.

usefulness of taking one choice rather than the other may be admitted in place of such evidence. But that *The Ring and the Book* shows Browning at one with James over pluralism is certainly less acceptable. The monologues do not show *witnesses* (in the ordinary sense), for there were none: and it is the whole point of the poem that some of the speakers have various reasons, personal or professional, for quite deliberately juggling with the "facts" in decidedly interested fashion. To say that each speaker is sure that he is rendering them veraciously is to adapt the poem to the theory. Johnson's arguments do not really require that we believe Browning entertained pluralism and made it the structural principle of his poem.

All his parallel with William James brings out is that neither poet nor philosopher saw the need to impugn or deny God for the presence of evil in the world, but rather the reverse, since the saintly heroism of such as Pompilia was thereby generated, to the edification of all good people, even a Pope. To think that life is a vale of soul-making is a moral-cum-metaphysical act of faith: its status as true or false is not in question since it cannot be verified. Browning asserts his faith in the poem, just as Carlyle did before him: their theme is the assertion of the will—heroism in fact. Both, unlike Pater, long for action, not thought. That faiths, all faiths, may not be versions of truth but only "precious as memorials of a class of sincere and beautiful spirits" is a reflection which haunts the work of both men as they strive to recreate, in *Past and Present,* and *The Ring and the Book,* the sense of the past: but they both do their best to exorcise it, rather than permit, in the modern manner, the presence always to cast its shadow.

Mr. Robert Langbaum is most careful in his chapter on the poem in his admirable book *The Poetry of Experience* to give full recognition to the fact that Browning makes it abundantly clear, both in his own preliminary summary in the first book, and in the monologues that follow, that Pompilia is indubitably saintly and Franceschini indubitably wicked. When he speaks of the poem as "relativist" he appears to mean something much less challenging than Mr. Johnson does when he uses the expression pluralist. "It is relativist," he writes, "in that the social and religious absolutes are not the means for understanding the right and wrong of the poem; they are for the most part barriers to understanding."[5] He means by this, it seems, that the poem relates to unique people and circumstances. Ordinarily if a priest ran away with the wife of a nobleman one might think they could only be guilty. But this priest, this wife, this nobleman are to be judged for what they really are, and not simply in their life-roles:

> Browning is not saying that all discontented wives are to be rescued from their husbands, but just this particular wife from her particular husband. Why? Because of what we understand Pompilia and Guido to *be*. Hence the use of repetition and the dramatic monologue—not because the judgments are a matter of opinion but because we must judge what is being said by who is saying it. The point is that all the speakers are eloquent to a fault and make the best possible case consistent with their own prepossessions and the facts accessible to them. Our judgments depend, therefore on what we understand of them as people— of their motives, sincerity, and innate moral quality. Judgment goes on, in other words, below the level of the argument and hence the dramatic monologue, which makes it possible for us to apprehend the speaker totally, to subordinate what he says to what we know of him through sympathy.[6]

This argument overlooks that it is a quality of all fiction to deal with individual persons and events, and that in some degree we must always be guided by the author's revelations concerning his characters what to think of their actions. Some authors do admittedly leave us to work out from various sorts of clue what to think, but Browning luridly directs us at the very beginning how to judge the people in *The Ring and the Book*. Mr. Langbaum freely concedes that "we would probably not discern the limitations of the pro-Pompilia speaker were we not specifically alerted to look for them." So clearly it is impossible also to accept that we have to sympathise with them, that is, "enter into their motives, sincerity and innate moral quality," before we can judge them. Yet Langbaum presses this interpretation of the poem more and more in order that it may serve as one more piece of evidence in support of his broader arguments on the subject of the poetry of experience. Thus he writes that Browning means that "truth depends upon the

[5]Robert Langbaum, *The Poetry of Experience* (1957), p. 113.
[6]Ibid., pp. 114-15.

nature of the theorising and ultimately upon the nature of the soul of which the theorising is a projection" and "What we arrive at in the end is not *the* truth, but truth as the worthiest characters of the poem see it." This view is not very far from Johnson's idea of pluralism after all.

The kind of theory I have been discussing does supply an answer to the question that is bound to occur to any reader of *The Ring and the Book,* and to treat it with skepticism imposes the obligation to supply an alternative. That question—to what end did Browning make *The Ring and the Book* an assemblage of dramatic monologues?—is intimately bound up with his remarks in the first and last books, including the metaphor of gold, alloy and ring on which so much has been written.

Browning's famous ring-metaphor has struck some critics as a curiosity of literature in that it is at variance with the facts of artistic creation. Its requiring us to replace the common phrase "hard fact" with, as it were, "soft fact" is curious, and it does rather suggest moral relativism, the idea that facts are malleable, and that each of us is free to impress our own meaning or sense of truth upon them. Yet at the same time Browning identifies facts with the truth, and uses the image of an alloy to suggest quite the contrary, that is, that he, at any rate, confronted with the facts of the old Yellow Book, kept exactly to them, and in no way tampered with them by adapting them to a work of art. It is tempting to see Browning's ambiguity on this question of "truth" and "fact" also to suggest that he somehow entertained the possibility that historical or legal evidence could not in itself supply the truth: for that one needs knowledge of character: and that he also must have meant his readers to see that the truth about human behaviour and motive is really inaccessible, a matter of personal judgment. Indeed, this view has been put forward.[7]

The whole matter is complicated by the nature of the law-

[7]George Levine, writing of Carlyle's growing concern, shortly after *Sartor Resartus,* with history and the primacy of fact, observes: "At best the turn was an expression of willed faith in the notion that the world and experience are under some supernatural moral control. Although he was too scrupulously honest a man to have been able to distort his sources consciously, he never wrote a history in which the facts had not already led him to his desired conclusions." See his "*Sartor Resartus* and the balance of fiction," *Victorian*

case given in the Book, for, rather exceptionally, the main facts of Pompilia's death were not disputed. The difficulty of judgment turned only on motive. Theoretically, as Langbaum notices, the truth of this is *really* inaccessible; there have been miscarriages of justice in plenty. But Browning removes this possibility from the minds of his readers altogether. He knows for certain that Guido was guilty, for the truth lay in the Book for him to extract. He dug it, as it were, "bit by bit," a "piece-meal gain" from the Book. He knew it was the truth, an ingot of gold, not merely by assaying it (whatever that means), but from "something else surpassing that,"

> Something of mine which, mixed up with the mass,
> Made it bear hammer and be firm to file.

This makes the alloy simultaneously a touchstone of a novel kind. He knew that the Book contained truth because he could "combine" with it, fusing his live soul with the inert stuff. It represented to him, in a manner familiar to us from accounts by Conrad and James of their sudden apprehension of a "sub-ject," a body of matter into which he could breathe his par-

---

Studies VIII, No. 2 (Dec. 1964), pp. 155-156. The final sentence, it seems to me, can apply also to Browning and *The Ring and the Book*. But Mr. Levine also connects (p. 157) Carlyle (in *Sartor*) with Browning in having it that we lean substantially upon the "character" (i.e. the good qualities, and notably sincerity) of Teufelsdrokh when we are trying, as we read, to assess the truth (in a relativist sense, of course) of the "clothes-philosophy." He goes on to speak of the "obvious connection of elements of this vision with the later work of James and Conrad—indeed with much of the modern novel." This part of his article, arguing that Carlyle and Browning are akin in coming "perilously close to relativism," staying clear of it largely in the same way too, seems to me ill-grounded, and particularly so in making further connection with the highly objective fiction of our present century. It seems to go back on the fact, which Mr. Levine properly emphasizes, that *Sartor Resartus* does not progress, that is, has no action; it employs a biographical method (the resemblances of which to fiction must, *pace* Northrop Frye, be discounted) not in the way a novelist does, but as a means of skillfully disguising what is in the last resort, doctrine. In this, surely, is the resemblance with *The Ring and the Book* and the majority of Browning's other monologues. The presence of doctrine without action is a feature which makes any connection of elements in these works with the novels of James and Conrad of minor importance at most.

ticular spirit. His reaction to the recognition is one of exhilaration, again a familiar enough response:

> A spirit laughs and leaps through every limb,
> And lights my eye, and lifts me by the hair,
> Letting me have my will again with these. . . .

It is not hard to see that Browning means by "truth" what the creative artist often means—that the facts of a "story" which have accidentally come to his attention exert an enormous appeal to his sense of life and its workings. So strong is his feeling that he can "see" what must have happened that he has no doubt at all of the rightness of his interpretation. In this sense the original facts and the divined "truth" are naturally one and the same. What is unusual is that Browning found his "truth" (a goldmine of a subject, as he might have said) in such a large body of fact. As James observed in the Preface to *The Aspern Papers,* an historian cannot have too many facts, an artist too few—as a rule.

The first Book of the poem describes the long reverie in which the poet re-enacted the scenes of the crime in imagination, driven on by his sense of the perfect subject. It goes on to a highly censorious judgment of Guido and his brothers, and then, to make doubly sure that the reader makes no mistake about the motives of each of those whose speech the poet is imaginatively to create, gives a brief description of them in turn. It is quite clear, therefore, that he did not mean us to form our own judgments about the significance of a crime as in a novel of Dostoevsky. Nor are we reading an early version of *Rashomon.* The attraction of the subject consisted in the demonstration it offered of the wickedness of Guido, which is the central part of a picture made up of "depth below depth of depravity," as Browning put it in his letter of 19 November 1868, to Julia Wedgwood.[8] "I was struck with the enormous wickedness and weakness of the main composition of the piece" he wrote. That Guido is to be taken as the centre of interest is clear from the final book of the poem which describes "our glaring Guido" as a soaring rocket, now declining into oblivion. (Perhaps this image reveals something of Browning's

[8]*Robert Browning and Julia Wedgwood,* ed. Richard Curle (1937), p. 159.

ambiguous conception of the man.) In the first book, Guido's second monologue is called "the summit of so long ago."

Another obvious attraction to Browning must have lain in the "drama" of the case having been "live fact deadened down," that is, not what really happened during the killing but what was laid before the judges as a set of documents. Browning's cry,

> Let this old woe step on the stage again!
> Act itself o'er anew for men to judge,

is quickly qualified—"Not by the very sense and sight indeed." The interest is not in the murder reconstructed, but in the *trial.* In his letter to Miss Wedgwood, Browning states: "The whole of his speech, as I premise, is untrue—cant and cleverness—as you see when the second speech comes...." In other words, Browning's interest lies in exposing wickedness through irony, an irony directed at the extreme lengths to which love of self will go, and the equal lengths to which speech will be abused to justify it. Browning makes it plain that one lesson we are to learn is that

> our human speech is naught,
> Our human testimony false, our fame
> And human estimation words and wind.

Obviously Browning could not have meant that speech is to be invariably so regarded, or he could not have been able himself to decide upon Guido's guilt and Pompilia's innocence. The suggestion is no more than that truth is very often abused because our gift of language is so capable of furthering lies and deceit that we can even persuade ourselves of our innocence. This apercu is peculiarly Browning's own, and nowhere is it better illustrated than in his account of the ending he would have given to Tennyson's *Enoch Arden*—whereby we are to enjoy the irony of overhearing high-minded reflections upon the evil life of Enoch as his funeral-cart passes.[9]

Browning justifies his excessively liking the study of "morbid cases of the soul" ("I thought that, since I could do it, and even liked to do it, my affair it was rather than another's") by a love

[9]Curle, op. cit., p. 75 (letter of Sept. 2, 1864).

of truth—God made men like this. "Before I die, I hope to purely invent something,—here my pride was concerned to invent nothing: the minutest circumstance that denotes character is *true:* the black is so much—the white, no more."[10] The remark that his pride was concerned to *invent nothing* brings us round to the question we started with. What it means is that to Browning wickedness justifying itself seemed particularly characteristic of human behaviour, and that this needed pointing out. Unfortunately the very nature of this truth means that the *hypocrite lecteur* would prefer to talk it away, so that the only way to authenticate it is by demonstration of the way in which excellent exculpations and evasions (such as a reader might himself use) are thought up by one indisputably guilty of crime. This is where fact comes in. What better "argument" in support of the point could be adduced than being able to show that the fiction is also fact, attented by authentic documents?

This no doubt explains the artistic reasons Browning had for maintaining that the art-object, his poem (symbolised by a ring), was made from the gold of crude fact. But there is a psychological aspect of the matter too. Browning's creative energy found its natural outlet in irony of various kinds. In *Pippa Passes* it is an intricate irony of situation, involving various kinds of wickedness frustrated by chance. But its most remarkable form is the monologue of self-justification. (Conrad, incidentally, saw his creative power to be connected with self-justification.) This doubtless had its origin in the powerful confessional strain in Browning, illustrated in his earliest compositions, written before he had recognised that "Art may tell a truth obliquely." It seems reasonable, on the evidence of the number of monologues based on real people, that Browning felt most able to write when he had most assurance that he was not confessing, that is, when he was able to see himself "reanimating" rather than inventing.[11] This would mean that the long passage in the first book of the poem to the effect that only

[10] Ibid., pp. 158-159.

[11] Miss Wedgwood argued that Browning was not truly dramatic because his thoughts intruded so often. Guido was stupid and brutal, not ingenious and wily. Browning replied "Why I almost have you at an unfair advantage, in the fact that the whole story is *true!*" ibid., p. 188.

God can create and man but "project his surplusage of soul" is
really a piece of self-justification on Browning's part. He appears to be making a case for those artists (and Joyce and Shakespeare, in some degree, are others) who are not good at inventing *ex nihilo,* but need "documents" or verifiable data to set
them off and to sustain their imagination.

Browning, both in the poem and in his letter to Miss Wedgwood, makes it clear that he sees wickedness and hypocrisy to
be inescapable facts of the life God has created: he is one possessed of "a temper perhaps offensively and exaggeratedly
inclined to dispute authoritative tradition, and all concessions
to the mere desires of the mind." Among the desires of the
mind he counts the employment of poetic art to idealise human beings. The facts, he says, want explaining, not altering.
He insists in the face of Miss Wedgwood's appeal to Sir Francis
Bacon's notion of poetry, that he feels himself right in his very
severe judgment upon men. So it is abundantly clear that *The
Ring and the Book* was *intended* (at any rate) to impress this
upon his readers. The climax of the poem, "the summit of so
long ago," is Guido's second appearance, revealing that he was
indisputably guilty, the occasion when, in prison

> death's breath rivelled up the lies,
> Left bare the metal thread, the fibre fine
> Of truth, i' the spinning: the true words shone last.
> How Guido to another purpose quite,
> Speaks and despairs, the last night of his life,
> In that New Prison by Castle Angelo
> At the bridge foot: the same man, another voice.

His companions, the Cardinal and Abate, former friends, are
awe-struck, "So changed is Franceschini's gentle blood." Bearing this in mind a later passage about the poem's method capable of misconstruction takes on a precise meaning.

Speaking of the country, or world, he is to create in the poem,
he explains that it is his deliberate intention not to write it from
a single point of view:

> A novel country: I might make it mine
> By choosing which one aspect of the year
> Suited mood best, and putting solely that
> On panel somewhere in the House of Fame,

Landscaping what I saved, not what I saw:
—Might fix you, whether frost in goblin-time
Startled the moon with his abrupt bright laugh,
Or August's hair afloat in filmy fire,
She fell, arms wide, face foremost on the world,
Swooned there and so singed out the strength of things.
Thus were abolished Spring and Autumn both,
The land dwarfed to one likeness of the land,
Life cramped corpse-fashion. Rather learn and love
Each facet-flash of the revolving year!—
Red, green and blue that whirl into a white,
The variance now, the eventual unity,
Which make the miracle. See it for yourselves,
This man's act, changeable because alive!
Action now shrouds, nor shows the informing thought;
Man, like a glass ball with a spark a-top,
Out of the magic fire that lurks inside,
Shows one tint at a time to take the eye:
Which, let a finger touch the silent sleep,
Shifted a hair's-breadth shoots you dark for bright,
Suffuses bright with dark, and baffles so
Your sentence absolute for shine or shade.
Once set such orbs,—white styled, black stigmatized,—
A-rolling, see them once on the other side
Your good men and your bad men every one
From Guido Franceschini to Guy Faux,
Oft would you rub your eyes and change your names.

The Ring and the Book, 1348-1378

We notice that the image of the glass ball's changing from bright to dark illustrates a change in men from seeming innocence to proven guilt, namely in Guido and Guy Faux: the point being made is that innocent appearances are deceptive. We can easily be taken in by the Guidos of the world; the point is made again in the last book when the Augustinian preacher (on the text of "Let God be true and every man a liar") asserts that Pompilia was lucky to be vindicated: many like her are not.

The passage is not very happily expressed, but that it relates simply to "*this* man's act," Guido's, is clear enough from the context. E. D. H. Johnson quotes from it to explain why Browning composed the poem as a series of monologues representing "kaleidoscopic views." Confronted by first one, then another aspect of the story, the reader will be baffled in his inclination to settle for easy answers, to cast his "sentence absolute for shine or shade."[12] This suggests that the poem leaves the truth in doubt: but it demonstrates simply that many pretenders to innocence are truly guilty. Johnson's argument does not take sufficient account of Guido's speaking twice to different effect, and so showing that he was not (on the first occasion) impressing his own truth on the world, but was simply lying. The "shine or shade" in any case relates to the image of the glass ball, not the "views." The "views" are the separate dramatic monologues, and are necessary for Browning's particular gift to exercise itself—a gift not for showing that we make our own truths but for ironical exposure[13] of human failings. Browning supports his own Augustinian monk's text, "Let God be true and every man a liar," and agrees with him that Pompilia's case showed that although human testimony was more often than not false, the truth abided with God. The glass ball is an obscure image for human beings who, by lying, put on a false appearance to the world. Browning appears to

[12]Johnson, loc, cit., p. 23.

[13]I prefer to use this phrase to describe Browning's single monologues because the alternative, used by Dowden, "intellectual sympathy" can lead, as I venture to suggest it does in Mr. Langbaum's book *The Poetry of Experience*, to the idea that they take us into a new category of poetic art in the nineteenth century, an art depending upon a special willingness to enter into the minds of wicked and ignorant men and *ipso facto* to suspend one's normal moral attitudes. This seems to me to overlook the fact that not only all drama, but also all works employing irony—those, say, of Chaucer and Swift, to take obvious examples—have always depended upon a pretended "sympathy." The claim that the sympathy is, in Browning, genuine, seems to me to remove an obvious cause of our satisfaction in his poems. Langbaum's case is that we are expected to show sympathy towards his erring apologists in a manner analogous to the scientific attitude of mind. Historical or psychological considerations, he suggests, cause us to suspend our moral judgment of the duke in "My Last Duchess." This seems to me quite fallacious. Our moral feelings are not, admittedly, like those we would have if we were in reality the envoy *encountering* the duke, but then in art they never are. Our moral indignation is *used* by the poet, nevertheless, as an essential element in the poem's power.

allude to the "electric egg," an instrument used to show the
effect of an electric discharge in a glass vessel partially exhausted of air. This effect was produced by passing a charge
from an electric machine across a gap between metal or carbon
rods enclosed in a glass chamber of ellipsoidal shape attached
to an air pump. It consisted of a bright, reddish-purple glow,
spreading out from the points of the rods, forming dark and
light striations as the glass "globe" is more and more exhausted.
The machine could be set up with only one rod connected with
the electric machine (e.g., Holtz's machine); if the other were
earthed by touching it, the glow would appear in its characteristically variegated and uncertain form. This seems to be the
effect Browning describes as deriving from "the magic fire that
lurks inside" (the MS has "rolls" corrected to "lurks"), an effect which

> baffles so
> Your sentence absolute for shine or shade,

a phrase which recurs several times in the poem. The Pope, we
should notice, has no more doubt of his ability to see through
the false lights and shades of Guido, than has Browning his
creator. He dismisses the Comparini thus:

> Go!
> Never again elude the choice of tints!
> White shall not neutralize the black, nor good
> Compensate bad in man, absolve him so:
> Life's business being just the terrible choice.
>
> So do I see, pronounce on all and some
> Grouped for my judgment now, — profess no doubt
> While I pronounce: dark, difficult enough
> The human sphere, yet eyes grow sharp by use,
> I find the truth, dispart the shine from shade,
> As a mere man may, with no special touch
> O' the lynx-gift in each ordinary orb. ...
> *The Pope*, 1234-1245

So the scientific metaphor is not a support for the relativist
argument, only for Browning's explicit meaning, that appear-

ances, helped out by lies and misconstructions, are surprising-
ly misleading.[14]

One point remains. Browning's rueful remarks about the
British public, "who like me not," but "may like me yet" show,
I think, that he had learned from experience that he had re-
lied too much upon his readers' ability to see through the irony
of his earlier monologues. This time he was going to spell it
out—

> Perchance more careful whoso runs may read
> Than erst when all, it seemed, could read who ran.

Browning, one infers, far from intending to create ambiguity
for his readers to penetrate, was bent, in *The Ring and the
Book,* on eliminating it. Nothing could be further from his
mind than the "pluralism" or "relativism" under discussion.
This is not to say that he may not have encouraged it in others,
only that he himself aimed at illustrating the evil that may
mask itself behind specious words. His own Christianity has
been shown by Hoxie N. Fairchild to be doubtful: but Browning appears to have believed that he was a Christian poet seeking to deal fairly with the world from his standpoint of special
inspiration. This makes him a Victorian, not a modern. ...

The conclusion I want to make is that Browning's strength as
a poet springs from the same source as his weakness. He is by
temperament, and by the forces of his time no doubt, com-
mitted to a faith in God as the prop for his moral being. His
strength lies in his confidence that suffering and passion have
value, and more particularly, in his feeling that he has an un-

[14]The electric egg was going out of use by about 1860 in favour of the "vac-
uum" or Geissler tube. But Faraday demonstrated the instrument at the
Royal Institution in one of the lectures in his Christmas lecture-series for
children (and parents) in 1859-1860. (A stenographic report of the lectures is
given in *Chemical News* [1860].) The lecture, delivered on Jan. 7, 1860 (pp.
126-129), contained the demonstration ("...we have that glorious electric
light; and the moment I cut off the connexion it stops"): the report illustrates
the instrument (fig. 4). The lectures were published as *A Course of six lectures on the various forces of Matter and their relations to each other,* with
numerous illustrations, edited by W. Crookes in 1860; they had several editions. They were then republished by Griffin, Bohn and Co. in 1863, together
with Faraday's more famous Christmas lecture on the chemical history of a
candle.

assailable position from which to create through irony. In my view, *The Ring and the Book* goes back on both, and shows the weak side of his art. The method of juxtaposing his monologues within a framework of explicit moral condemnation destroys the irony which elsewhere so stimulates the reader into admiration of his art. His explicitness really does substitute "galvanism for life" and a spark for the flame of true imagination. Fra Lippo Lippi, Browning's earlier spokesman, offered no apology for his art: nature and mankind are immensely worth the artist's labours:

> But why not do as well as say,—paint these
> Just as they are, careless what comes of it?
> God's works—paint anyone, and count it crime
> To let a truth slip. Don't object, 'His works
> 'Are here already; nature is complete:
> 'Suppose you reproduce her—(which you can't)
> 'There's no advantage! You must beat her then.'
> For don't you mark? We're made so that we love
> First when we see them painted, things we have passed
> Perhaps a hundred times nor cared to see.

The Ring and the Book sees art, Browning's art in that poem at any rate, to be a matter of contriving that "something dead may get to live again." But truth of fact is not truth of imagination. "Fra Lippo Lippi" lives: and it does so because Browning is not afraid to expose his doctrine (for the poem has doctrine enough) to the irony which the dramatic monologue excels in, that arising from having doctrine from a doubtful advocate. Lippi's love of the world and man as subjects for art seems not unlike the love of the world, the flesh and the devil masquerading as primal innocence:

> I always see the garden and God there
> A-making man's wife: and, my lesson learned,
> The value and significance of flesh,
> I can't unlearn ten minutes afterwards.

His worldliness persists even into heaven itself:

> So, all smile—
> I shuffle sideways with my blushing face

Under the cover of a hundred wings
Thrown like a spread of kirtles when you're gay
And play hot cockles, all the doors being shut,
Till, wholly unexpected, in there pops
The hothead husband!

Such frivolity permits us take or leave his claim that the
artist who represents men and women realistically serves God
quite as well as the conventional religious painter. It is con-
venient, we may think, for him to say so. In consequence, the
notion remains indissolubly associated with Fra Lippo himself, part of his being like his wenching, not floating free as
doctrine—even though we may recognize it as in fact part of
the complex of *Browning's* "ideas" on religion and self-ex-
pression. The "freedom" of the reader, as Sartre puts it, is un-
compromised. The delicate balance of this irony is tipped ever
so slightly by our externally derived knowledge that the
painter who loves women so well—

If you get simple beauty and nought else
You get about the best thing God invents

—is the Fra Lippo Lippi whose work has come down to us, and
whose claim to be on the right course in religious painting has
been validated by history. This historical testimony is a hundred times more eloquent than Browning's perfervid assertions in *The Ring and the Book*. The reader's own knowledge
of the historical outcome of the events can contribute nothing
to the recognition of truth in that poem, for the characters and
incidents are unfamiliar. Browning has worked exceedingly
hard, but his reader has nothing to do save watch a demonstration. The doctrine it conveys is commended to us not by irony
but by exposure, and its culminating monologue is delivered
not by a doubtful advocate but by a proclaimed liar. Moreover
Browning feels himself, I suggest, so safely hedged about by
his moral frame that he can admit into Guido's first monologue,
and that of the Pope, "arguments" which are more subversive
of the faith supporting that moral frame than he could permit
himself in any other context. Guido's monologue in particular
really does point towards moral relativism if it is considered in
purely intellectual terms, without respect to his known guilt.

Yet the contemporary estimate of the poem is not surprising. It must have seemed to many readers who found subversive arguments attributed to the wicked Guido and moral confidence to the Pope a *counterblast* to the relativism making itself felt in that decade. It stands, in my view, as an elaborate Victorian monument to the faith that truth does not depend upon human testimony, but is absolute. Its method, that of juxtaposing dramatic monologues, serves a purpose quite contrary to that proposed by its modern apologists. Today we may find it less impressive because it has lost imaginative force as it has gained in moral explicitness,[15] an explicitness which intensifies the pessimism the poem finally displays.

---

[15]A. K. Cook in *A Commentary upon Browning's "The Ring and the Book"* (1920), p. 3, anticipates the conclusion of this essay in arguing against G. K. Chesterton's claim that *The Ring and the Book* could be regarded as "the epic of free speech." He points out that while Browning may have seen the possibility of encouraging this interpretation in Book I, lines 1348-1378, he was fully conscious even as early as *Sordello* that the "setters-forth" of unexampled themes had "best chalk broadly on each vesture's hem / The wearer's quality."

Robert Browning: The Music of Music

by John Hollander

English Romantic poetry is strangely unconcerned with actual instrumental or vocal music. Musical imagery occurs frequently in Wordsworth, Coleridge, Keats and Shelley when a response to the perception of some noise in nature is to be rhetorically or conceptually heightened. But their imaginative concern is largely with the music, as it were, of sound. With one notable exception in English nineteenth-century poetry, the tradition of attention to this concern persists well into the period of dawning symbolist influence, when the music of poetry itself would come to triumph in power and universality over the most abstract of quartets, the most visionary of symphonic poems, which language began striving to emulate. Browning is that exception. His knowledge and experience of, and his lifelong interest in music have been widely discussed, and recently there has been Professor Ridenour's profound and acute study of some of the ways in which Browning abstracted from his experience of music modes for representing experience of the world in general.[1] Browning's detailed musical images are almost unique in English poetry, however, and they are all the more remarkable when read against the poet's Romantic heritage. It is easy to describe them as emblematic,

"Robert Browning: The Music of Music" by John Hollander is reprinted from *Strivers' Row* by permission of John Irwin, editor and publisher, and by the author.

[1]George M. Ridenour, "Browning's Music Poems: Fancy and Fact," PMLA LXXVIII (1963), 369-377; this article remains one of the most impressive apprehensions that exists of Browning's mind at work. William C. DeVane's pages on "Charles Avison" in *Browning's Parleyings* (New Haven, 1927), pp. 252-282, are basic to a study of the poet's sense of musical culture.

as generating not only new analogies but new grounds for analogy with each turn of explication. One is reminded of some of the more conventional musical conceits in seventeenth-century poems: the sympathetic vibration of two perfectly tuned strings as a type of love, for example, or even Alciati's venerable emblem of the stringed instrument, well-tuned, as political unification. But the ways in which Browning's imaginative use of music depart from his heritage are more elusive.

Sometimes, in fact, English Romantic sound imagery will actually take up a Renaissance musical emblem and naturalize it; this is particularly frequent in Shelley, whose imaginative energies delighted in transforming pastoral images of sound into the heightened underscoring of a more immediately envisioned landscape. Even an unacknowledged historical semantic change can serve as a pivoting point, as with the shift of meaning in "sweet" from the seventeenth-century musical sense of "in perfect tune" (cf. modern "sour note" and see Jessica in *The Merchant of Venice* [V,1] : "I am never merry when I hear sweet music") to the continuing olfactory one, in these lines from *Epipsychidion:*

> And from her lips, as from a hyacinth full
> Of honey-dew, a liquid murmur drops,
> Killing the sense with passion: sweet as stops
> Of planetary music heard in trance. ...
>
> (83-6)

Here the two meanings blend the human physical senses and reanimate, along with the psychologizing about the trance, what would otherwise be a seventeenth-century cliché. Or even more obviously, about 60 lines further on, a conceit bordering on the quibbling—"We are we not formed, as notes of music are, / For one another, though dissimilar"—becomes transformed, in the appositive paraphrase of the following lines, from a homely, almost technical musical trope into an image lying in the mainstream of English Romantic musical expression:

> Such difference without discord, as can make
> Those sweetest sounds, in which all spirits shake
> As trembling leaves in a continuous air? (144-6)

The figure is that of musical sound blending with the natural
noise of leaves moving in the air, the mingled measure of human music and the voice of nature. Whether specifically embodied in the symbol of the Aeolian harp (or even more
ubiquitous from the mid-eighteenth century on, in complex
and surrogate forms of that symbol), the truest music, in
English Romantic tradition, was always the least feigning.
Eighteenth-century nature poetry had brought a new poetic
recognition to the consciousness of outdoor sound, employing
both neoclassical and pastoral images of music to describe what
was not music after all, but, acoustically speaking, noise. Rooted
in pastoral conventions in which natural noises of wind and
water and amplifying echo authenticated the poetical truth of
utterance within the *locus amoenus,* the music of natural sound
in Wordsworth and Coleridge, and in a renewed way in Keats
and Shelley, drowns out the sound of cultural music. German
Romantic writing is full of deep musico-literary connections,
but in England a combination of the backward state of British
music and the prime involvement of Romantic vision with the
discovery of consciousness by, and in, the open hall of the rural, contribed to trivialize the concert hall, the drawing-room
and the opera house as far as the poetic imagination was
concerned.[2]

Browning's earliest musical imagery reflects this English
tradition, and Shelley in particular, in unsurprising ways. In
Pauline, the "sweet task" of reading Shelley himself becomes

> To disentangle, gather sense from song:
> Since, song-inwoven, lurked there sense which seemed
> A key to a new world, the muttering
> Of angels, something yet unguessed by man.[3]
>   (413-416)

[2]For a detailed introduction to this matter, see my *Images of Voice: Music
and Sound in Romantic Poetry,* Churchill College Overseas Lecture No. 5
(Cambridge, England, 1970); and "Wordsworth and the Music of Sound" in
Geoffrey H. Hartman, ed., *New Perspectives on Coleridge and Wordsworth*
(New York, 1972), 41-84.

[3]This and subsequent quotations are from the Centenary Edition of Browning's works, ed. F. G. Kenyon (London, 1912). The problematic relations between language and music in *Pauline* also yield the more Keatsian image of
ll. 377-9: "And first I sang as I in dream have seen / Music wait on a lyrist
for some thought / Yet singing to herself until it came."

Text and music, braided together like thought and feeling in an image of a secondary harmonizing that goes back to Milton's "At a Solemn Music," here yield up a truth that Wordsworth's American progeny would forever strain to hear in the half-decipherable whisperings of nature. In a more German mood, at the end of *Pauline,* the protagonist invokes the inaccessibility of music's transcendent truth, a truth seen to be so much like the power of an eroticized but unyielding nature:

> kissing me when I
> Look up—like summer wind! Be still to me
> A help to music's mystery which mind fails
> To fathom, its solution no mere clue!
> (928-931)

In Part II of *Paracelsus,* that ghost of Alastor, the young poet Aprile, limns his vision of the life of art, transforming the world by the very act of describing it in a sequence of projects moving from the sculptural, to the plastic, to the verbal ("Now poured at once forth in a burning flow, / Now piled up to a grand array of words"). The sequence concludes with a final creative act, like a sigh of completion as a maker breathes upon his perfected but still lifeless shapes:

> This done, to perfect and consummate all,
> Even as a luminous haze links star to star,
> I would supply all chasms with music, breathing
> Mysterious motions of the soul, no way
> To be defined save in strange melodies.
> (II, 475-479)

Here is another of the core musical images of Romantic tradition—the cave, shell or chasm embodying a spirit of sound. Like the mysterious eloquence of music in *Pauline,* these lines invoke a background of visionary music in its relation to landscape, a background extending back past Shelley to Wordsworth and the eighteenth century. This *musique en plein air,* heard at a distance, remembered from the past dominating English poetry, might have remained the conceptual source of later musical imagery in Browning, as, in transformations worked upon Keats' versions of it, it was for Tennyson. But under the pressure of a number of forces, it virtually disap-

peared from Browning's world of images, reappearing only at
the end of his career, in the language of the sentimentalist "He"
who hears flute-music through the trees in one of the poems of
A solando. The forces which banish it are various: the developing interest in the minute particulars of cultural and historical
fact under the rhetorical control of dramatic monologue, for
one; a fascination, mentioned earlier, with an almost seventeenth-century emblematic mode of thought, for another, and
withal Browning's own love and knowledge of music, and the
ways in which this knowledge shaped his listening ear.

This last is a most elusive matter. There has been a good deal
of dispute about the order and depth of Browning's technical
musical skill, and it has been fashionable to deride it.[4] Baldas-
sare Galuppi, for example, was a Venetian composer of opera
primarily, and there seem to be no known "toccatas" by him.
Almost any cultured reader today knows that, had said protagonist indeed played "stately at the clavichord," he would
have been inaudible in a room full of even temporarily silenced masquers—a clavichord's tiny, private, touch-responsive
tinkle was almost for the ear of the performer alone. Abt Vogler's descending chromatic sequences are, in the words of a
prominent and prolific Victorian composer, "the refuge of the
destitute amateur improviser." These crude dismissals are
easily answered. In the first place, Browning cannot be judged
by fairly sophisticated, twentieth-century musicological standards; after all, his own contemporaries conventionally mis-
translated the last word in the title of Bach's *Das Wohltempierte
Klavier* as "clavichord" (it means, generically, "keyboard").
Although Browning later claimed to have known actual Galup-
pian toccatas from ms. volumes,[5] we may assume that he was in

[4]Aside from DeVane, *Parleyings*, see, for example, Herbert E. Greene,
"Browning's Knowledge of Music," PMLA LXII (1947), 1095-99, containing
the remark by Sir Charles Villiers Stanford quoted above. More sophisticated
in its own musical knowledge is W. Wright Roberts, "Music in Browning,"
Music and Letters XVII (1936), 237-248.

[5]See Browning's letter of June 30, 1887 to the Rev. Henry G. Spaulding of
Boston, reprinted in Greene, "Browning's Knowledge of Music," pp. 1098-
1099. In this communication, the poet also explains what he meant by such
phrases as "mode Palestrina" and "Elizabethan plainsong" which had been
seized upon by musicians as evidence that he knew nothing of music.

[6]DeVane, *Parleyings*, p. 260.

fact filling in, a la Borges, a historical lacuna, and that the stop consonants of the Italian polysyllable "toccata" tripped across the tongue with an appropriate gallop. And again, the cavalier attribution of works to early composers was ubiquitous in the nineteenth century (the reader with some pianism of his own may observe that the first of the two popular volumes entitled *Early Keyboard Music,* originally compiled in 1904 and still kept in print by Schirmer, contains what purports to be a *"Fuga"* by Frescobaldi: a moment's inspection will reveal that it is a fine academic pastiche of Bach — composed, in fact, by Clementi!). Similarly, the scraps of music Browning himself undoubtedly composed — for the children to sing in *Strafford,* for example ("suitable for children," as DeVane[6] characterized it, but no more "historically accurate" for the seventeenth century than a similar song at an equivalent moment in Donizetti might have been), or for "the lilt (Oh, not sung!)" to which Pietro of Abano's tale is crooned — are amateurish. But not mindlessly so, for they betoken the kind of intimate acquaintance with the actualities of composition and performance that transform musical listening from a passive condition of being played upon, to a kind of active engagement with the flow of structured sound. Compared with selectively hearing melody, or responding to "a rattling good tune" — that curse of the English musical sensibility, as De Quincey so tellingly observed[7] — that active faculty of energized listening is like following a sophisticated argument or thread of discourse, as opposed to understanding merely the spoken language of an utterance. This faculty Browning not only possessed, but wrote about as if he possessed. A mere technical allusion to musical

---

[7]Thomas De Quincey, "Style," in *Works* (Edinburgh, 1862), X, 160-1. Part of this passage deserves quotation: "A song, an air, a tune; that is, a short succession of notes revolving rapidly upon itself, how could that, by possibility, offer a field of compass for the development of great musical effects? The preparation pregnant with the future, the remote correspondence, the questions, as it were, which to a deep musical sense are asked in one passage and answered in another...these and ten thousand forms of self-conflicting musical passion, what room could they find, what opening, what utterance in so limited a field as an air or song?" One needs to know enough about music to raise such a question before he can know that there are, indeed, circumstances under which a single melodic line can contain, or outline, or imply such effects. My point is only that Browning knew at least that much.

practice, even a clever conceit based on it, is one thing. A grasp of, for example, the dialectic of vertical and horizontal in analytic or even compositional schemata, is another.

For example, when Milton writes in Book XI of *Paradise Lost* about the music of Jubal—Michael is showing Adam a projected vision of the dangers and possibilities of human culture—he reveals tents

> whence the sound
> Of instruments that made melodious chime
> Was heard, of Harp and Organ; and who mov'd
> Their stops and chords was seen: his volant touch
> Instinct through all proportions high and low
> Fled and pursu'd transverse the resonant fugue.
>   (XI, 558-63)

Mostly simply, this is an expansion of the Biblical text in which Jubal figures as the father "of all such as handle the harp and organ." But the virtuoso in the passage, improvizing polyphonic keyboard fantasias, is an actual seventeenth-century musician. "His *volant* touch / Instinct" is, given the now-obsolete sense of "touch" to mean a sounded musical phrase, almost synaesthetic, in applying to his flying fingers and the flights of sound which they elicit. The metaphor then follows music flight in another sense, "through all proportions high and low / Fled and pursu'd transverse the resonant fugue." Not only the flight of printed notes on a stave, but the abstract motion of the horizontal parts, the polyphonic voices, *through* high and low intervals (almost in the way that, we might say, a curve flies *through* higher and lower cartesian coordinates), are being figured here. The final revelation of the syntax is that his "volant touch...pursu'd transverse the resonant fugue," and the implied elusiveness of the fugue, the musical form, its structure and indeed its notational shape, is underlined by the semantic movement of the whole passage, through the "volant" to the "fled" and, finally, to the "fugue," both in object and in more than resonant name. Aside from all its other brillancies, the whole passage is mimetic of the act of hearing music when one knows how it is put together, and can perhaps even envision its notation. Such representations of musical experience are very rare indeed in English poetry, as are, in any language, poets capable of producing them.

Browning has almost no immediate predecessors with sufficiently available musical knowledge to enable them to mythologize listening to music as they could do to the wind in the trees, or, in particular, the experience of seeing through and behind the seen. One exception, however, is Leigh Hunt. As both connoisseur and practicing music critic, one might have expected Hunt to have essayed something on the subject of concert music, and indeed he did: "The Fancy-Concert" (1845), a serio-comic extravaganza, written in the anapestic tetrameters of incipient *vers de societe,* and conjuring up an imaginary perfect concert, embracing the history of music from the late Baroque to Beethoven.[8] Then, too, Hunt left some smaller pieces, including one, in a smarmy German manner on "the Lover of Music to His Pianoforte." Of most interest to the problem of getting sophisticated musical experience into poetry, however, are two blank-verse poems, one, a fragment called "Paganini" first published in 1834, and "A Thought on Music" with the subtitle "suggested by a Private Concert, May 13, 1815."

The first of these[9] starts out in the language of an almost conventional European contemporary Paganiniolatry, invoking

> the pale magician of the bow,
> Who brought from Italy the tales, made true,
> Of Grecian lyres; and on his sphery hand,
> Loading the air with dumb expectancy,
> Suspended, ere it fell, a nation's breath.
>
> (3-7)

It then goes on to acknowledge the diabolic tincture in the violinist's nature by seeing him as "One that had parted with his soul for pride, / And in the sable secret lived forlorn." Continental romantic tradition made much of the demonic,

[8]"The Fancy-Concert," first published in 1845. In *Poetical Works,* ed. H. S. Milford (Oxford, 1923), pp. 374-377. "Fancy" in the title, of course, means "fantasied."

[9]Hunt, *Poetical Works,* pp. 255-257.

deracinated figure of the musician, from Diderot on. Even in
the English seventeenth century, stories were told of the composer and keyboard virtuoso John Bull that affirmed his cloven
hoof. Hunt does all but recite Paganiniana about fiddle-strings
made from the gut of a dead mistress; but after a while, the tone
changes and becomes a frantic, rather Shelleyan effusion of
straining effort to keep descriptive pace with the dazzling range
of effects of the master's playing. For about 75 lines, the images
proliferate in pursuit of the stream of sound, in a pattern perhaps most directly modelled upon the lyrical treatment of
mountain streams and cataracts moving rapidly through landscape (Hunt probably could not have known Crashaw's *Musicks
Duell*, some of whose descriptions of lute-playing and bird-
song his poem suggests). One may cut in almost at random:

> he would overthrow
> That vision with a shower of notes like hail,
> Or sudden mixtures of all difficult things
> Never yet heard; flashing the sharp tones now,
> In downward leaps like swords; now rising fine
> Into some utmost tip of minute sound,
> From whence he stepped into a higher and higher
> On viewless points, till laugh took leave of him:
> Or he would fly as if from all the world
> To be alone and happy, and you should hear
> His instrument become a tree far off,
> A nest of birds and sunbeams, sparkling both,
> A cottage-bower. ...   (50-63)

Or, perhaps later on, where the resources of Jacobean dramatic
verse are called out in aid of hearing and feeling:

> or some twofold strain
> Moving before him in sweet-going yoke,
> Ride like an Eastern conqueror, round whose state
> Some light Morisco leaps with his guitar;
> And ever and anon o'er these he'd throw
> Jets of small notes like pearl, or like the pelt
> Of lovers' sweetmeats on Italian lutes
> From windows on a feast-day, or the leaps
> Of pebbled water, sprinkled in the sun,
> One chord effecting all. ...   (72-81)

Toward the end of the piece, in its way, a kind of exercise, some attention is paid to the attending consciousness "when the ear / Felt there was nothing present but himself / And silence," for example—but by and large, the genre of the piece is low-mimetic, a step above the devices used by Southey to render the waters coming down at Lodore, perhaps. Much more interesting is the fragment of Hunt's written nearly twenty years earlier. "A Thought on Music"[10] struggles, against what proves to be the ultimately overwhelming power of conventionalized rhetoric about music, epithets and stock responses, to anatomize the act of informed listening. The first sixteen lines represent the English romantic musical experience in miniature, as the more or less specific (if not, in this instance, technical) observations move outdoors from the concert-room, and substitute for the dramaturgy of structure and style in the musical world, the cadences and closures of easily available myth:

> To sit with downward listening, and crossed knee,
> Half conscious, half unconscious, of the throng
> Of fellow-ears, and hear the well-met skill
> Of fine musicians,—the glib ivory
> Twinkling with numerous prevalence,—the snatch
> Of brief and birdy flute, that leaps apart,—
> Giddy violins, that do whate'er they please,—
> And sobering all with circling manliness,
> The bass, uprolling deep and voluble;—
> Well may the sickliest thought, that keeps its home
> In a sad heart, give gentle way for once,
> And quitting its pain-anchored hold, put forth
> On that sweet sea of many-billowed sound,
> Foating and floating in a dreamy lapse,
> Like a half-sleeper in a summer boat,
> Till heaven seems near, and angels travelling by.
>   (1-16)

The second part of the poem moves beyond even this, back into the recesses of German romantic musical theory where the very referential vagueness of music, its lack of quasi-linguistic mean-

---

[10]*Poetical Works*, pp. 254-255.

ing, is held to make it the most universal and poetic of arts. The following lines openly deny the possibility of just the kind of listening a character in Browning, for example, will express:

> For not the notes alone, or new-found air,
> Or structure of elaborate harmonies,
> With steps that to the waiting treble climb,
> Suffice a true-touched ear. ...   (17-20)

—and as the meditation resumes, the language, the cadence, the movement of image and example through the argument, become unabashedly Wordsworthian:

>   To that will come
> Out of the very vagueness of the joy
> A shaping and a sense of things beyond us,
> Great things and voices great: nor will it reckon
> Sounds, that so wake up the fond-hearted air,
> To be the unmeaning raptures they are held,
> Or mere suggestions of our human feeling,
> Sorrow, or mirth, or triumph. Infinite things
> There are, both small and great, whose worth were lost
> On us alone,—the flies with lavish plumes,—
> The starry-showering snow,—the tints and shapes
> That hide about the flowers,—gigantic trees,
> That crowd for miles up mountain solitudes,
> As on the steps of some great natural temple,
> To view the godlike sun:—nor have the clouds
> Only one face, but on the side of heaven
> Keep ever gorgeous beds of golden light.
>
> Part then alone we hear, as part we see;
> And in this music, lovely things of air
> May find a sympathy of heart or tongue,
> Which shook perhaps the master, when he wrote,
> With what he knew not,—meanings exquisite,—
> Thrillings, that have their answering chords in heaven,—
> Perhaps a language well-tuned hearts shall know
> In that blest air, and thus in pipe and string
> Left by angelic mouths to lure us thither.   (20-45)

The poem has moved from a brief encounter with the attempt to render the experience of aware listening, through the evasions of merely literary writing about musical instruments

("And virgin trebles wed the manly bass"—so Marvell in "Music's Empire," and so the cliché thereafter), out to the dream journey in "a summer boat," and finally to a Wordsworthian recognition of the superior power of mythologized nature in accounts of heightened moments of consciousness. Willy-nilly, the English romantic poet, no matter how profound his immersion in the world of musical art, will succumb to the force of the image of the mingled measure, the dispersion of the sounds of human music, vocal or instrumental, in the moving air of landscape. Even the hint of neoplatonizing myth at the end (it combines an older image of sympathetic resonance with association of a spirit of music with moving air imprisoned in a cavity)—and even the cancelled line in Hunt's manuscript (the text given is the published one of 1875) so reminiscent of German romantic musical theory: "Music's the voice of Heaven without the words"—cannot overpower the larger natural vision.

In this vision in eighteenth- and nineteenth-century English poetry, the music of order and of Orphean power, so celebrated in the Renaissance and Baroque, gives way to and attention to the music of sound. Romantic myths of consciousness first introduce us to the music of silence—silence in an acoustical, rather than a rhetorical sense: the soundless, rather than the tacit. But in Browning's mature poetry we are aware of a musical sensibility of a very different sort. What his monologuists hear is the music of music itself; what concerns him is by no means raw sound, nor even embodied feeling—indeed, he is acutely aware of how reductive so many usual readings of musical significances can be. Rather is he attentive to the full flux of musical experience, the apprehension of meanings not in musical sounds themselves, not in modalities of major and minor, rapid and slow alone, but in the very structures of musical art, understood in their stylistic and historical dimensions.

From an early observation, like one of *Paracelsus* about the wind passing "like a dancing psaltress" over the breast of the earth in springtime (a tamed Coleridgean "mad lutanist" and an Aeolian harp image of a conventional type), he can move eventually to a total avowal of the power and significance of instrumental music. It is important to note the distinction be-

tween, on the one hand, an older, emblematic concept of instrumental music, by which an Orphean instrument stood for
the emotive and persuasive power of music, poetry and eloquence itself, and, on the other, the elevation of "pure"—that
is, instrumental—music to a position of highest importance in
Continental romantic aesthetic theory. The common view that
textless music, being more general, was therefore more universal even than song, depended upon an association of vagueness of referential meaning with states of feeling; it is almost as
if, in the frantic quest for pictorial and musical correspondences
that we find in some of speculations of a Wackenroder, of a
Runge, instrumental music is doing the imaginative work of
landscape, of uninhabited natural scenery, in representing the
continuingly unfolding epic of human awareness. A notion
far less common in Continental aesthetic tradition, however,
gives to the flow of music in time a meaning much more discursive. "Must pure instrumental music not make of itself a
text? and does not a theme in it get as developed, confirmed,
varied and contrasted as the object of meditation in a philosophical argument?" asks Friedrich Schlegel[11] in a remark
somewhat uncharacteristic of a historical moment which proclaims music's flights above and beyond the discursive.

What is ultimately so remarkable about Browning's use of
the act of comprehending music listened to, rather than merely
heard, is its ability to operate with both of these opposed
views. Along with the dialectic of the spatial and temporal
images which harmonic and melodic, vertical and horizontal
modes of musical perception tend to project; along with music's
ability, as Ridenour has so brilliantly shown, to function for
Browning as an emblem in the representation of a theory of
fictions; we find the more mature musical imagery in Browning's poetry mediating between the lyrical and the discursive

---

[11] F. W. Schlegel, *Athenaums-Fragmente*, in *Kritische Schriften* (Munchen,
1964), p. 87 (my translation). The whole preceding sentence is of great interest
in this respect, and I am indebted to Charles Rosen for pointing it out to me:
*Wer aber Sinn für die wunderbaren Affinitäten aller Künste und Wissen-
schaften hat, wird die Sache wenigstens nicht aus dem platten Gesichtspunkt
der sogenanten Natürlichkeit betrachten, nach welcher die Musik nur die
Sprache der Empfindung sein soll, und eine gewisse Tendenz aller reinen
Instrumentalmusik zur Philosophie an sich nicht unmöglich finden."*

even on a theoretical level. "Ah, Music, wouldst thou help!" murmurs Don Juan in *Fifine at the Fair* (ll. 943-945). "Words struggle with the weight / So feebly of the False, thick element between / Our soul, the True, and Truth!"—but the point of the whole following passage is not that music floats above meanings, but that it can sometimes do the work of signifying more effectively, and it concludes with the strange ascription to music of a usually unacknowledged attribute: "And since to weary words recourse must be, / At least permit they rest their burden here and there, / Music-like: cover space!" (ll. 961-963) *"Cover space!"*—not by flying above it, nor by being audible at a distance, but rather by filling room: this is conceptual possibility, not a phonetic nor even an auditory phenomenon. The movement of thought, not merely feeling, often seems more like music than like sequences of words. In addition, it is confusing, if not actually ironic, that such a notion would occur only to someone able to grasp, in a concrete and "technical" sense, the nature of purely musical thought—someone who, whether or not he might have erred in reading "sixths diminished" into his fictive Galuppi toccata, certainly understood the syntax of sonata-form, the unfolding logic of variation, the architechtonics of structural harmony to any degree.

It is this sense of music's meaning which gradually comes to inform the musical imagery in Browning's poetry.[12] Even where his toying with a conceit is closest to the Donne and Quarles he admired, even where his interlocutors will turn a comparison which they have already faceted like a jewel over and over, that it may catch the light differently, an interest lying behind that of the capability of emblems will be at work. "Clash forth life's common chord, whence, list how there ascend / Harmonics far and faint, till our perception end,— / Reverberated notes whence we construct the scale / Embracing what we know and feel and are!" proposes Don Juan a bit further on in *Fifine at the Fair* (ll. 968-971). The image he uses anticipates what would become in twentieth-century

---

[12]Rather than, for example, borrowings imagined by William Lyon Phelps in a simplistic essay on "Browning, Schopenhauer and Music," *North American Review* CCVI, 622-627.

English the cliche of "overtones" (a word introduced into the language only in the 1860's, in fact, to translate Helmholtz's *Oberton,* "harmonic partial") as a German musical parallel to the French, pictorial term "nuances" of significance. But it is not only that acoustical phenomena—harmonics, combination tones, etc., like echoes — or Doppler-effect dying wails of train whistles in nineteenth- or twentieth-century poetry—are figures for meanings, but that the relational connotations of *musical tones,* rather than acoustical noises, have been affirmed in the vehicle of the metaphor itself. It represents the phenomenology of experience in a powerful way: first, there is the almost crude trope, reworked from the earlier "Abt Vogler," of "life's common chord"—the givens of feelings, the routines of sensation—from which emanate the harmonics, barely heard or recorded only in what Leibniz called music's "unconscious arithmetic," reaching up into physical inaudibility as they simultaneously increase in frequency beyond about 15,000 cycles per second, and drop below the threshhold of audible amplitude. And yet, and yet...it is the harmonics, not the gross packagings of them we discern as tones or triads, which are the atoms of acoustical and hence of musical experience. And so the rumbling of the ordinary world seems to release the increasingly faint ideas, the overtones of consciousness, out of which it is itself ultimately composed.

Such an image, both forceful and accurate, must also be understood as coming from a special kind of experience of listening to music—from brooding over the act of listening through an understanding of the structural causes of the music's sensuous and emotive effects. It is this aspect of listening which Leigh Hunt was unable or unconcerned to figure forth in the early fragment previously noted. We may observe a moment toward the representation of sophisticated listening in all of Browning's music poems. "A Toccata of Galuppi's," to start with, is all talk over music, although there are several levels of audible or fancied discourse, and which is background, which moving against it—which is underscoring and sounding through holes in the other, music or chatter—is always nicely in question.[13] If it were only a matter of his moral about cultural history, Browning might as well have chosen, say, a masque of Inigo Jones' being performed for its doomed Caroline court. The specific function of the music in the poem is to be mimetic of chatter, as the poem's chatter is, indeed, to sound like rapid passage-work (with the brilliant prosodic conflict producing a *ritardando* at its coda: "Dear, dead women, with such hair, too" is jammed into the otherwise unvarying trochaic rhythm). The listener here is an over-hearer of both music and talk.

In "Master Hugues of Saxe-Gotha" the monologuist is the listening musician, responding to the consequences of his own playing; his meditation starts from the historical donné of the exercise by an old master whose very name rhymes with "fugues." The dramaturgy of fugal entrances, of which any listener would be aware, is heightened for the performer by the visual and kinetic dimensions of notational pattern and actual fingerings. In the poem, they are all at work to strengthen the imaginative difference between the execution and the architecture of formal structure, on the one hand, and the final human function, whatever or wherever it may be, on the other. Again, though, it is clear that throughout "Master Hugues" the organist is anchored to a moment in his own musical culture in which "Counterpoint glares like a Gorgon" (as opposed, say, to the taste of the second third of the twentieth century for polyphonic styles of the past in themselves). The intellectual web is spun out, rises, and drapes itself, in an unstated pictorial correspondence, over the tracery and other carved stonework in the church's interior, and whether its veil protects, obscures, obliterates, or even creatively mediates, remains the unanswered question about tradition and imagination, dwelling in the air like the overhang of echo.

In "Abt Vogler" the meditative structure grows out of the overhang of echoing in the vault of memory; the poem follows

[13]Wendell Stacy Johnson, "Browning's Music," *Journal of Aesthetics and Art Criticism* XII (Winter, 1963), 203-207, goes into this other aspect of metaphorical or "verbal" music in Browning's music poems.

the improvisation in time, and the emblematic readings of harmonic progressions in the famous final stanza lead toward a traditional meditative coda, a descent to the ground of ordinary life from the mind's flights, even as the flights of life alight on the beds of sleep and death. Chromatic descent then pauses for a moment on the last momentary peak of a suspension:

> Give me the keys. I feel for the common chord again,
>   Sliding by semitones till I sink into the minor,—yes,
> And I blunt it into a ninth, and I stand on alien ground,
>   Surveying awhile the heights I rolled from into the deep;
> Which, hark, I have dared and done, for my resting-place
>   is found,
>   The C Major of this life: so, now I will try to sleep.
>
>   (XII)

"Dared and done," but without the first "determin'd" from the triad in Smart's "A Song to David" which he is echoing—and now even the gross obviousness is appropriate to the image of the quotidian as C Major, easy, "normal," its signature uncluttered with sharps and flats, the Dorian tonality of march, power, order and health translated into classical diatonic conventions. But in an image when the extempore meditation is at its heights, "such gift be allowed to man, / That out of three sounds he frame, not a fourth sound, but a star," there is greater emblematic subtlety: a fundamental process of musical conceptualization, whereby the harmonic triad becomes not only an aural organism more significant than the sum of the meanings of its parts, but a self-sustaining object of attentive wonder, transcending even the embodying medium which generated it. The leap from tone to star is accomplished in something very like a conceit with a hole in it, and itself occurs at a high point of the poem's imaginative structure, paralleling perhaps a tonal peak in the composer's still-resounding improvisation on that small, private organ "of his own invention."

> Consider it well: each tone of our scale in itself is naught:
>   It is everywhere in the world—loud, soft, and all is said:
> Give it to me to use! I mix it with two in my thought:
>   And there!...   (VII)

Tones are ordinary particulars: music, like architectural structures, like poetry, builds upward as well as outward from its elements, and only from the tops of such buildings can their strength, and their fragility, be perceived.

In his "Parleying with Charles Avison" Browning himself becomes one of his monologuist listeners-to-music, but his discourse is with musicology, rather than with any performed composition. It is a moralization of the ruins of the simplistic ancestors of those structural and harmonic complexities of a later age which themselves have caused the crumbling. The presiding muse of the art here is Clio, not Euterpe or Terpsichore; the historical dialectic of stylistic succession as against a mysterious invariance, of attenuation and complexity, finally devolves upon the history of music. But for Browning, music's history is now and England, and Avison's trivial and silly little march tune becomes important because of its author's connection to Browning through a chain of teachers. The Avison poem is very explicit about how "There is no truer truth obtainable / By Man than comes of music." It is also very insistent upon resurrecting the Dorian ethos for a C Major march that can, like most marches, organize human life around it with a crudely Orphean force that all art envies.

But as an involved listener, there is no figure to challenge the Don Juan of *Fifine at the Fair*. He is a musical sophisticate like the others, capable of expressing a continuing wonder at the reductions which occur in moving from "Effect, in Art, to cause," still marvelling how music,

> that burst of pillared cloud by day
> And pillared fire by night, was product, must we say,
> Of modulating just, by enharmonic change,—
> The augmented sixth resolved,—from out the straighter
> range
> Of D sharp minor—leap of disemprisoned thrall—
> Into thy light and life, D major natural?   (639-641)

The actual harmonic resolution here—a conventional "Italian sixth," probably, pivoting around an enharmonic rewriting of D sharp/E flat—attests less to a musical sensibility than a feeling for the brightness, the "light and life" of the resolved D major.

But Don Juan's listening ear is most aware, both of what it hears and of itself, in the remarkable long section that weaves in and out of memories of Schumann's *Carnaval* (Op. 9). The monologuist has turned to it at a crucial point in his thoughts, hung somewhere between what Kierkegaard's protagonist of the "Either/Or" calls rotation of field and rotation of crops.[14] If Elvire's firmness makes his circle just, he can roam through many arcs, including, for example, Fifine's; a sensibility that knows its Raphael to be central and unwobbling can let its eyes sip Dore. The Fair through which he is walking leads, by a bit of involuntary memory, to the *Carnaval,* and the technique of musical variation as employed in that romantic potpourri becomes the correlative for the wandering eros. In lines 1515 to 1636 of *Fifine at the Fair* we are introduced to what I think is one of the very few anticipations in nineteenth-century literature of Swann's chasing down of his *petite phrase* through the corridors of sentimental association. The Don rehearses his recent keyboard reading of *Carnaval* not merely for its associations with the Pornic Fair, but as a model of an erotic rhythm of sharpened desire and satiation on the familiar:

> I somehow played the piece, remarked on each old theme
> I'the new dress; saw how food o' the soul, the stuff that's
> Made to furnish man with thought and feeling, is purveyed
> Substantially the same from age to age, with change
> Of the outside only for successive feasters. ...
>
> (1612-1616)

He is thinking of Schumann's generation of moods, of the successive "scenes mignonnes" from the "quatre notes" of the anagrammatic "sphinx" motives, of the very assemblage of the character pieces of the work. But he soon concentrates on the desire's banquet of sense, and on the history of taste as its projected image, tracing it along until

> one day, another age by due
> Rotation, pries, sniffs, smacks, discovers old is new,
> And sauce, our sires pronounced insipid, proves again
> Sole piquant, may resume its titillating reign —
> With music, most of all the arts, since change is there

---

[14] Soren Kierkegaard, *Either/Or,* tr. D. F. and L. M. Swenson (New York, 1959), I, 281-296.

> The law, and not the lapse: the precious means the rare,
> And not the absolute in all good save surprise.
> So I remarked upon our Schumann's victories
> Over the commonplace, how faded phrase grew fine,
> And palled perfection. ...   (1645-1654)

And when he turns to *Carnaval* in detail, it is, as he says, to Elvire's favorite portion of it,

> that movement, you prefer,
> Where dance and shuffle past, — he scolding while she pouts,
> She canting while he clams, — in those eternal bouts
> Of age, the dog — with youth, the cat — by rose-festoon
> Tied teasingly enough — Columbine, Pantaloon:
> She, toe-tips and *staccato*, — *legato*, shakes his poll
> And shambles in pursuit, the senior. *Fi la folle!*
> Lie to him! get his gold and pay its price! begin
> Your trade betimes, nor wait till you've wed Harlequin
> And need, at the week's end, to play the duteous wife,
> And swear you still love slaps and leapings more than life!
> Pretty, I say.   (1658-1669)

The Don is, of course, reading himself and his dancing gypsy girl into Schumann's *"Pantalon et Columbine"* piece, and, as in so many other great moments of self-betrayal by speakers in Browning, he is quite unaware of what he is doing. "And so I somehow-nohow played / The whole o'the pretty piece; and then..." he continues; if he means here the whole of *Carnaval* (rather than merely the *"Pantalon et Columbine"*), a startling and poignant memory-lapse underlines the authenticity of his proclaimed self-knowledge in a little epiphany of error. "Whatever weighed / My eyes down, furled the films about my wits?" he asks, and immediately goes on to essay an uneasy answer:

> suppose,
> The morning-bath, — the sweet monotony of those
> Three keys, flat, flat and flat, never a sharp at all, —
> Or else the brain's fatigue, forced even here to fall
> Into the same old track, and recognize the shift
> From old to new, and back to old again, and, — swift
> Or slow, no matter, — still the çertainty of change,
> Conviction we shall find the false, where'er we range,
> In art no less than nature. ...   (1671-1679)

His memory slips. There is indeed a B major section of the *"Reconnaissance"* piece, enharmonically arrived at through the C-flat in an A-flat minor close, and Don Juan's harping on the "sweet monotony" underlines the unavowed self-revelation earlier on. Whether desiring to eat the cake had, or to have the cake eaten, Browning's Don Juan has something of the same relation to Kierkegaard's, of Mozart's, as the protagonist of *Maude* to Hamlet. And though his reading of Schumann may be both consciously tendentious and unknowingly self-absorbed, it is never reductive, as reverie over familiar music can seldom be.[15] In this again, he is one of Browning's most mature listeners.

In Don Juan's available experience, as throughout his work, Browning was using the world of music in all its aspects—those of stylistic history, simpler acoustic theory, the facts of amateur and professional performance, and so forth—much as he could call up those other realms of art and historical melodrama. Particularly in its historical dimension, the spread of formal music lay before him like landscape; and, much like landscape in the poetry of some of his predecessors, provided not merely examples, but modes of exemplification of creative acts of knowledge—mappings as well as maps of the course of truth through the shadowed visible. By the end of his career, the earlier Romantic treatment of music as a conceptual and semantic instrument for the amplification of nature's susurrus might seem simplistic.

It is all the more interesting, then, to turn to "Flute-Music, With an Accompaniment" from the *Asolando* volume, where the entire poem is set in a typical Romantic outdoor musical environment, and "the bird-like fluting / Through the ash-tops yonder" of the opening lines is in itself like an archaic dance or aria theme picked up for a set of *variations brilliantes.* But the old theme is in itself merely archaistic, a clever pastiche

[15] I don't really believe that the error is Browning's, rather than his character's; if it is, however, its association with Don Juan's self-revelation would be of interest at another, deeper level. But this might be connected with the personal reminiscence of the amateur pianist when, in the final phases of the reverie, the realm of the ear sinks down to the sense of touch, and muscles "taxed by those tenths' and twelfth's unconscionable stretch," make for an impressive close.

—this is not the true mingled measure as one might hear it in Collins, or Bowles, or Wordsworth or Coleridge, the blending of a singer's or instrumentalist's voice with natural sound, or the filtering of that voice through the objects of landscape. This is not the post-pastoral natural music, unruined because never having been brought indoors; it is, rather, the high, formal musical art with which Browning was concerned throughout his career, now, literally, *asolate* — brought outdoors for recess and free play.

As the poem unrolls, *"He"* hears a neighbor's flute-playing, and hears it sentimentally and / as it were, picturesquely: he is a literary listener, and has an ear only for the Love, Hope, Musing and, finally, Acquiescence which, by turns, emanate from the inner source of sound curtained by the ash-tops. *"She,"* on the other hand, hears the music of music, none the less so because, having heard the amateur flautist practice before, she recognizes one of his five easy pieces—in this case, some etude or other by Jean Louis Tulou (a flautist and maker of flutes—whose trademark, one learns from Grove's *Dictionary,* was a nightingale). *She* is amused at what *He* concludes from what his "ear's auxiliar / —Fancy—found suggestive"; *She* can ask

> So, 't was distance altered
>   Sharps to flats? The missing
> Bar when syncopation faltered
>   (You thought—paused for kissing!)
> Ash-tops too felonious
>   Intercepted? Rather
> Say—they well-nigh made euphonious
>   Discord, helped to gather
> Phrase, by phrase, turn patches
>   Into simulated
> Unity which botching matches,—
>   Scraps reintegrated.   (133-144)

This is like the half-serious reductiveness of Aldous Huxley's itself reductive version of D. H. Lawrence, Mark Rampion, purporting to hear only the "horsehair on catgut" in Beethoven's quartet Op. 132, as an ad hoc response to Spandrell's mystical reading of it in *Point Counterpoint.* The dialectic is indeed of "fact and fancy" here, as several critics have pointed out. But it also handles, brilliantly as well as playfully, two contrasted versions of the role of music in an imaginative universe. *She* hears the music that goes on in Browning's poetry; *He* hears music of a more visionary sort, taking up, for example, the older theme of "Notes by distance made more sweet"—

> Distance—ash-tops aiding
> Reconciled scraps less contrarious,
> Brightened stuff fast fading.
>   (170-172)

Nevertheless, he is more aware of the human nuances, of the factuality of his visionary hearing for which there is no word. The separate responses of the two are polarized across a line cut by domestic comedy (and by the assignment of the reductive reading to the woman and the problematic one to the man, in a tradition that goes back at least as far as Chaucer's Chaunteclere and Pertelote). Those responses bifurcate a fiction which, in Browning's own rich sense of music, remains uncloven—a blended involvement with musical actuality and with the Imagination's lust for the discovery of signification in all experience. A Browning monologuist would hear all that *He* hears but *in*, not apart from, what *She* does. Their argument can be abandoned, not resolved, in bed; its resolution could only occur in that highest and most self-aware act of listening to music which becomes, through—not despite—its technical consciousness, an attention to the music of humanity.

Browning: Good Moments
and Ruined Quests

by Harold Bloom

One of the principles of interpretation that will arise out
of the future study of the intricacies of poetic revisionism,
and of the kinds of misreading that canon-formation engenders, is the realization that later poets and their critical
followers tend to misread strong precursors by a fairly consistent mistaking of literal for figurative, and of figurative for
literal. Browning misread the High Romantics, and particularly his prime precursor, Shelley, in this pattern, and through
time's revenges most modern poets and critics have done and
are doing the same to Browning. I am going to explore Browning, in this chapter, as the master of misprision he was, by attempting to show our tendency to read his epiphanies or
"good moments" as ruinations or vastations of quest, and our
parallel tendency to read his darkest visions-of-failure as if
they were celebrations.

I will concentrate on a small group of Browning's poems including *Cleon, Master Hugues of Saxe Gotha, A Toccata of
Galuppi's, Abt Vogler,* and *Andrea del Sarto,* but I cannot
evade for long my own obsession with *Childe Roland to the
Dark Tower Came,* and so it and its contrary chant, *Thamuris
Marching,* will enter late into this discourse. Indeed, I want to
end with a kind of critical self-analysis, and ask myself the
question: why am I obsessed by the *Childe Roland* poem, or

rather, what does it *mean* to be obsessed by that poem? How is
it that I cannot conceive of an antithetical practical criticism
of poetry without constantly being compelled to use *Childe
Roland* as a test case, as though it were the modern poem
proper, more even than say, *Tintern Abbey* or *Byzantium* or
The Idea of Order at Key West? Is there a way to make these
questions center upon critical analysis rather than upon psychic self-analysis?

In Browning's prose *Essay on Shelley,* there is an eloquent
passage that idealizes poetic influence:

> There is a time when the general eye has, so to speak, absorbed
> its fill of the phenomena around it, whether spiritual or mate-
> rial, and desires rather to learn the exacter significance of what
> it possesses, than to receive any augmentation of what is pos-
> sessed. Then is the opportunity for the poet of loftier vision, to
> lift his fellows.... The influence of such an achievement will
> not soon die out. A tribe of successors (Homerides) working
> more or less in the same spirit, dwell on his discoveries and
> reinforce his doctrine; till, at unawares, the world is found to be
> subsisting wholly on the shadow of a reality, on sentiments
> diluted from passions, on the tradition of a fact, the convention
> of a moral, the straw of last year's harvest.

Browning goes on to posit a mighty ladder of authentic
poets, in an objective and subjective alternation, who will
replace one another almost endlessly in succession, concerning which, "the world dares no longer doubt that its gradations
ascend." Translated, this means: "Wordsworth to Shelley to
Browning," in which Browning represents a triumph of what
he calls the objective principle. Against Browning's prose
idealization, I will set his attack upon the disciples of Keats in
his poem *Popularity:*

> And there's the extract, flasked and fine,
>   And priced and saleable at last!
> And Hobbs, Nobbs, Stokes and Nokes combine
>   To paint the future from the past,
>   Put blue into their line.

For "Hobbs, Nobbs, Stokes and Nokes" we might read Tennyson, Arnold, Rossetti, and whatever other contemporary
Keatsian, whether voluntary or involuntary, that Browning

wished to scorn. But the next stanza, the poem's last, would surely have cut against Browning himself if for "John Keats" we substituted "Percy Shelley":

> Hobbs hints blue,—straight he turtle eats:
> Nobbs prints blue,—claret crowns his cup:
> Nokes outdares Stokes in azure feats,—
> Both gorge. Who fished the murex up?
> What porridge had John Keats?

The vegetarian Shelley, according to his friend Byron, tended to dine on air and water, not fit fare for the strenuously hearty Browning, who in his later years was to become London's leading diner-out. But though Browning seems not to have had the slightest *personal* consciousness of an anxiety of influence, he wrote the most powerful poem ever to be explicitly concerned with the problem. This is the dramatic monologue *Cleon,* in which the imaginary jack-of-all-arts, Cleon, is in my judgment a kind of version of Matthew Arnold, whose *Empedocles on Etna* Browning had been reading. Arnold's Empedocles keeps lamenting his own and the world's belatedness, a lament that becomes a curious kind of inauthentic overconfidence in Cleon's self-defense:

> I have not chanted verse like Homer, no—
> Nor swept string like Terpander, no—nor carved
> And painted men like Phidias and his friend:
> I am not great as they are, point by point.
> But I have entered into sympathy
> With these four, running these into one soul,
> Who, separate, ignored each other's art.
> Say, is it nothing that I know them all?

Browning could enjoy the belatedness of Arnold or Rossetti, because no poet ever felt less belated than this exuberant daemon. We remember the malicious epithet applied to him by Hopkins: "Bouncing Browning." I think we can surmise that poetic belatedness as an affliction, whether conscious or unconscious, always rises in close alliance with ambivalence towards the prime precursor. Browning felt no ambivalence towards Shelley, such as Yeats had towards Shelley, or Shelley towards Wordsworth, or Wordsworth towards Milton. Brown-

ing loved Shelley unbrokenly and almost unreservedly from
the age of fourteen, when he first read him, until his own
death at the age of seventy-seven. But ambivalence is not the
only matrix from which the anxiety of influence rises. There is
perhaps a darker source in the guilt or shame of identifying
the precursor with the ego-ideal, and then living on in the
sense of having betrayed that identification by one's own
failure to have become oneself, by a realization that the ephebe
has betrayed his own integrity, and betrayed also the covenant
that first bound him to the precursor. That guilt unmistak-
ably was Browning's, as Betty Miller and others have shown,
and so the burden of belatedness was replaced in Browning
by a burden of dissimulation, a lying-against-the-self, rather
than a lying-against-time.

But is not that kind of shame only another mask for the
guilt-of-indebtedness, the only guilt that ever troubles a poet-
as-poet? Certainly, Shelley for Browning was precisely the
"numinous shadow" or ancestor-god whose baleful influence is
stressed by Nietzsche. Rather than demonstrate this too obviously, whether by recourse to Browning's poem *Pauline* or
by an examination of the unhappy episode in which the young
Browning yielded to his stern mother's Evangelical will, I
think it more interesting to seek out what is most difficult in
Browning, which is the total contrast between his optimism, a
quality both temperamental and theoretical, and the self-
destructive peculiarities of his men and women. I want to start
by puzzling over the grotesque and unique poem, *Master
Hugues of Saxe-Gotha,* with its curious and central contrast
between the charming organist who speaks the monologue and
the heavy pseudo-Bachian composer, also invented by Browning, whose name is the poem's title. The relationship between
performer and composer *is* the poem. This relationship is *not*
a displaced form of the ambivalence between ephebe and precursor, because the performer's reading/misreading of the
composer is very different from the later poet's interpretation
of an earlier one, or anyone's reading/misreading of any poet.
It is true that a performance is an interpretation, but a performance lacks the vital element of revisionism that makes for
fresh creation. The charm of the poem *Master Hugues of Saxe-*

G otha, like the chill of the somewhat similar but greater poem. *A Toccata of G aluppi's,* is precisely that we are free of the burden of misprision and that the performer in each poem is more like a reciter of a text than he is like a critic of a text. Yet it remains true that you cannot recite any poem without giving some interpretation of it, though I would hazard the speculation that even the strongest recital, acting, or performance is at best a weak reading/misreading, in the technical antithetical senses of "weak" and "strong," for again there is no strength, poetic or critical, without the dialectics of revisionism coming into play.

The organist earnestly wants to understand Hugues without revising him, but evidently the world is right and the poor organist wrong, in that less is meant than meets the ear in Hugues' mountainous fugues. Hugues is a kind of involuntary musical nihilist, who in effect would rather have the void as purpose than be void of purpose. The organist is not only old-fashioned in his devotion to Hugues but, as we might say now, old-fashioned in his devotion to meaning. Yet skepticism, a suspicion concerning both meaning-in-Hugues and meaning-in-life, has begun to gain strength in the organist, despite himself. His quasi-desperate test-performance of Hugues, thematically racing the sacristan's putting-out of the light, moves from one sadly negative conclusion to a larger negation, from "But where's music, the dickens?" to:

> Is it your moral of Life?
>   Such a web, simple and subtle,
> Weave we on earth here in impotent strife,
>   Backward and forward each throwing his shuttle,
> Death ending all with a knife?

The very reluctance of the organist's interpretation convinces us of its relevance to Hugues. Hugues will not "say the word," despite the organist's plea, and the organist lacks the strength to break out on his revisionary own and do what he wants to do, which is "unstop the full-organ, / Blare out the *mode Palestrina,*" akin to the gentle simplicity of his own nature. Yet we must not take the organist too literally; after all, there is nothing whatsoever to prevent him from playing

Palestrina to his own satisfaction in the moments of light that
remain to him. But it is the problematical, cumbersome, absurdly intricate Hugues who obsesses him, whose secret or lack
of a secret he is driven to solve. Despite himself, the organist
is on an antithetical quest, like absolutely every other monologist in Browning. The luminous last line of the poem is to be
answered, emphatically: "Yes!"

> While in the roof, if I'm right there,
>   ...Lo you, the wick in the socket!
> Hallo, you sacristan, show us a light there!
>   Down it dips, gone like a rocket.
> What, you want, do you, to come unawares,
> Sweeping the church up for first morning-prayers,
> And find a poor devil has ended his cares
> At the foot of your rotten-runged rat-riddled stairs?
>   Do I carry the moon in my pocket?

If the organist is right, then the gold in the gilt roof is a
better emblem of a final reality than the spider web woven by
Hugues. But fortunately the darkening of the light breaks in
upon an uneasy affirmation, and leaves us instead with the
realization that the organist is subject as well as object of his
own quest for meaning. Hugues goes on weaving his intricate
vacuities; the organist carries the moon in his pocket. Has the
poem ended, however humorously, as a ruined quest or as a
good moment? Does Browning make it possible for us to know
the difference between the two? Or is it the particular achievement of his art that the difference cannot be known? Does the
organist end by knowing he has been deceived, or does he end
in the beautiful earliness of carrying imagination in his own
pocket, in a transumptive allusion to the Second Spirit in one
of Browning's favorite poems, Shelley's *The Two Spirits:
An Allegory*? There the Second Spirit, overtly allegorizing
desire, affirms that the "lamp of love," carried within, gives
him the perpetual power to "make night day." Browning is
more dialectical, and the final representation in his poem is
deeply ambiguous. But final representation in his poem is
deeply ambiguous. But that is a depth of repression that I
want to stay with, and worry, for a space, if only because it

bothers me that *Master Hugues of Saxe-Gotha,* like so many of Browning's poems, ends in an *aporia,* in the reader's uncertainty as to whether he is to read literally or figuratively. Browning personally, unlike Shelley, was anything but an intellectual skeptic, and that he should create figures that abide in our uncertainty is at once his most salient and his most challenging characteristic.

A Toccata of Galuppi's can be read as a reversal of this poem, since it appears to end in the performer's conscious admission of belatedness and defeat. But Browning was quite as multiform a maker as poetic tradition affords, and the *Toccata* is as subtle a poem as ever he wrote. It invokes for us a grand Nietzschean question, from the Third Essay of *On the Genealogy of Morals:* "What does it mean when an artist leaps over into his opposite?" Nietzsche was thinking of Wagner, but Browning in the *Toccata* may be another instance. Nietzsche's ultimate answer to his own question prophesied late Freud, if we take the answer to be: "All great things bring about their own destruction through an act of self-overcoming." I think we can say rather safely that no one was less interested in *Selbstaufhebung* than Robert Browning; he was perfectly delighted to be at once subject and object of his own quest. Like Emerson, whom he resembles only in this single respect, he rejoiced always that there were so many of him, so many separate selves happily picnicking together in a single psyche. From a Nietzschean point of view, he must seem only an epitome of some of the most outrageous qualities of the British empirical and Evangelical minds, but he is actually more sublimely outrageous even than that. There are no dialectics that can subsume him, because he is not so much evasive as he is preternatural, wholly daemonic, with an astonishing alliance perpetual in him between an impish cunning and endless linguistic energy. I think we can surmise why he was so fascinated by poets like Christopher Smart and Thomas Lovell Beddoes, poets who represented the tradition of Dissenting Enthusiasm carried over into actual madness. With energies like Browning's, and self-confidence like Browning's, it took a mind as powerful as Browning's to avoid being carried by Enthusiasm into alienation, but perhaps the oddest of all

Browning's endless oddities is that he was incurably sane, even
as he imagined his gallery of pathological enthusiasts, mono-
maniacs, and marvelous charlatans.

There are at least four voices coldly leaping along in *A
Toccata of Galuppi's,* and only one of them is more or less
Browning's, and we cannot be certain even of that. Let us break
in for the poem's conclusion, as the monologist first addresses
the composer whose "touch-piece" he is playing, and next the
composer answers back, *but only through the monologist's
performance,* and finally the speaker-performer acknowledges
his defeat by the heartlessly brilliant Galuppi:

[Stanzas XI-XV have been deleted from text.]

The "swerve" *is* the Lucretian *clinamen,* and we might say
that Galuppi, like Lucretius, assaults the monologist-performer
with the full strength of the Epicurean argument. One possible interpretation is that Browning, as a fierce Transcen-
dentalist of his own sect, a sect of one, is hammering at the
Victorian spiritual compromise, which his cultivated speaker
exemplifies. That interpretation would confirm the poem's
seriocomic opening:

> Oh Galuppi, Baldassaro, this is very sad to find!
> I can hardly misconceive you; it would prove me deaf and
>   blind;
> But although I take your meaning, 'tis with such a heavy
>   mind!

Galuppi's triumph, on this reading, would be the dramatic
one of shaking up this cultivated monologist, who first half-
scoffs at Galuppi's nihilism, but who ends genuinely frightened
by the lesson Galuppi has taught which is a lesson of mortality
and consequent meaninglessness. But I think that is to under-
estimate the monologist, who is a more considerable temperament even than the organist who plays Hugues and can bear
neither to give Hugues up nor accept Hugues' emptiness.
Galuppi is no Hugues, but a powerfully sophisticated artist
who gives what was wanted of him, but with a Dance-of-Death
aspect playing against his audience's desires. And the speaker,
who knows physics, some geology, a little mathematics, and will
not quite abandon his Christian immortality, is at least as

enigmatic as the organist, and for a parallel reason. Why cannot he let Galuppi alone? What does he quest for in seeing how well he can perform that spirited and elegant art? Far more even that Galuppi, or Galuppi's audience, or than Browning, the speaker is obsessed with mortality:

> Then they left you for their pleasure: till in due time,
> one by one,
> Some with lives that came to nothing, some with deeds
> as well undone,
> Death stepped tacitly and took them where they never see
> the sun.

One of the most moving elements in the poem is its erotic nostalgia, undoubtedly the single sphere of identity between the monologist and Browning himself. Eros crowds the poem, with an intensity and poignance almost Shakespearean in its strength. Nothing in the poem is at once so moving and so shocking as the monologist's final "Dear dead women, with such hair, too —," for this spiritual trimmer is very much a sensual man, like his robust creator. It is the cold Galuppi who is more the dualist, more the artist fulfilling the Nietzschean insight that the ascetic ideal is a defensive evasion by which art preserves itself against the truth. But where, as readers, does that leave us, since this time Browning elegantly has cleared himself away? His overt intention is pretty clear, and I think pretty irrelevant also. He wants us — unlike the monologist, unlike Galuppi, unlike Galuppi's hard-living men and women — to resort to his ferocious version of an antithetical Protestantism, which is I think ultimately his misprision of Shelley's antithetical humanism. Yet Browning's art has freed us of Browning, though paradoxically not of Shelley, or at least of the strong Lucretian element in Shelley. Has the monologist quested after Galuppi's truth, only to end up in a vastation of his own comforting evasions of the truth? That would be the canonical reading, but it would overliteralize a metaleptic fuguration that knowingly has chosen not to attempt a reversal of time. When the speaker ends by feeling "chilly and grown old," then he has introjected Galuppi's world and Galuppi's music, and projected his own compromise formulations. But this is an *illusio*, a metaleptic figuration that is on the verge of becoming an opening irony or reaction-formation again, that is, rejoining the tone of jocular evasion that began the poem. Nothing has happened because nothing has changed, and the final grimness of Browning's eerie poem is that its speaker is caught in a repetition. He will pause awhile, and then play a toccata of Galuppi's again.

Let us try a third music-poem or improvisation, the still more formidable *Abt Vogler*, where the daemonic performer is also the momentary composer, inventing fitfully upon an instrument of his own invention, grandly solitary because there is nothing for him to interpret except his own interpretation of his own creation. The canonical readings available here are too weak to be interesting, since they actually represent the poem as being pious. The historical Vogler was regarded by some as a pious fraud, but Browning's Vogler is too complex to be regarded either as an impostor or as sincerely devout. What matters most is that he is primarily an extemporizer, rather than necessarily an artist, whether as performer or composer. The poem leaves open (whatever Browning's intentions) the problem of whether Vogler is a skilled illusionist, or something more than that. At the least, Vogler is self-deceived, but even the self-deception is most complex. It is worth knowing what I must assume that Browning knew; Vogler's self-invented instruments sounded splendid only when played by Vogler. Though the great temptation in reading this poem is to interpret it as a good moment precariously attained, and then lost, I think the stronger or antithetical reading here will show that this is very nearly as much a poem of ruined quest as *Childe Roland* or *Andrea del Sarto* is.

Abt Vogler is one of those poems that explain Yeat's remark to the effect that he feared Browning as a potentially dangerous influence upon him. If we could read *Abt Vogler* without interpretative suspicion (and I believe we cannot), then the poem would seem to be a way-station between the closing third of *Adonais* and Yeats's Byzantium poems. It establishes itself in a state of being that seems either to be beyond the antithesis of life and death, or else that seems to be the state of art itself. Yet, in the poem *Abt Vogler,* I think we have neither, but something more puzzling, a willed phantasmagoria that is partly Browning's and partly an oddity, a purely visionary dramatic monologue.

Vogler, we ought to realize immediately, does not seek the purposes of art, which after all is hard work. Vogler is day-dreaming, and is seeking a magical power over nature or super-nature, as in the debased Kabbalist myth of Solomon's seal. Vogler is not so much playing his organ as enslaving it to his magical purposes, purposes that do not distinguish between angel and demon, heaven and hell. Vogler is no Blakean visionary; he seeks not to marry heaven and hell, but merely to achieve every power that he can. And yet he has a moving purpose, akin to Shelley's in *Prometheus Unbound,* which is to aid earth's mounting into heaven. But, is his vision proper something we can grant the prestige of vision, or is there not a dubious element in it?

Being made perfect, when the subject is someone like Vogler, is a somewhat chancy phenomenon. Unlike the sublimely crazy Johannes Agricola, in one of Browning's earliest and most frightening dramatic monologues, Vogler is not a genuine Enthusiast, certain of his own Election. Stanza VI has a touch of *Cleon* about it, and stanza VII is clearly *unheimlich,* despite the miraculous line: "That out of three sounds he frame, not a fourth sound, but a star." But with Stanzas VIII and IX, which are this poem's *askesis* or sublimation, it is not so easy to distinguish Vogler from Browning, or one of the beings always bouncing around in Browning, anyway:

VIII

Well, it is gone at last, the palace of music I reared;
    Gone! and the good tears start, the praises that come too
      slow;
For one is assured at first, one scarce can say that he feared,
    That he even gave it a thought, the gone thing was to go.
Never to be again! But many more of the kind
    As good, nay, better perchance: is this your comfort to
      me?
To me, who must be saved because I cling with my mind
    To the same, same self, same love, same God: ay, what
      was, shall be.

IX

Therefore to whom turn I but to thee, the ineffable Name?
   Builder and maker, thou, of houses not made with hands!
What, have fear of change from thee who art ever the same?
   Doubt that thy power can fill the heart that thy power
      expands?
There shall never be one lost good! What was, shall live as
      before;
   The evil is null, is nought, is silence implying sound;
What was good shall be good, with, for evil, so much good
      more;
   On the earth the broken arcs; in the heaven, a perfect
      round.

The poem, from here to the end, in the three final stanzas, is
suddenly as much Browning's Magnificat as the *Song to David,*
which is deliberately echoed in the penultimate line, is Smart's.
But what does that mean, whether in this poem, or whether
about Browning himself? Surely he would not acknowledge,
openly, that his is the art of the extemporizer, the illusionist
improvising? Probably not, but the poem may be acknowledging an anxiety that he possesses, to much that effect. Whether
this is so or not, to any degree, how are we to read the final
stanza?

Well, it is earth with me; silence resumes her reign:
   I will be patient and proud, and soberly acquiesce.
Give me the keys. I feel for the common chord again,
   Sliding by semitones, till I sink to the minor,—yes,
And I blunt it into a ninth, and I stand on alien ground,
   Surveying awhile the heights I rolled from into the deep;
Which, hark, I have dared and done, for my resting-place
      is found,
   The C Major of this life: so now I will try to sleep.

This descent to C Major separates Vogler totally from Browning again, since of the many keys in which the genuinely musical
Browning composes, his resting place is hardly a key without
sharps or flats. Browning has his direct imitation of Smart's
Song to David in his own overtly religious poem, *Saul,* and so
we can be reasonably certain that Vogler does not speak for

Browning when the improviser belatedly stands on alien ground, surveying the Sublime he had attained, and echoes Smart's final lines:

Thou at stupendous truth believ'd; —
And now the matchless deed's atchiev'd,
DETERMINED, DARED, and DONE.

What Vogler has dared and done is no more than to have dreamed a belated dream; where Browning is, in regard to that Promethean or Shelleyan a dream, is an enigma, at least in this poem. What *Abt Vogler,* as a text, appears to proclaim *is* the impossibility of our reading it, insofar as reading means being able to govern the interplay of literal and figurative meanings in a text. Canonically, in terms of all received readings, this poem is almost an apocalyptic version of a Browningesque "Good Moment," a time of privilege or an epiphany, a sudden manifestation of highest vision. Yet the patterns of revisionary misprision are clearly marked upon the poem, and they tend to indicate that the poem demands to be read figuratively against its own letter, as another parable of ruined quest, or confession of imaginative failure, or the shame of knowing such failure.

I turn to *Andrea del Sarto,* which with *Childe Roland to the Dark Tower Came,* and the meditation entitled *The Pope* in *The Ring and the Book,* seems to me to represent Browning at his greatest. Here there would appear to be no question about the main issue of interpretation, for the canonical readings seem fairly close to the poem in its proclamation that this artist's quest is ruined, that Andrea stands self-condemned by his own monologue. Betty Miller has juxtaposed the poem, brilliantly, with this troubled and troublesome passage in Browning's *Essay on Shelley:*

Although of such depths of failure there can be no question here we must in every case betake ourselves to the review of a poet's life ere we determine some of the nicer questions concerning his poetry, —more especially if the performance we seek to estimate aright, has been obstructed and cut short of completion by circumstances, —a disastrous youth or a premature death. We may learn from the biography whether his spirit invariably saw and spoke from the last height to which it had attained. An absolute vision is not for this world, but we are permitted a continual approximation to it, every degree of which in the individual, provided it exceed the attainment of the masses, must procure him a clear advantage. Did the poet ever attain to a higher platform than where he rested and exhibited a result? Did he know more than he spoke of?

On this juxtaposition, Andrea and Browning alike rested on a level lower than the more absolute vision they could have attained. Certainly Andrea tells us, perhaps even shows us, that he knows more than he paints. But Browning? If he was no Shelley, he was also no Andrea, which in part is the burden of the poem. But only in part, and whether there is some level of *apologia* in this monologue, in its patterning, rather than its overt content, is presumably a question that a more antithetical practical criticism ought to be capable of exploring.

Does Andrea overrate his own potential? If he does, *then there is no poem,* for unless his dubious gain-in-life has paid for a genuine loss-in-art, then he is too self-deceived to be interesting, even to himself. Browning has complicated this matter, as he complicates everything. The poem's subtitle reminds us that Andrea was called "The Faultless Painter," and Vasari, Browning's source, credits Andrea with everything in execution but then faults him for lacking ambition, for not attempting the Sublime. Andrea, in the poem, persuades us of a wasted greatness not so much by his boasting ("At any rate 'tis easy, all of it! / No sketches first, no studies, that's long past: / I do what many dream of, all their lives..."), but by his frightening skill in sketching his own twilight-piece, by his showing us how "A common greyness silvers everything—." Clearly, this speaker knows loss, and clearly he is the antithesis of his uncanny creator, whose poetry never suffers from a lack of ambition, who is always Sublime where he is most Grotesque, and always Grotesque when he storms the Sublime. Andrea does not represent anything in Browning directly, not even the betrayed relationship of the heroic precursor, yet he does represent one of Browning's anxieties, an anxiety related to but not identical with the anxiety of influence. It is an anxiety of representation, or a fear of forbidden meanings, or in Freudian language precisely a fear of the return-of-the-repressed, even though such a return would cancel out a poem-as-poem, or is it *because* such a return would end poetry as such?

Recall that Freud's notion of repression speaks of an unconsciously *purposeful* forgetting, and remind yourself also that what Browning could never bear was a sense of *purposelessness*. It is purposelessness that haunts Childe Roland, and we remember again what may be Nietzsche's most powerful insight, which closes the great Third Essay of *Towards the Genealogy of Morals*. The ascetic ideal, Nietzsche said, by which he meant also the aesthetic ideal, was the only *meaning* yet found for human suffering, and mankind would rather have the void *for* purpose than be void *of* purpose. Browning's great fear, purposelessness, was related to the single quality that had moved and impressed him most in Shelley: the remorseless purposefulness of the Poet in *Alastor*, of Prometheus, and of Shelley himself questing for death in *Adonais*. Andrea, as an artist, is the absolute antithesis of the absolute idealist Shelley, and so Andrea is a representation of profound Browningesque anxiety.

But how is this an anxiety of representation? We enter again the dubious area of *belatedness*, which Browning is reluctant to represent, but is too strong and authentic a poet to avoid. Though Andrea uses another vocabulary, a defensively evasive one, to express his relationship to Michelangelo, Raphael, and Leonardo, he suffers the burden of the latecomer. His Lucrezia is the emblem of his belatedness, his planned excuse for his failure in strength, which he accurately diagnoses as a failure in will. And he ends in deliberate belatedness, and in his perverse need to be cuckolded:

> What would one have?
> In heaven, perhaps, new chances, one more chance—
> Four great walls in the New Jerusalem,
> Meted on each side by the angel's reed,
> For Leonard, Rafael, Agnolo and me
> To cover—the three first without a wife,
> While I have mine! So—still they overcome
> Because there's still Lucrezia,—as I choose.
>
> Again the Cousin's whistle! Go, my Love.

Can we say that Andrea represents what Shelley dreaded to become, the extinguished hearth, an ash without embers? We know that Shelley need not have feared, yet the obsessive, hidden fear remains impressive. Browning at seventy-seven was as little burned out as Hardy at eighty-eight, Yeats at seventy-four, or Stevens at seventy-five, and his *Asolando,* his last book, fiercely prefigures Hardy's *Winter Words,* Yeats's *Last Poems,* and Stevens's *The Rock,* four astonishing last bursts of vitalism in four of the strongest modern poets. What allies the four volumes (*The Rock* is actually the last section of Steven's *Collected Poems,* but he had planned it as a separate volume under the title *Autumn Umber*) is their overcoming of each poet's abiding anxiety of representation. "Representation," in poetry, ultimately means self-advocacy; as Hartman says: "You justify either the self or that which stands greatly against it: perhaps both at once." We could cite Nietzsche here on the poet's Will-to-Power, but the more orthodox Coleridge suffices, by reminding us that there can be no origination without discontinuity, and that only the Will can interrupt the repetition-compulsion that *is* nature. In the final phases of Browning, Hardy, Yeats, and Stevens, the poet's Will raises itself against Nature, and this antithetical spirit breaks through a final anxiety and dares to represent itself as what Coleridge called self-determining spirit. Whether Freud would have compounded this self-realizing instinct with his "detours towards death" I do not know, but I think it is probable. In this final phase, Browning and his followers (Hardy and Yeats were overtly influenced by Browning, and I would suggest a link between the extemporizing, improvising aspect of Stevens, and Browning) are substituting a transumptive representation for the still-abiding presence of Shelley, their common ancestor.

I want to illustrate this difficult point by reference to Browning's last book, particularly to its *Prologue,* and to the sequence called *Bad Dreams.* My model, ultimately, is again the Lurianic Kabbalah, with its notion of *gilgul,* of lifting up a precursor's spark, provided that he is truly one's precursor, truly of one's own root. *Gilgul* is the ultimate *tikkun,* as far as an act of representation can go. What Browning does is fascinatingly like the pattern of *gilgul,* for at-the end he takes up precisely Shelley's dispute with Shelley's prime precursor, Wordsworth.

By doing for Shelley what Shelley could not do for himself, overcome Wordsworth, Browning lifts up or redeems Shelley's spark or ember, and renews the power celebrated in the *Ode to the West Wind* and Act IV of *Prometheus Unbound.* I will try to illustrate this complex pattern, after these glances at *Asolando,* by returning for a last time (I hope) to my personal obsession with *Childe Roland to the Dark Tower Came,* and then concluding this discourse by considering Browning's late reversal of *Childe Roland* in the highly Shelleyan celebration, *Thamuris Marching.*

The *Prologue* to *Asolando* is another in that long series of revisions of the *Intimations* Ode that form so large a part of the history of nineteenth- and twentieth-century British and American poetry. But Browning consciously gives a revision of a revision, compounding *Alastor* and the *Hymn to Intellectual Beauty* with the parent poem. What counts in Browning's poem is not the Wordsworthian gleam, called here, in the first stanza, an "alien glow," but the far more vivid Shelleyan fire, that Browning recalls seeing for the first time, some fifty years before:

> How many a year, my Asolo,
>   Since—one step just from sea to land—
> I found you, loved yet feared you so—
>   For natural objects seemed to stand
> Palpably fire-clothed! No—
>
> No mastery of mine o'er these!
>   Terror with beauty, like the Bush
> Burning but unconsumed. Bend knees,
>   Drop eyes to earthward! Language? Tush!
> Silence 'tis awe decrees.
>
> And now? The lambent flame is—where?
>   Lost from the naked world: earth, sky,
> Hill, vale, tree, flower,—Italia's rare
>   O'er-running beauty crowds the eye—
> But flame? The Bush is bare.

When Shelley abandoned the fire, then it was for the transumptive trumpet of a prophecy, or in *Adonais* for the same wind rising ("The breath whose might I have invoked in song / Descends on me") to carry him beyond voice as beyond

sight. Browning, as an Evangelical Protestant, fuses the Shelleyan heritage with the Protestant God in a powerfully in-
congruous transumption:

> Hill, vale, tree, flower—they stand distinct,
>   Nature to know and name. What then?
> A Voice spoke thence which straight unlinked
>   Fancy from fact: see, all's in ken:
> Has once my eyelid winked?
>
> No, for the purged ear apprehends
>   Earth's import, not the eye late dazed:
> The voice said 'Call my works thy friends!
>   At Nature dost thou shrink amazed?
> God is it who transcends.'

This is an absolute logocentrism, and is almost more than
any poem can bear, particularly at a time as late as 1889. Browning gets away with it partly by way of a purged ear, partly because his Protestantism condenses what High Romanticism
normally displaces, the double-bind situation of the Protestant believer whose God simultaneously says "Be like Me in My
stance towards Nature" and "Do not presume to resemble Me in
My stance towards nature." The sheer energy of the Browningesque daemonic Sublime carries the poet past what ought
to render him imaginatively schizoid.

But not for long, of course, as a glance at *Bad Dreams* will
indicate, a glance that then will take us back to the greatest of
Browning's nightmares, the demonic romance of *Childe
Roland. Bad Dreams III* is a poem in which the opposition between Nature and Art *has* been turned into a double-bind, with
its contradictory injunctions:

> This was my dream! I saw a Forest
>   Old as the earth, no track nor trace
> Of unmade man. Thou, Soul, explorest—
>   Though in a trembling rapture—space
> Immeasurable! Shrubs, turned trees,
> Trees that touch heaven, support its frieze
> Studded with sun and moon and star:
> While—oh, the enormous growths that bar
> Mine eye from penetrating past

Their tangled twine where lurks—nay, lives
Royally lone, some brute-type cast
In the rough, time cancels, man forgives.
On, Soul! I saw a lucid City
Of architectural device
Every way perfect. Pause for pity,
Lightning! Nor leave a cicatrice
On those bright marbles, dome and spire,
Structures palatial,—streets which mire
Dares not defile, paved·all too fine
For human footstep's smirch, not thine—
Proud solitary traverser,
My Soul, of silent lengths of way—
With what ecstatic dread, aver,
Lest life start sanctioned by thy stay!
Ah, but the last sight was the hideous!
A city, yes,—a Forest, true,—
But each devouring each. Perfidious
Snake-plants had strangled what I knew
Was a pavilion once: each oak
Held on his horns some spoil he broke
By surreptiously beneath
Upthrusting: pavements, as with teeth,
Griped huge weed widening crack and split
In squares and circles stone-work erst.
Oh, Nature—good! Oh, Art—no whit
Less worthy! Both in one—accurst!

In the sequence of *Bad Dreams,* Browning himself, as interpreter of his own text, identifies Nature with the husband, Art
with the wife, and the marriage of Art and Nature, man and
woman—why, with Hell, and a sadomasochistic sexual Hell,
at that. But the text can sustain very diverse interpretations, as
the defensive intensity of repression here is enormously strong.
The City is of Art, but like Yeats's Byzantium, which it
prophesies, it is also a City of Death-in-Life, and the previous
vision of the forest is one of a Nature that might be called
Life-in-Death. Neither realm can bear the other, in both senses
of "bear"—"bring forth" or "tolerate." Neither is the other's
precursor, and each devours the other, if they are brought
together. This is hardly the vision of the *Prologue* to *Asolando,*
as there seems no room for either Browning or God in the

world of the final stanza. Granted that this is nightmare, or severe repression partly making a return, it carries us back to Browning at his most problematic and Sublime, to his inverted vision of the Center, *Childe Roland to the Dark Tower Came.*

As the author of two full-scale commentaries on this poem (in *The Ringers in the Tower*, 1971, and in *A Map of Misreading*, 1975) I reapproach the text with considerable wariness, fairly determined not only that I will not repeat myself, but also hopefully aiming not merely to uncover my own obsessional fixation upon so grandly grotesque a quest-romance. But I recur to the question I asked at the start of this discourse; is there an attainable *critical* knowledge to be gathered from this critical obsession?

Roland, though a Childe or ephebe on the road to a demonic version of the Scene of Instruction, is so consciously belated a quester that he seems at least as much an obsessive interpreter as anything else purposive that he might desire to become. He out-Nietzsches Nietzsche's Zarathustra in his compulsive will-to-power over the interpretation of his own text. It is difficult to conceive of a more belated hero, and I know of no more extreme literary instance of a quest emptying itself out. Borges accurately located in Browning one of the precursors of Kafka, and perhaps only Kafka's *The Castle* rivals *Childe Roland* as a Gnostic version of what was once romance. Nearly every figuration in the poem reduces to ruin, yet the poem, as all of us obscurely sense, appears to end in something like triumph, in a Good Moment carried through to a supreme representation:

> There they stood, ranged along the hill-sides, met
>   To view the last of me, a living frame
>   For one more picture! in a sheet of flame
> I saw them and I knew them all. And yet
> Dauntless the slug-horn to my lips I set,
>   And blew, '*Childe Roland to the Dark Tower came.*'

Surely it is outrageous to call this a Supreme or even a Good Moment? The stanza just before ends with the sound of loss: "one moment knelled the woe of years." Wordsworth and Coleridge had viewed the Imagination as compensatory, as trading off experiential loss for poetic gain, a formula that we can begin to believe was an unmitigated calamity. It is the peculiar fascination of *Childe Roland,* as a poem, that it undoes every High Romantic formula, that it exposes the Romantic imagination as being merely an accumulative principle of repression? But such negation is itself simplistic, and evades what is deepest and most abiding in this poem, which is the representation of *power.* For here, I think, is the kernel of our critical quest, that Kabbalistic point which is at once *ayin,* or nothingness, and *ehyeh,* or the representation of Absolute Being, the rhetorical irony or *illusio* that always permits a belated poem to begin again in its quest for renewed strength. Signification has wandered away, and Roland is questing for lost and forgotten *meaning,* questing for *representation,* for a seconding or re-advocacy of his own self. Does he not succeed, far better than Tennyson's Ulysses and Percivale, and far better even than the Solitaries of the High Romantics, in this quest for representation? Let us grant him, and ourselves, that this is a substitute for his truly impossible original objective, for that was the *antithetical,* Shelleyan dream of rebegetting oneself, of breaking through the web of nature and so becoming one's own imaginative father. Substitution, as Roland shows, needs not be a sublimation, but can move from repression *through* sublimation to climax in a more complex act of defense.

Psychoanalysis has no single name for this act, unless we were willing (as we are not) to accept the pejorative one of paranoia for what is, from any point of view that transcends the analytic, a superbly valuable act of the will. Roland teaches us that what psychoanalysis calls "introjection" and "projection" are figurations for the spiritual processes of identification and apocalyptic rejection that exist at the outer borders of poetry. Roland leans, and we learn with him, that the representation of power *is* itself a power, and that this latter power or strength is the only purposiveness that we shall know. Roland, at the close, is re-inventing the self, but at the considerable expense of joining that self to a visionary company of loss, and loss means loss of *meaning* here. The endless fascination of his poem, for any critical reader nurtured upon Romantic tradition, is that the poem, more clearly than any other, neverthe-

less does precisely what any strong Romantic poem does, at
once de-idealizes itself far more thoroughly than we can de-
idealize it, yet points also beyond this self-deconstruction or
limitation or reduction to the First Idea, on to a re-imagining,
to a power-making that no other discursive mode affords. For
Roland, as persuasively as any fictive being, warns us against
the poisonous ravishments of truth itself. He and his reader
have moved only through discourse together, and he and his
reader are less certain about what they know than they were as
the poem began, but both he and his reader have endured unto
a representation of more strength than they had at the start,
and such a representation indeed turns out to be a kind of
restitution, a *tikkun* for repairing a fresh breaking-of-the-
vessels. Meaning has been more curtailed than restored, but
strength is revealed as antithetical to meaning.

I conclude with a great poem by Browning that is his conscious revision of *Childe Roland:* the marvelous late chant,
Thamuris Marching, which is one of the finest unknown, unread poems by a major poet in the language. Twenty-two
years after composing *Childe Roland,* Browning, not at the
problematic age of thirty-nine, but now sixty-one, knows well
that no spring has followed or flowered past meridian. But
Childe Roland is a belated poem, except in its transumptive
close, while all of *Thamuris Marching* accomplishes a metaleptic reversal, for how could a poem be more overwhelmingly early than this? And yet the situation of the quester is
objectively terrible from the start of this poem, for Thamuris
knows he is marching to an unequal contest, a poetic struggle
of one heroic ephebe against the greatest of precursors, the
Muses themselves. "Thamuris marching," the strong phrase
repeated three times in the chant, expresses the *exuberance
of purpose,* the Shelleyan remorseless joy in pure, self-
destructive poetic quest, that Browning finally is able to
grant himself.

Here is Browning's source, *Iliad* II, 594 ff:

> ...and Dorion, where the Muses
> encountering Thamyris the Thracian stopped him from
> singing, as he came from Oichalia and Oichalian Eurytos;

> for he boasted that he would surpass, if the very Muses,
> daughters of Zeus who holds the aegis, were singing
>   against him.
> and these in their anger struck him maimed, and the
>   voice of wonder
> they took away, and made him a singer without memory;
>
> [Lattimore version]

Homer does not say that Thamyris lost the contest, but rather that the infuriated Muses lost their divine temper, and unvoiced him by maiming his memory, without which no one can be a poet. Other sources, presumably known to Browning, mention a contest decided in the Muses' favor by Apollo, after which those ungracious ladies blinded Thamyris, and removed his memory, so as to punish him for his presumption. Milton, in the invocation to light that opens Book III of *Paradise Lost*, exalted Thamyris by coupling him with Homer, and then associated his own ambitions with both poets:

> Nightly I visit: nor sometimes forget
> Those other two equall'd with me in Fate,
> So were I equall'd with them in renown,
> Blind Thamyris and blind Maeonides.

Milton presumably had read in Plutarch that Thamyris was credited with an epic about the war waged by the Titans against the Gods, the theme that Browning would associate with Shelley and with Keats. Browning's Thamuris marches to a Shelleyan *terza rima,* and marches through a visionary universe distinctly like Shelley's, and overtly proclaimed as being *early:* "From triumph on to triumph, mid a ray / Of early morn—." Laughing as he goes, yet knowing fully his own doom, Thamuris marches through a landscape of joy that is the deliberate point-by-point reversal of Childe Roland's self-made phantasmagoria of ordeal-by-landscape:

> Thamuris, marching, laughed 'Each flake of foam'
> (As sparklingly the ripple raced him by)
> 'Mocks slower clouds adrift in the blue dome!'
>
> For Autumn was the season; red the sky
> Held morn's conclusive signet of the sun
> To break the mists up, bid them blaze and die.

Morn had the mastery as, one by one
All pomps produced themselves along the tract
From earth's far ending to near Heaven begun.

Was there a ravaged tree? it laughed compact
With gold, a leaf-ball crisp, high-brandished now,
Tempting to onset frost which late attacked.

Was there a wizened shrub, a starveling bough,
A fleecy thistle filched from by the wind,
A weed, Pan's trampling hoof would disallow?

Each, with a glory and a rapture twined
About it, joined the rush of air and light
And force: the world was of one joyous mind.
                                                    (19-36)

From Roland's reductive interpretations we have passed to
the imagination's heightened expansions. And though this
quest is necessarily for the fearful opposite of poetic divination,
we confront, not ruin, but the Good Moment exalted and
transfigured, as though for once Browning utterly could fuse
literal and figurative:

Say not the birds flew! they forebore their right—
Swam, reveling onward in the roll of things.
Say not the beasts' mirth bounded! that was flight—

How could the creatures leap, no lift of wings?
Such earth's community of purpose, such
The ease of earth's fulfilled imaginings—

So did the near and far appear to touch
In the moment's transport—that an interchange
Of function, far with near, seemed scarce too much;
                                                    (37-45)

Roland's band of failures has become the glorious band of
precursors among whom Thamuris predominates. The
Shelleyan west wind of imagination rises, Destroyer and
Creater, as Thamuris, eternally early, stands as the true
ephebe, "Earth's poet," against the Heavenly Muse:

Therefore the morn-ray that enriched his face,
If it gave lambent chill, took flame again
From flush of pride; he saw, he knew the place.

What wind arrived with all the rhythms from plain,

Hill, dale, and that rough wildwood interspersed?
Compounding these to one consummate strain,

It reached him, music; but his own outburst
Of victory concluded the account,
And that grew song which was mere music erst.

'Be my Parnassos, thou Pangaian mount!
And turn thee, river, nameless hitherto!
Famed shalt thou vie with famed Pieria's fount!

'Here I await the end of this ado:
Which wins—Earth's poet or the Heavenly Muse.'

There is the true triumph of Browning's art, for the ever-early Thamuris is Browning as he wished to have been, locked in a solitary struggle against the precursor-principle, but struggling *in* the visionary world of the precursor. Roland rode through a Gnostic universe in which the hidden God, Shelley, was repressed, a repression that gave Browning a negative triumph of the Sublime made Grotesque. In *Thamuris Marching*, the joyous struggle is joined overtly, and the repressed partly returns, to be repressed again into the true Sublime, as Browning lifts up the sparks of his own root, to invoke that great mixed metaphor of the Lurianic Kabbalah. There is a breaking-of-the-vessels, but the sparks are scattered again, and become Shelley's *and* Browning's words, mixed together, among mankind.

Browning and the Question of Myth

by Robert Langbaum

The history of criticism is largely the history of the changing questions we ask about works of art. The pre-eminence in
our time of Yeats, Eliot and Joyce, and the connection of these
writers with an aristic method and a mode of thought that Eliot,
in reviewing Joyce's *Ulysses,* has himself called *mythical—*
all this leads me to ask about Browning's use of myth. The
question seems particularly relevant since Yeats and Browning
had in common an intense admiration for Shelley. Now Yeats,
we know, admired not Shelley the Godwinian radical, but
Shelley the Platonist and mythmaker—the Shelley who, in the
manner of Blake, used archetypal symbols.[1] The question is
whether Browning—who did for a time admire Shelley the
Godwinian radical—had affinities also with Shelley the mythmaker and (the two terms are inextricably connected) symbolist.

It is certainly the visionary whom Browning praises in the
essay he wrote on Shelley in 1852. "I would rather consider
Shelley's poetry as a sublime fragmentary essay towards a
presentment of the correspondency of the universe to Deity, of
the natural to the spiritual, and of the actual to the ideal, than
I would isolate and separately appraise the worth of many
detachable portions which might be acknowledged as utterly

"Browning and the Question of Myth," by Robert Langbaum. Reprinted
from *PMLA,* 81 (1966), 575-85 by permission of the Modern Language Association of America and by the author. Copyright © 1966 by MLA. The
essay also appears in *The Modern Spirit: Essays on the Continuity of Nine-
teenth- and Twentieth-Century Literature* (New York: Oxford University
Press, 1970).

[1]See W. B. Yeats, "The Philosophy of Shelley's Poetry," *Essays and Introductions* (New York, 1961).

perfect in a lower moral point of view, under the mere conditions of art." Shelley's main excellence is "his simultaneous
perception of Power and Love in the absolute, and of Beauty
and Good in the concrete, while he throws, from his poet's
station between both, swifter, subtler, and more numerous
films for the connection of each with each, than have been
thrown by any modern artificer of whom I have knowledge;
proving how, as he says, — 'The spirit of the worm within the
sod / In love and worship blends itself with God.'"[2]

Those lines might have been written by Blake — a sign that
Browning comes in this passage very close to Yeats's appreciation of Shelley in terms applicable to a mythmaking poet like
Blake. Browning offers, in defining Shelley's main excellence,
a good definition of the myth-making poet — of the poet who
does not merely make decorative allusions to an established
literary mythology, but who actually *sees* the world as mythical,
who sees man, nature, and God as intimately engaged in a
natural-supernatural story.

To ask about Browning's use of myth is to ask two questions.
The first is whether Browning believed in using — as Arnold
did in *Sohrab* and *Merope,* and Tennyson did in the *Idylls* —
the grand old enduring subjects that have come down to us in
the literary tradition. The answer to the first question is no.
Browning agreed with Miss Barrett, when she said in that
often-quoted letter to him: "I am inclined to think that we want
new *forms,* as well as thoughts. The old gods are dethroned.
Why should we go back to the antique moulds, classical moulds,
as they are so improperly called?"[3] Browning himself said as
much and more when, at the end of his life, he dealt, in "Parleying With Gerard de Lairesse," with the question of how far
the Greeks ought to be used as models for modern art: We have
gone beyond the Greeks, he concluded, in religion and in
moral and psychological insight. Modern poets should not,

[2]The "Essay on Shelley" is quoted from the "Florentine Edition" of Browning's *Works,* ed. Charlotte Porter and Helen A. Clarke (New York, 1898),
XII, 299. Browning's verse is quoted from the Centenary Edition of his *Works,*
introductions by F. G. Kenyon, 10 vols. (London, 1912).

[3]*The Letters of Robert Browning and Elizabeth Barrett Barrett 1845-1846,*
ed. Elvan Kintner, 2 vols. (Cambridge, Mass., 1969), 20 March 1845, I, 43.

therefore, pour new wine into old bottles. They should no longer

> Dream afresh old godlike shapes,
> Recapture ancient fable that escapes,
> Push back reality, repeople earth
> With vanished falseness, recognize no worth
> In fact new-born unless 'tis rendered back
> Pallid by fancy, as the western rack
> Of fading cloud bequeaths the lake some gleam
> Of its gone glory!   (382-389)

We should not ignore reality in favor of old subjects from mythology. Nor should we render modern facts poetical by decorating them with outworn mythological allusions.

On the issue raised by Arnold in the Preface to his *Poems* of 1853—the issue as to which subjects are better for modern poetry, the grand, enduring subjects or subjects drawn from modern life—Browning stood against Arnold and with the modern realists.[4] It is true that Browning himself almost always used subjects drawn from the past. But he used them as history rather than myth. This explains his taste for little-known characters and incidents out of the past. For such characters and incidents have clearly not come down to us through the literary tradition. We can believe in the factuality of characters and incidents whose existence is authenticated even though they are no longer remembered. The forgotten historical character is the very opposite of the mythical character whose historical existence is doubtful even though he is vividly "remembered."

The historical attitude suggests that the past was as confused and unglamorous as the present. The historical attitude is also interested in tracing change—in showing how different were the ideas and values of the past from ours, in showing that the past was itself in the process of change. Yet the historical change is apparent because we can measure it against a recog-

---

[4]All this has been made abundantly clear by W. C. DeVane in his excellent essay, "Browning and the Spirit of Greece," *Nineteenth-Century Studies*, ed., Herbert Davis et al. (Ithaca, N.Y., 1940), as well as in his *Browning's Parleyings* (New Haven, 1927), and his *Browning Handbook*, 2nd ed. (New York, 1955).

nizably continuous human or psychological reality. This again is opposite to the mythical attitude, which idealizes the past in order to set it up as a permanent criterion of value. At the same time, the mythical attitude makes the people of the past seem different from us, larger, sometimes superhuman. It is the past as permanent criterion that Arnold had in mind in the Preface. In his very use of the past, then, Browning disagreed with Arnold. And he disagreed, too, on that other important issue of the Preface—Arnold's attack on internal drama, on the idea that modern poetry ought to treat, in Browning's phrase, "the incidents in the development of a soul."

On the issues raised by Arnold in the Preface and elsewhere, Browning was mainly right. For it is surely a weakness in Arnold's critical position that, while he could see art as dependent on the power of both the man and the moment, he should have supposed that the masterwork of one historical moment could or should have the virtues of the masterwork of another historical moment. Browning, on the other hand, was wrong in not understanding the importance of an action or of some external mechanism for portraying an internal state. Browning's poems fail just to the extent that his characters describe and analyze their thoughts and emotions, without any vividly apparent external reason for doing so. Browning was interested in talking about both history and psychology, and his problem as an artist was to find a means for doing so. Now a *mythos* or action, properly understood, is a way of accomplishing this end. For the kind of action we call mythical, just because it does not imitate a strictly external reality, is the kind that can speak with one voice of both internal and external reality. The problem is to use myth or the mythical method without archaizing—to use them in a distinctively modern way.

We have here a criterion for understanding the course of Browning's development and for assessing his work. For while he failed in *Paracelsus* and *Sordello* to reconcile internal and external reality, the two are successfully brought together in the best dramatic monologues. In *Paracelsus,* Browning fails because he has pushed offstage just those historical events that might have given outline and interest to his obscure historical character. What we get through a long poem is a continuing high-pitched reaction to we hardly know what; and we find ourselves longing for those vulgar events that Browning was so proud to have excluded.

In his long labors over *Sordello,* however, Browning apparently wrestled with the problem of reconciling internal and external reality. As DeVane has shown in his *Browning Handbook, Sordello* was written in four different periods, in each of which Browning took a quite different view of his subject. In the first version, Browning treated his obscure historical character in the manner of *Paracelsus*—he gave us the history of a soul. In the second version, he made Sordello a man of action, a warrior and lover, thus showing Sordello's impact on the world around him. In the third version, he neglected Sordello himself and concentrated on the historical events of the period. In the fourth version, he rounded out his plot by making Sordello the champion of the masses and Salinguerra's son. The four Sordellos, which are imposed one upon the other, never do add up to a single *Sordello.*

It is just the elements of the first three *Sordellos* that are brought together in the best dramatic monologues. They are not brought together by plot—if by plot we mean a complete action, the kind that ties all the threads together and therefore seems to modern writers, especially novelists, who judge by the criteria of realism, to offer too neat a rationalization of the material. But the three elements are nonetheless brought together by an action—a direction of the speaker's energies outward. It is because the speaker is not trying to tell the truth about himself, but is trying to accomplish something or make an impression, that he actually does reveal himself truly. This is the way characters reveal themselves in drama.

As in drama, the speaker has outline because we see him not, as we see Paracelsus, in a confiding relation; we see him rather in a conflicting relation with another person. And we get, therefore, through the contrast, a sense of how he looks from the outside. The speaker also has outline because his fundamental human energies are clothed in the predilections peculiar to his age—as in "The Bishop Orders His Tomb," where the Italian Renaissance bishop manifests his competitiveness and desire for immortality by ordering for himself a more expensive tomb than his rival's. A whole way of seeing, thinking and feeling is manifested through that aim; so that we get through one action the man and the age, the man as he looks to others and himself, the outer and the inner reality. The action is, however, incomplete. That is the price Browning pays for using a realistic action; for the characteristically realistic action is the slice-of-life.

His best dramatic monologues entitle Browning to his rank among the two or three best Victorian poets. But is he also — as he certainly aimed to be — one of the great poets of English literature? In trying to answer, we have to admit that even in his best volume, *Men and Women,* Browning was tempted — in dramatic monologues like "Cleon" and "Bishop Blougram" — to slip back to the analytic, discursive style of the earlier, the *Paracelsus* period. And we know how, in the later dramatic monologues — in "Mr. Sludge," Prince Hohenstiel-Schwangau," "Fifine" — he did slip back, without even the lyric fire of the *Paracelsus* period.

We have also to admit that even his very best dramatic monologues remain, after all, only splendid vignettes — "prismatic hues," as he himself called them. They do not add up to what Browning called "the pure white light,"[5] the total vision of life that the greatest poets give us, and that Browning from the start — from the time of *Sordello* — intended to give us. *The Ring and the Book,* of course, is Browning's climactic attempt to give us a total vision of life. He brings several dramatic monologues, several points of view together, in order to collapse the "prismatic hues" into "the pure white light" — in order to make explicit what is implicit in all the dramatic monologues, that the relative is an index to the absolute, that the relative is our way of apprehending the absolute.

This brings us to the second question about Browning's use of myth, the question that arises from our experience of Yeats, Eliot and Joyce. In reviewing *Ulysses* for *The Dial* of November 1923, Eliot argues that Joyce is not as people think a "prophet of chaos," but that he has given us the materials of modern disorder and shown us how to impose order upon them. He has done this by what Eliot calls "the mythical method." Eliot is referring to the continuous parallel between

[5]*Letters R.B.-E.B.B.,* 13 January 1845, I. 7.

the trivial and apparently meaningless events of Joyce's novel
and the events in the *Odyssey*.

> In using the myth, in manipulating a continuous parallel be-
> tween contemporaneity and antiquity, Mr. Joyce is pursuing
> a method which others must pursue after him. ... It is simply
> a way of controlling, of ordering, of giving a shape and a sig-
> nificance to the immense panorama of futility and anarchy
> which is contemporary history. It is a method already adum-
> brated by Mr. Yeats. ... It is a method for which the horoscope
> is auspicious. Psychology...ethnology [i.e., anthropology],
> and *The Golden Bough* have concurred to make possible what
> was impossible even a few years ago. Instead of narrative
> method, we may now use the mythical method. It is, I seriously
> believe, a step toward making the modern world possible for at,
> toward...order and form.

With the mythical method, the modern writer can render the
disordered surface of modern life, while showing how nevertheless the mythical patterns inevitably reassert themselves at
the unconscious roots of existence. This is the method Eliot
himself uses in *The Waste Land*.

Now the whole point of *The Ring and the Book* was to pull
out of a forgotten and sordid old Roman murder case the Christian scheme of sin and redemption. Having himself, in an experience of illumination, seen through to the *truth* of the case,
Browning's artistic strategy for conveying that truth was to
restore *The Old Yellow Book* in which he had found the documents of the case. He wanted to give us the experience of reading the raw documents, to give us the jumbled real-life surface
of the case and yet make us see through the facts—the facts so
peculiar to the place and time—an eternal pattern. This is
something like what Eliot says Joyce does.

Something, but not quite. For the case, as Browning renders
it, does not really present a surface of ambivalence; and the
pattern is rather too explicitly a moral pattern. We feel, as a
result, that we are getting not the absolute truth, but Browning's
notions about absolute truth. *The Ring and the Book*, therefore, in spite of the many great things in it, does not in the end
quite come off. Browning is more convincing in the best dramatic monologues, where he gives us truth as simply a relative

manifestation that points somehow to the absolute. How? Through the fundamental human energy of the speaker, that seems to lead back to an unconscious ground of existence where all energies merge and are justified.

It is out of this unconscious ground that myths, according to twentieth-century theory, arise.[6] And there remains, in *The Ring and the Book,* a pattern which is in Eliot's sense mythical because underlying. I mean the pattern of the Andromeda-Perseus myth and its Christian analogue, the myth of St. George and the dragon. We know that Browning's imagination was dominated throughout his career by the image of the beautiful Andromeda, chained naked to the rock, waiting helplessly for the serpent to come out of the sea to devour her, but waiting also—though she does not consciously know this—for Perseus to descend miraculously—to "come," as Browning puts it in *Pauline,* "in thunder from the stars"—to rescue her. The combination of sexual and spiritual ramifications gives the image its strength and validity.

The Andromeda—St. George myth connected Browning's life and art, giving him, as only myths can, what Yeats called Unity of Being. In the greatest event of his life, he repeated the mythical pattern by rescuing Miss Barrett. And there is no doubt that he recognized the same mythical pattern when he read in *The Old Yellow Book* about Caponsacchi's rescue of Pompilia. He even changed the date of the rescue to make it fall on St. George's Day. It was because Browning was able to assimilate the murder case to the myth that *The Ring and the Book* is at once a very personal and a very impersonal poem.

There are many references throughout *The Ring and the Book* to the Andromeda—St. George myth, and it is used rather as the vegetation myth is used in *The Waste Land.* We are made to see a continuity between the pagan and Christian versions of the same myth. And all the characters seem inevitably to have some memory of the myth—though the debased characters remember it in a debased form; while the cynical characters, who see Caponsacchi's rescue as an abduction, turn the

[6]See, for example, Kerényi's Prolegomena to C. G. Jung and C. Kerényi, *Essays on a Science of Mythology,* trans. R. F. C. Hull, rev. ed. (New York and Evanston: Harper Torchbooks, 1963).

myth into its obverse, the myth of Helen and Paris.[7] Nevertheless, the references remain only references—mythological
allusions to illustrate points that are really being made
discursively.

The Ring and the Book is an important poem, because it
moves in the right direction. It moves away from myth as overt
subject matter; yet it goes so far as to bring back the mythical
pattern—not the particular events and characters of the Andromeda story, but the pattern—as inherent in the very structure of the mind, in what we would nowadays call the
unconscious. *The Ring and the Book* does the same thing for
the Christian pattern of sin and redemption—bringing Christian virtue alive again out of what Miss Barrett, in the letter I
have quoted, calls "this low ground," and through circumstances, like Caponsacchi's abduction of Pompilia, which would
seem the reverse of virtuous. The fact that Miss Barrett goes on,
after inveighing against subjects drawn from classical mythology, to say that "Christianity is a worthy *myth,* and poetically
acceptable,"[8] shows that she and Browning were against the
classical mythology of the official literary tradition, because it
projects obsolete meanings we only pretend to believe in as a
literary game. It is because Browning did not go far enough in
his use of mythical pattern, did not allow the meaning of his
poem to rest in the pattern, that he considered that myths could
grow obsolete.

Browning's idea of progress would seem to prevent a complete reliance on mythical pattern. For Yeats, the symbols and
myths are permanent, and the ideas about them change. But
for Browning, the myths change; myths are the progressively
changing symbolic language for the same continuing idea. In
"Parleying With Charles Avison," Browning takes off from the
idea, expressed forty years earlier in a letter to Miss Barrett,
that "in Music, the Beau Ideal changes every thirty years."[9]
Music, like Avison's, of a generation or two ago, seems so obsolete; yet the thing music talks about remains the same, and it
requires only a few technical adjustments to translate from an

[7]See DeVane, "Browning and the Spirit of Greece," *Nineteenth-Century Studies,*pp. 485-490.

[8]*Letters R.B.-E.B.B.,* I, 43.

[9]*Letters R.B.-E.B.B.* [7 March 1846] , I, 523.

old to a new musical idiom. We need the ever-changing idioms to startle us over and over again into ever new apprehensions of the old truth. For "Truths escape / Time's insufficient garniture: they fade, / They fall"—when the old garniture seems to turn into a lie. In the same way,

> Soon shall fade and fall
> Myth after myth—the husk-like lies I call
> New truth's corolla-safeguard.
>   (371-373, 378-380)

Certainly, the mythical method as practiced by Yeats, Eliot and Joyce depends on an idea or recurrence, on a cyclical rather than a linear view of history.[10] The idea of progress requires that you keep track of time; while the mythical method requires that you collapse time. Browning does collapse time whenever he writes about Andromeda, and it is significant that he always writes well on that subject. The Andromeda passage in his first poem, *Pauline* (656-667), is one of the finest passages he ever wrote. The passage is quite remarkably echoed by Hopkins's "Andromeda" sonnet.

I mention the similarity to suggest that Hopkins, in spite of the many nasty things he said about Browning (things that show a minute knowledge of the older poet's work), must to some extent have learned his music from Browning. Both poets are obscure because they are trying to use words in such a way as to overcome the analytic effect of language—the effect Browning has in mind when he talks about Sordello's failure to create a satisfactory poetic language,

> Because perceptions whole, like that he sought
> To clothe, reject so pure a work of thought
> As language: thought may take perception's place
> But hardly co-exist in any case,

[10]Hence Joyce's interest in Vico's cyclical theory of history. In commenting on Vico's cyclical theory, Yeats writes: "though history is too short to change either the idea of progress of the eternal circuit into scientific fact, the external circuit may best suit our preoccupation with the soul's salvation, our individualism, our solitude. Besides we love antiquity, and that other idea—progress—the sole religious myth of modern man, is only two hundred years old" (Introduction to "The Words Upon the Window-Pane," *Explorations*, London, 1962, p. 355).

Being its mere presentment—of the whole
By parts, the simultaneous and the sole
By the successive and the many.

(589-595)

The crowd, Browning goes on to say, which deals in ready-
made thoughts, has merely to tack them together; and presumably the crowd can be lucid. But for Sordello, thought and
language are the things perception has been rent into. They are
the diffusion and destruction of perception; and it is the point
of poetic language to give that sense of itself.[11] Both Browning
and Hopkins break up conventional syntax and multiply associations with bewildering rapidity, in order to make us feel that
the things language has laid out in space and time and in an
order of succession are really happening simultaneously—in
order to restore the instantaneous, orchestrated quality of the
original perception. Both poets are working for an effect characteristic of symbolism and the mythical method.

In defending himself in a letter to Ruskin against Ruskin's
charge of obscurity, Browning explains that the poetry or effect of simultaneity lies precisely in the jumps that the reader
is forced to make for himself.

> I *know* that I don't make out my conception by my language,
> all poetry being a putting the infinite within the finite. You
> would have me paint it all plain out, which can't be; but by
> various artifices I try to make shift with touches and bits of out-
> lines which *succeed* if they bear the conception from me to you.
> You ought, I think, to keep pace with the thought tripping from
> ledge to ledge of my "glaciers," as you call them; not stand
> poking your alpenstock into the holes, and demonstrating that
> no foot could have stood there;—suppose it sprang over there?
> In *prose* you may criticise so—because that is the absolute repre-
> sentation of portions of truth, what chronicling is to history—

[11]Park Honan sees in Browning's pessimism about the possibilities of language a sign that he was experimenting in *Sordello* toward a new poetic style
(*Browning's Characters*, New Haven, 1961, p. 37). J. Hillis Miller sees Browning's language as approximating "whole perceptions," because so "often close
to the inarticulate noise which is the source of all words" (*Disappearance of
God*, p. 90). This can be true of Browning but, as Miller's examples show, not
at his best; it is sometimes true of Hopkins at his best—e.g., "The Windhover."

> but in asking for more *ultimates* you must accept less *mediates*, nor expect that a Druid stone-circle will be traced for you with as few breaks to the eye as the North Crescent and South Crescent that go together so cleverly in many a suburb.

And he says of a poem of his: "Is the jump too much there? The whole is all but a simultaneous feeling with me."[12]

Browning sketches out what has come to be the dominant twentieth-century theory about poetry — that it makes its effect through the association in the reader's mind of disparate elements, and that this process of association leads to the recognition, in what has been presented successively, of static pattern. The recognition is often in the twentieth century called "epiphany." It is the recognition of what Hopkins calls the "inscape" of the object in poetry.

The difference between Browning and Hopkins is that Hopkins dislocates language in order to make his *image* more palpable — to make us feel the force of the bird's soaring in "The Windhover," and the even greater force of its falling movement. The meaning emerges as paradox, and then only by implication — the implication that the active and passive life are equally intense, that Christ triumphed through failure. Browning, on the other hand, tries to achieve the effect of simultaneity through discursive thought itself. That is why Browning is hardly ever at his best where he is obscure; while Hopkins is often at his best where he is obscure. Hopkins goes farther than Browning in symbolizing and myth-making.

Yet if you can get certain knotty passages of Browning sufficiently well in mind to leap playfully from idea to idea with the swiftness and freedom of Browning's mind, you actually start a process of association that turns the discursive thought into poetry. Swinburne gives the best descriptions of the pleasure to be derived from the discursive Browning. In comparing Browning with a really obscure poet like Chapman, Swinburne denies that Browning is obscure at all. For obscurity is the product of a confused and chaotic intellect; whereas

[12]Quoted in W. G. Collingwood, *The Life of John Ruskin* (Boston and New York, 1902), pp. 164-165.

if there is any great quality more perceptible than another in
Mr. Browning's intellect it is his decisive and incisive faculty
of thought, his sureness and intensity of perception, his rapid
and trenchant resolution of aim.... He is something too much
the reverse of obscure; he is too brilliant and subtle for the ready
reader of a ready writer to follow with any certainty the track of
an intelligence which moves with such incessant rapidity, or
even to realize with what spider-like swiftness and sagacity his
building spirit leaps and lightens to and fro and backward and
forward as it lives along the animated line of its labour, spring
from thread to thread and darts from centre to circumference of
the glittering and quivering web of living thought woven from
the inexhaustible stores of his perception and kindled from the
inexhaustible fire of his imagination.... It is hopeless to enjoy
the charm or to apprehend the gist of his writings except with a
mind thoroughly alert, an intention awake at all points.[13]

To return then to our two questions about Browning and
myth, we might say that Browning defined his realism precisely
through opposition to myths as overt subject matter. He was,
however, feeling his way to the twentieth-century development,
through realism and psychology, to a psychological use of
myth. In rejecting myth in "Parleying With Gerard de
Lairesse," Browning asks whether he would do better to tell
two stories—to repeat the old myth through realistically apprehended modern circumstances, repeat the myth of Dryope
plucking the lotus blossoms through the story of an English
girl plucking "fruit not fabulous" but "Apple of English home-
steads." "Advantage would it prove or detriment / If I saw
double?" (118-126).

It is through just such double vision that twentieth-century
writers have returned to myth. Browning's phrase recalls
Blake's distinction between single vision, which is Newton's
way of seeing facts as just facts, and double vision, which is the
capacity to read facts symbolically.[14] "Oh, we can fancy too!"
Browning continues,

[13]*George Chapman* (London, 1875), pp. 16-17. For a detailed analysis of
associationism and speed in Browning, see Robert Preyer, "Two Styles in the
Verse of Robert Browning," *ELH*, XXXII (March 1965), 62-84.

[14]See Blake's poem "With happiness stretched across the hills," in the letter
to Thomas Butts [22 November 1802].

but somehow fact
Has got to—say, not so much push aside
Fancy, as to declare its place supplied
By fact unseen but no less fact the same,
Which mind bids sense accept.

(149-153)

We have here the modern distinction, derived from Coleridge, between neoclassical fancy and romantic or modern imagination. The neoclassicist went on using the old myths, not because he believed in them, but because they were decorative and poetical. The neoclassical painter Lairesse could, in the walk described in his book on painting, maintain the old mythical view because he was blind. But the modern artist insists on the truth of his mythical vision—his perception of "the links," in Browning's words, that "blind / Our earth to heaven" (145-147)—because it evolves out of direct perception of the facts. The modern artist creates his own myths and symbols by bringing to the sensuous apprehension of reality the whole mind or imagination.

This is the essence of modern symbolist theory. Not only "Lairesse" and "Avison," but the whole *Parleyings* can best be understood as Browning's verse essay on symbolism. In "Bernard de Mandeville," we are told to read the opposition between good and evil as symbolic of the absolute design of things, and not to take evil as in itself a substantial reality. If in a ground-plan we were told that A is the house, we would be foolish to ask where's the roof to A. But

Why so very much
More foolish than our mortal purblind way
Of seeking in the symbol no mere point
To guide our gaze through what were else inane,
But things—their solid selves?

(184-188)

"A myth may teach," says Browning, "Only, who better would expound it thus / Must be Euripides not Aeschylus" (204-206). Euripides did not, like Aeschylus, take myth literally, but understood it as symbolic, as a way of talking about life. Euripides was, in other words, a realist and therefore a symbolist.

Browning then makes a myth. In the morning of creation, only man was sullen, because he could not like the plants and animals enjoy the sun unconsciously. Man yearned to understand the sun, both in its visible aspect and as an all-informing principle of energy. Man yearned, in other words, to make contact through his mind with the "outside mind" behind the sun, and so love the sun consciously through his understanding. Finally, "Prometheus helped him,"

> Offered an artifice whereby he drew
> Sun's rays into a focus,—plain and true,
> The very Sun in little: made fire burn
> And hence forth do Man service—glass-conglobed
> Though to a pin-point circle—all the same
> Comprising the Sun's self, but Sun disrobed
> Of that else-unconceived essential flame
> Borne by no naked sight.
>
> (301-309)

Prometheus is conceived as having taught man to draw down through a magnifying glass a symbolic representation of the sun, which could be looked at, understood, and used to start a fire, as the sun itself could not. From the symbol, we can "infer immensity," but only the symbol can engage our affection: "In little, light, warmth, life, are blessed— / Which, in the large, who sees to bless?" (317-319). The whole crucial passage recalls Coleridge's dictum that a true symbol "always partakes of the reality which it renders intelligible."[15]

In "Daniel Bartoli," Browning rejects a kind of symbolism quite different from the modern—the kind set forth in Bartoli's *Dei Simboli Trasportati al Morale,* where the seventeenth-century Jesuit historian does two things Browning does not like. Bartoli repeats implausible legends, and uses them to teach moral lessons; whereas for Browning "historical fact had," as DeVane puts it, "a righteousness of its own."[16] Bartoli is represented as telling an absurdly miraculous legend of a female saint, in order that Browning may, by way of contrast,

---

[15]*The Statesman's Manual, Works,* ed. Shedd, I, 437. Roma A. King, Jr., derives from the Prometheus passage the title of his latest book on Browning, *The Focusing Artifice* (Athens, Ohio, 1968). See Ch. VII on the *Parleyings.*
[16]*Browning's Parleyings,* p. 53.

tell a story from a memoir, in which a real girl, acting in plausible circumstances, shows herself to be a saint in a far more important sense than Bartoli's Saint Scholastica.

In "Christopher Smart," Browning draws from the case of the poet who once and once only wrote a great poem, and then when he was in the madhouse, the essential doctrine of symbolist poetry—the doctrine that poetry is, as Yeats put it, a revelation and should make the effect of a revelation. Smart achieves his effect not by giving an exhaustive catalogue of details like modern naturalists, nor by concerning himself like the aesthetes with appearances only. Smart uses his *selected* details as symbols—making them stand for the rest and imbuing them with ideas and moral meaning. He does not, on the other hand, like the scientists and their followers, start with abstract laws that when applied to nature must inevitably devalue it. Smart's ideas are inseparable from the palpably rendered objects that embody them. He gives in his "Song to David" the truth about nature, because he gives "her lovelinesses infinite / In little" (144-145).

In "George Bubb Dodington," Browning shows that this second-rate Machiavellian failed in politics, because he operated by rational laws of calculated self-interest that we all understand too well. But the great Machiavellian—Browning has Disraeli in mind, the whole parleying is an attack upon him— is the great charlatan who, like the artist, knows how to turn himself and his work into a symbol. He does this by wrapping himself in mystery, operating by motives we cannot understand.

> No animal—much less our lordly Man—
> Obeys its like. . . .
>   Who would use
> Man for his pleasure needs must introduce
> The element that awes Man. Once for all,
> His nature owns a Supernatural.
>   (134-135, 183-191)

In "Francis Furini"—the parleying that makes the most complete statement of symbolist doctrine—Browning is doing something more important than just defending his son's nude paintings. Browning defends the nude in painting by showing

that the nude figure is more symbolic than the clothed figure,
and symbolic precisely of soul. The artist agonizes

> to adumbrate, trace in dust
> That marvel which we dream the firmament
> Copies in star-device when fancies stray
> Outlining, orb by orb, Andromeda —
> God's best of beauteous and magnificent
> Revealed to earth — the naked female form.
>
> (138-143)

The artists who see most clearly God's purpose — to dispense
"all gifts / To soul through sense" — are those who "bid us
love alone / The type untampered with [i.e., the archetype],
the naked star!" (233-247).[17]

In symbolism, there is no high or low; symbolism demonstrates that we can know the so-called high only by knowing the
so-called low. There you have the error of the Darwinians —
and it is no digression for Browning to associate them with the
prudish enemies of the nude — who think that their knowledge
of man's low origin negates his spirituality. Once we see that
the large subject of "Furini" is symbolism, then the attack on
the Darwinians has even more cogency, and Browning's de-
preciation of man's cognitive faculties has more philosophical
justification that DeVane in his book on the *Parleyings* make
out. We can see how Browning's relativism leads to symbolism
when, in criticizing in a letter of 1881 the Darwinian idea that
evolution is ungoverned by intelligence, Browning says that
"time and space" are "purely conceptions of our own, wholly
inapplicable to intelligence of another kind."[18]

The Darwinians do not realize, Browning implies in
"Furini," that their theory is itself, by its hierarchical arrangement of nature, an anthropomorphizing symbol system based
on intuition of a perfection from which all nature can be scaled
downward. The Darwinians, who take an abstract view of na-

[17]For an elaboration of Browning's argument, see Sir Kenneth Clark, *The
Nude: A Study in Ideal Form* (New York, 1956). "The Greeks," Clark concludes, "perfected the nude in order that man might feel like a god, and in a
sense this is still its function, for although we no longer suppose that God is
like a beautiful man, we still feel close to divinity in those flashes of self-
identification when, through our own bodies, we seem to be aware of a universal order" (p. 370).

ture, looking downward from the top, see only what is lacking. An artist like Furini, instead, who takes his stand within nature, can through loving penetration of a particular living thing uncover "Marvel at hiding under marvel, pluck / Veil after veil from Nature" (395-396), and thus see the living thing as pointing upward, as symbolizing the whole perfect scheme.

The pre-eminence that the Darwinians themselves give man derives not from man's power or even from his knowledge. For the proportions of nature are so incommensurate with our cognitive faculties that we can never know nature as it is in itself:

> ...what *is* minuteness—yonder vault
> Speckled with suns, or this the millionth—thing,
> ...that on some insect's wing
> Helps to make out in dyes the mimic star?
>
> (293-296)

The thing that gives us pre-eminence is our moral sense, our intuition of perfection; and all the individual knows for sure is his consciousness of himself as having that sense. The individual finds in and through his self-consciousness what we should call anthropomorphizing images—"thus blend / I, and all things perceived, in one Effect" (361-362)—which, by some mysterious law, he understands as corresponding to the external world. What the individual knows, in other words—and here Browning comes close to Blake's "Where man is not, nature is barren"[19]—is *imagined* nature.

Like Andromeda, the individual clings to his "rock-split of self-knowledge" (410), with the sea of ignorance surging round. Art teaches him about spirit by directing his gaze precisely toward the body, toward

> Those incommensurably marvellous
> Contrivances which furnish forth the house
> Where soul has sway! Though Master keep aloof,

[18] To Dr. F. J. Furnivall, 11 October 1881, *Letters of Robert Browning,* collected by Thomas J. Wise, ed. T. L. Hood (New Haven, 1933), p. 200. Browning's argument would be stronger if he had not confused Darwinian theory with the Lamarckian, which actually does find intelligence in the evolutionary process.

[19] *The Marriage of Heaven and Hell,* "Proverbs of Hell."

> Signs of His presence multiply from roof
> To basement of the building. ...
>   He's away, no doubt,
> But what if, all at once, you come upon
> A startling proof — not that the Master gone
> Was present lately — but that something — whence
> Light comes — has pushed Him into residence?
>
> (533-543)

Suddenly, in what we should call an epiphany, the physical details light up from within, manifesting the invisible in the visible, turning into what we should call a symbol.

Browning is trying to say what Yeats says more pithily — that "Man can embody truth but he cannot know it."[20] The passage even concludes with Yeats's favorite circular symbol of the serpent with its tail in its mouth.

> Was such the symbol's meaning, — old, uncouth —
> That circle of the serpent, tail in mouth?
> Only by looking low, ere looking high,
> Comes penetration of the mystery.
>
> (544-547)

In the *Parleyings* — which is the most complete statement of his maturest thought — Browning answers the problems of his time by suggesting that we change the nature of the questions we put to the universe, that we turn upon all aspects of life double rather than single vision. Had Browning been able to realize such doctrine in his art, had he been able to make his fragmentary glimpses of life symbolic of the whole, of an absolute vision, he would have broken through to the modern mythical method. He would have broken through to a final clarity of vision and style and been one of the great. poets of English literature. As it is, he is a poet of enduring interest — partly because his very faults show that he was turning analytic thought against itself, that he understood what had to be done.

---

[20]To Lady Elizabeth Pelham, 4 January 1939, *The Letters of W. B. Yeats*, ed. Allan Wade (London, 1954), p. 922.

Troops of Shadows: Browning's Types

by Adrienne Munich

> Printing is God's latest and best work to spread the true
> religion throughout the world.
>
> MARTIN LUTHER, Table Talk

> Give chase, soul! Be sure each new creature consigned
>   To my Types will go forth to the world, like God's bread
> —Miraculous food not for body but mind,
>   Truth's manna!
>
> BROWNING, "Fust and His Friends"

I

Browning began his literary career with *Pauline: A Fragment of a Confession,* a disorderly apprentice work which both celebrates and laments the profound effect upon him of his secular reading.[1] *Parleyings With Certain People of Importance in Their Day,* written toward the end of his life, completes the fragmentary confession in similar terms. In this literary retrospective he justifies his work by struggling, debating, and coping—various senses of "parleying"—with its artistic influences. Although deeply impressed by all the arts, he ultimately subordinated them to his poetry. But in his first poem he cannot make a clear choice, feeling that all arts light his aesthetic passion:

"Troops of Shadows: Browning's Types" by Adrienne Munich. This article appears for the first time in this volume.

[1] For expert advice I thank Rachel Jacoff of Wellesley College and Liliane Greene and Ruth Hein of the Center for Independent Study.

My life has not been that of those whose heaven
Was lampless, save where poesy shone out;
But as a clime, where glittering mountain-tops,
And glancing sea, and forests steeped in light,
Give back reflected the far-flashing sun.[2]

This dissipation of Apollonian energies lies at the center of
Browning's aesthetic and gives all his poems an unsettled quality, a refusal to be content with "one rapture" (l. 610). But an
even greater conflict troubles his art. His dual allegiance to
God and to Shelley caused him more distress than his multiple
allegiances to the arts. How to present and reconcile what he
saw as internal polarities, how to come to terms with his own
sensibility posed a problem which Browning grapples with in
these two antipodal works.

By reading these two works as a pair, as forming a parenthesis
enclosing the major works, it becomes clear that Browning
represented himself by using a typological framework. Although conventional autobiography disgusted him and caused
him to assert that the voices of his monologues were not his
own, both *Pauline* and the *Parleyings* reveal the poet himself.
By breaking parts of himself into types, he shows how characteristic this kind of projection was to his imagination. He
thought of his works as beamed through a prism, the pure white
light of truth broken into separate colors. But these facets of
truth can more accurately be described as types, a word he himself used in the *Parleyings* to characterize his work. His tendency to portray individuals as types suggests an approach to
his work as a whole. He himself indicated this mode of thought
in the original title of "Italy" for "My Last Duchess." The
scope of the present inquiry, however, can only suggest this
figural approach to his oeuvre. Concentrating upon the two
works at either end of his career will indicate ways in which
Browning himself leads his readers to this largely uncon-
sidered context for placing his poetry in a tradition of figural
representation.

[2]Lines 360-64 Quotations from *Pauline* are taken from the original published edition (London: Saunders and Otley, 1833). Quotations from *Parleyings* are taken from *The Works of Robert Browning*, ed. F. G. Kenyon, vol.
10 (London, 1912), known as the Centenary Edition.

The concept of types—as in emblems and as in Biblical typology—is a confused and confusing tradition.[3] Since it came down to Browning through his own reading, through his listening to sermons, and by following a characteristic mode of thought of his times it cannot be ordered into an internally consistent system. It is not only more helpful but more accurate to acknowledge that Browning, rather than offering a coherent system, displays a strong tendency to organize his poetry in terms of types. In thus conceiving of his literary antecedents, Browning draws upon the typological tradition of Biblical exegesis, his knowledge of emblem literature,[4] his familiarity with Renaissance iconography, and his intimate knowledge of Dante.[5] By borrowing at will from various traditions of figural representation and by applying the method of interpretation to his own life, he found a way of acknowledging his pagan debt while saving his evangelical soul.

II

In *Pauline,* Browning's hero predicts his own literary birth even as he mourns the ordinary pain of loss attending any birth. The poet describes his passage into poethood with the

[3]Browning's use of typology is perhaps most conventionally Biblical in "Saul." See Ward Hellstrom, "Time and Type in Browning's *Saul,*" *ELH,* 33 (1966): 370-89. On more general uses of Victorian typology, see George P. Landow, "Moses Striking the Rock: Typological Symbolism in Victorian Poetry," *Literary Uses of Typology,* ed. Earl A. Miner (Princeton, 1977): 315-44; Ian Fletcher, "Some Types and Emblems in Victorian Poetry," *The Listener* LXXVII (May 25, 1967): 680-81.

[4]Mrs. Sutherland Orr, *Life and Letters of Robert Browning,* Second Edition rev. F. G. Kenyon (Boston; 1908), p. 30 tells of Browning's early familiarity with Quarles. The Sotheby sale catalogue of Browning's library of 1913 records the following Quarles volumes: two copies, *Divine Poems,* 1633, 1669; *Divine Fancies,* 1723 (dated Nov. 19, 1837); *Emblems Divine and Moral, together with Hieroglyphics of the Life of Man,* 1777; *Judgment and Mercy for Afflicted Souls.* The best evidence of Browning's knowledge of emblems, however, is in his poems.

[5]Browning studied Dante with a tutor, Angelo Cerutti, who edited Danielo Bartioli's *De' Simboli Trasportati al Morale,* the subject of a parleying. Furthermore, there are frequent references in his letters to rereading Dante.

[6]William Clyde DeVane, *A Browning Handbook* (New York, 1955), p. 42.

Biblical image of leaving "a walled garden, thick with trees /
Where singing goes on." Since the poet planned "to look on
real life," he had to leave this Romantic paradise. The pain
comes primarily from the necessity of differentiating himself
from Shelley, whom he sees both as a radiant Sun-Treader and
as an atheist whose sensuous pagan values cannot be reconciled
with Browning's own evangelical Protestantism. Because of
this clash, *Pauline* is a guilty poem—guilty about having
strayed from the straight path to heaven, but also guilty about
the inability to renounce the glorious intensities that were part
of straying. The hero turns from his "wild" pagan dream of
intense idealism to Pauline, his muse and confessor, to shelter
him, to accept his confession, and to help him to rebirth.

Pauline's role in the poem cannot be satisfactorily glossed by
biographical information. J. S. Mill was only the first critic to
recognize that she was a "mere phantom,"[6] her presence seem-
ingly dictated by the dramatic necessity of conceiving an alternative to Shelley. But the brilliant pun of the title also betrays
his project as a Pauline one. As St. Paul found a way of sub-
suming Old Testament texts into New Testament reality by
reading them figurally, so Browning will find a way of valid-
ating and transcending Shelley by reading him as a figure of
Browning himself.

But this Pauline enterprise is audacious, and Browning
senses that such a self-promoting proclamation may expose him
to ridicule. He attempts to protect himself with a long Latin
epigraph from Agrippa. The quotation warns off the unwary
but biased reader by telling him that "we are teaching forbidden things." This is no poem for those of comfortable,
established beliefs, it somewhat pretentiously implies. The
passage recalls Dante's grave and portentious warning at the
beginning of Inferno III: "the gate of Hell is in this book."

A powerful feeling of having been elected places this speaker
close to the heresy of "Johannes Agricola in Meditation": The
announcement of grand aspiration is one of the dangerous elements of Browning's confession. But his terrible conflict comes
from a feeling, not so much of having been chosen, but having
been chosen twice. He senses himself the elected inheritor both
of Shelley and of God. Hence, the chaotic quality of his yearn-

ing. Even as he feels the "glow of HIS award"—that is, of Shelley's award—he recognizes another claim: "I felt as one beloved." Here he acknowledges God's love as he also acknowledges his need for God:

> This is 'myself'—not what I think should be,
> And what is that I hunger for but God?
> My God, my God! let me for once look on thee
> As tho' nought else existed: We alone.
>
> (ll. 820-23)

This appetite for sanctity battles with his conviction that he is heir to mighty pagan poets. They live inside him: to deny them would mean to reject part of himself. Acceptance of what he was meant to be emerges as an inner response to a higher law.

> So, as I grew, I rudely shaped my life
> To my immediate wants, yet strong beneath
> Was a vague sense of powers folded up—
> A sense that tho' those shadowy times were past,
> Their spirit dwelt in me, and I should rule.
>
> (ll. 339-43)

By the end of the poem however, he accedes to his own hunger for immortality. Henceforth his path must be directed to the heavenly gates.

> And one dream came to a pale poet's sleep,
> and he said, 'I am singled out by God,
> No sin must touch me.'
>
> (ll. 922-24)

This resolution is partial, even in the poem itself, as the poet vacillates. Since his pagan self can be denied only at a terrible price, it must be redefined and given a new validation.

By identifying Shelley with Apollo, god of all arts, Browning uses a typical image by which to bring about this accommodation. Very early in church history, Apollo had been turned into a type of Christ,[7] and by at least as early as the seventeenth

---

[7]Jean Seznec, *The Survival of the Pagan Gods* (Princeton, Bollingen Series XXXVIII, 1972), particularly Chapter One, "The Historical Tradition" and Chapter Two, "The Physical Tradition."

century in England, the precise image of a sun-treader had
been used to effect a religious revision of a Platonic philosophy.
In his devotional poem "The World," Vaughan uses the image
of treading the sun as an Apollonian figure which is itself
transcended by a brighter light:

> O fools (said I,) thus to prefer dark night
>   Before true light,
> To live in grots, and caves, and hate the day
>   Because it shews the way,
> The way which from this dead and dark abode
>   Leads up to God.
> A way where you might tread the Sun, and be
>   More bright than he.[8]

Though Browning applies the transformation to autobiography
rather than to theology, his purpose is similar. He suggests
that he, too, would like to find a way to tread the sun but to
shine with a brighter light. Then, his light would make a
shadow of the sun. The conversion, part of a confession, is ambiguous, however, since the poet cannot whole-heartedly renounce this radiant type. The force of Browning's adulation
modifies the implication that, however magnificent, the Sun-
Treader is an insufficient light to follow.

In an important scene mid-way through the poem, Browning suggests a similar transformation of pagan learning into a
Christian universe. This scene recalls an audacious moment in
Canto IV of Dante's *Inferno* and sets out to accomplish a similar
purpose: not only to assure a place in the canon for virtuous
pagans, but to insure the lineage of the poet himself as part of
this honorable company. Dante both writes himself into classical literary tradition and redeems that tradition for Christianity.

The canto opens with Dante being awakened out of a deep
sleep by a heavy thunder clap. Virgil then leads the pilgrim to
the first circle, inhabited by those who have not sinned but have
not been baptized. Some could not have been Christian because
they lived before Christ. "I myself am one," explains Virgil.
Dante also encounters four master poets of antiquity — Homer,

[8]Lines 49-56, *The Works of Henry Vaughan* ed. L. C. Martin, second edition (Oxford, 1957), p. 467.

Horace, Ovid, and Lucan—who honor Virgil as the loftiest of poets. In a dramatic act of proleptic praise, Dante has the four poets include him in their company. By placing the virtuous pagans in Limbo, Dante attempts to fit a valued tradition into a Christian framework. In this sense, Canto IV is his Pauline act.

Seen retrospectively, Canto IV is also Dante's Browninesque canto. It expresses his own longing for immortality. Without giving credit to Browning's "Two in the Compagna," Sinclair notes in his gloss on this scene: "It is Dante's version of 'the pain / Of finite hearts that yearn.'"[9] Browning felt this yearning for infinity so profoundly that most of his characters express madly, deviously, piously, humorously, or sadly their desire to prolong to eternity a valued aspect of their lives. The scene in *Pauline* endows this longing with supernatural authority.

For all its discontinuities, most of *Pauline* treats aspects of the problems raised in this passage of Canto IV, specifically the problem of literary continuity as one individual "of intensest life" feels and experiences it. Almost as if Browning were writing an extensive gloss on this scene, he gives us the experience of reading the powerful poets of antiquity. Then Browning's hero reenacts a version of the moment of poetic election.

Browning remembers his joyously active participation in reading Books mingled with self: "I myself went with the tale." He emphasizes the concreteness of imaginative reality:

> And nothing ever will surprise me now—
> Who stood beside the naked Swift-footed,
> Who bound my forehead with naked Properpine's hair.
> (ll. 333-35)

These delightful experiences, however, were a preparation for a greater encounter. All was eclipsed by Shelley's poems:

> And woven with them there were words, which seemed
> A key to a new world; the muttering
> Of angels, of some thing unguessed by man.
> (ll. 414-16)

[9]John D. Sinclair, trans. (Oxford, 1933; rpt. 1977), p. 70. See also E. R. Curtius, "Dante and the Antique Poets," *Literature and the Latin Middle Ages,* trans. Willard R. Trask (Princeton, 1953), pp. 17-19.

Enchanted by his identification, in which he saw his own thoughts mirrored but more gloriously in Shelley's poetry, he blissfully lived "with Plato" and "deeply mused" about how to attain joy.

Suddenly, "without heart-wreck," he awakens "as from a dream." That there was no pain in this awakening is disproven by the rest of the poem. Nonetheless, the poet prepares himself for his future by giving up his past and leaving himself free—a blank page upon which to write. As he emerges from his enclosed Romantic garden which rings with fairy songs and laughter, like Dante at the gate of Hell, he abandons all hope:

> First went my hopes of perfecting mankind,
> And faith in them—then freedom in itself,
> And virtue in itself—and then my motives' ends,
> And powers and loves; and human love went last.
>
> (ll. 458-61)

Cleansed of false hopes, he is ready to view the true shadows. Renunciation has made him strong.

The scene which follows, although similar in aim to Dante's, is portrayed through a Romantic filter. It is clearly set in the inner terrain of the self:

> My powers were greater—as some temple seemed
> My soul, where nought is changed, and incense rolls
> Around the altar—only God is gone,
> And some dark spirit sitteth in his seat!
>
> (ll. 468-71)

The dreamer's movement represents a passing through literary history as he leaves behind this Romantic temple (a version appears in Keat's *Hyperion,* another poem about poetic election). Browning insists that the moment when he transcends his own literary heritage comes after he passes through this godless temple. Then, he can meet the shades who will honor him:

> So I passed through the temple; and to me
> Knelt troops of shadowsr and they cried 'Hail, King!
> 'We serve thee now, and thou shalt serve no more!
> 'Call on us, prove us, let us worship thee!'
>
> (ll. 473-76)

This band, like the "lost adventurers, my peers" in "Childe Roland," represents an admiring audience and an aesthetic tribunal. Later in the poem, we discover that these poets set standards: "Unconsciously I measure me by them." But here, judgement is subordinated to admiration. The shades beg the poet to join them. Rather than humbly accepting the honor, he who might be suppliant instead tests the loyalties of the troop by asking them to help him escape the past:

> And I said, 'Are ye strong—let fancy bear me
> 'Far from the past.'—And I was borne away....
>   (ll. 477-78)

In this moment of birth the new poet is "borne" by his ancestor figures of the past. The mighty shadows, undismayed by guilty confession, act as midwives to the newborn artist. The antiphonal dialogue, almost liturgical in its rhythms, characterizes the ensuing coronation.

> And I said, 'I have nursed up energies,
> They will prey on me.' And a band knelt low,
> And cried, 'Lord, we are here, and we will make
> 'A way for thee—in thine appointed life
> 'O look on us!' And I said, 'Ye will worship
> 'Me; but my heart must worship too.' They shouted,
> 'Thyself—thou art our king!'
>   (ll. 481-87)

In addition to his abandonment of maternal Christian values in favor of Shelleyan abandon, Browning alludes to those literary sins of nursing the energies of his mother tongue in order to aspire to be a god, one worshiped rather than a worshiper.

In *Pauline,* however, none of these suggestions lead to conviction. The poet is too young to make a complete confession, as he himself admits in the subtitle. Not until the *Parleyings* are these suspicions subjected to a more comprehensive scrutiny. And not until the *Parleyings* does Browning acknowledge his debt to Dante.

Nonetheless, the troop of shadows is the audience to which Browning's *dramatis personae* play their roles. And these

shadows—an original meaning of figura[10]—are themselves
types, those poets who will be fulfilled by Browning. In the last
lines of *Pauline,* the relationship between the poet and the Sun-
Treader has been reversed, the speaker dedicating himself to
prophesy as he joins an ancient priesthood:

> I shall again go o'er the tracts of thought,
> As one who has a right; and I shall live
> With poets—calmer—purer still each time,
> And beauteous shapes will come to me again,
> And unknown secrets will be trusted me,
> Which were not mine when wavering—but now
> I shall be priest and lover, as of old.
>
>   (ll. 1013-19)

He embarks upon his mission of figuring forth types, of insisting upon facts as the true basis for fancy (his word for the imagination). His task presented in typological terms, was to reconcile Apollo with Christ and to reconcile Shelley with Browning.

III

Browning completed his fragment of a confession in the
Parleyings. Intended as an indirect autobiography, this long
and ambitious work presents a portrait of the artist according
to the influences upon his intellect—largely the books he read,
but also the paintings he saw and the music he heard. The seven
parleyings are dramatic monologues in which Browning himself first conjures up and then argues with shades of his intellectual past. The monologues are carefully divided into
sections; then the seven are enclosed by a Prologue and
Epilogue, written in dialogue. With uncharacteristic care he
plotted the work with an almost mathematical precision reminiscent of Dante. In fact, Browning took his title from his
favorite passage in the *Vita Nuova,* a work concerned with the
art of poetry and its relationship to the experienced life of the
poet.

[10] Eric Auerbach, "Figura," *Scenes from the Drama of European Literature*
(Gloucester, Mass., 1973), pp. 11-76.

Browning organizes his work in order to chart the life of his mind. It is an allegory in the most general sense; the seven persons of each parleying represent influences upon the author's mind, characters or issues from contemporary Victorian England, and an aspect of the poet's aesthetic. Thus, while the figures are historically real as well, they also represent aspects of Browning—the self as seen through others who have influenced him. The choice of the seven is idiosyncratic in that they do not necessarily stand for the most important persons in his life, but their relative obscurity allows the poet to subsume them in his own self-portrait. Each parleying acts out a mental battle as the poet struggles to define elements of his poetry. Browning summons these particular shades, and by arguing with them, he assesses his mission as "a priest and a lover, as of old."

Browning also expressed his ambition to combine love with vision in *Paracelsus,* his second published work. He portrayed the hero as a failed prophet, but one who prefigures a greater poet, who would combine the knowing of Paracelsus with the loving of his friend, Aprile:

> Let men
> Regard me, and the poet dead long ago
> Who loved too rashly and shape forth a third
> And better-tempered spirit.
> (Part V, ll. 885-88)

The *Parleyings* assesses this prophesy; is Browning in fact this third spirit, better attuned by the creator to fulfill the promise? The work justifies the career according to the poet's claim that he can correctly read the emblematic truth figured in earthly facts and then to convey those truths to a select audience. Although most "misconstrue" the signs;

> still, some few
> Have grace to see Thy purpose, strength to mar
> Thy work by no admixture of their own,
> —Limn truth, not falsehood, bid us to love alone
> The type untampered with, the naked star!
> (*Parleying With Francis Furini,* ll. 243-47)

To limn truth by presenting an actual historical case study is the explicit project of *The Ring and the Book,* for example. To base allegory upon history was the project of the Church Fathers in regard to Biblical interpretation. In following this tradition of commentary, Browning insists upon history as a basis for spiritual truth—the Old Yellow Book containing the facts of the Roman murder case, for instance, rather than the legend of Saint Somebody. Historical veracity makes him locate the stall where he chose the Yellow Book; it stood "precisely on that palace step" (Book I, 1. 50). In order to fulfill his Pauline role, he needs to base spiritual interpretation upon historical, literal "pure crude fact."

The bearing of the Prologue and Epilogue upon the rest of the work is so obscure that DeVane was only able to suggest tenuous connections to the work as a whole and saw no relationship to each other.[11] When viewed as providing the allegorical tension which informs the work as a whole, however, it is clear they they are essential to establishing Browning's self-portrait in terms of his identifications. The oppositions between the Prologue and the Epilogue define the polarities of an allegorical mode—a mode both explained and illustrated in each individual parleying. The Prologue, "Apollo and the Fates," has a pagan theme from antiquity, an infernal setting, and a young hero. The Epilogue, "Fust and his Friends," has a religious theme from the Middle Ages, a figuratively celestial setting, and characters who are looking toward death. The opening is somber in tone and color, whereas the end is burlesque, with grotesque rhymes and comic figures.

The Apollo of the Prologue is a young god who descends to plead with the Fates for the life of Admetus. The movement downward resembles the inward movement in *Pauline,* where the poet confronts the dark shape residing in his soul. In this return to autobiography and inwardness after a career of writing about others, Browning compresses the action to three lines in a dizzying dive from the highest peak to the lowest hollow:

From above.

Flame at my footfall, Parnassus! Apollo,
Breaking a-blaze on thy topmost peak,

[11] William Clyde DeVane, *Browning's Parleyings* (New Haven, 1927), p. 284.

Burns thence, down to the depths—dread hollow—
Haunt of the Dire Ones.

(ll. 1-4)

Apollo arrives at the sacred place where the Fates dwell, "Dragonwise couched in the womb of our Mother." Both the setting and the figures—the bright, youthful, optimistic Apollo and the dark, aged, cynical Moirai—set up the classic poles of the dualism by which allegory is defined. As Angus Fletcher explains, this is "dualism in its theological sense, where it implies the radical opposition of two independent, mutually irreducible mutually antagonistic substances, in short the opposition of Absolute Good and Absolute Evil. . . . It is found in all allegories that thematic opposition of absolutes is expressed by an ordering of imagery and agents which is equally dualistic."[12]

The psychomachia of the *Parleyings* pits the artist against the oppositions of Good and Evil as he tries to reconcile himself to imperfection or at least to find a momentary permanence. Occasionally, when Browning is unable to bridge the poles, the work threatens to disintegrate as the poet frantically casts a span of words over the abyss. In each parleying an emblematic artifice temporarily stills the constantly shifting realities.

In the Prologue, a wine press is used emblematically; it produces the lihuid which warms the senses so that life can be viewed optimistically. The grapes are transformed by art— "earth's nature sublimed by Man's art." The pun describes the action of art, turning solid matter into spiritual truth. But this particular art owes more to a pagan than to a Christian god. Apollo brings the Fates a false and momentary warmth; while they are under the influence of Apollo's wine, they view mankind more optimistically. Their happier philosophy lasts only until the sobering shock of an "explosion from earth's center" restores their characteristic pessimism.

The explosion recalls the event suggested in *Pauline*— perhaps the maternal explosion which awakened the young poet from his idealistic dreams. At any rate, Apollo here is Browning's Shelleyan aspect, that period of his life when Shelley inspired him to renounce both meat and the Almighty in the name of proclaiming a brotherhood of all creatures. The

[12]Angus Fletcher, *Allegory* (Ithaca, N.Y., 1964), p. 222.

divinity of the Prologue is a young, early Apollo, whose naivete
and sunny disposition blind him to important, darker truths
even as his optimistic blindness adds to his appeal. The trusting
god ascends, confident that he has won life for Admetus; his
optimism leads him to believe in man's pure selfless actions.
Though splendid, Apollo takes his place among those of
Browning's figures who are self-deceived. By elaborating on
his early praise of Shelley in *Pauline,* Browning adds a
corrective.

The background to Browning's revision of his youthful
enthusiasm for Shelley can be discovered in Browning's life
at the time he was shaping the *Parleyings.* In the decade before he began "Apollo and the Fates," he had reason carefully
to reexamine his relationship to Shelley. The library edition
of Shelley's works, the labor of H. Buxton Forman, began to appear in 1876. Because Browning had supplied Forman with
some biographical and textual data and some references to
Shelley's continuing influence upon his own poetry, Forman
sent Browning each volume as it appeared, from 1876 to 1880.[13]

The process of reviewing and footnoting his own poetic
development from Shelley, a theme in *Pauline,* continued in
another way. In 1878, Browning added an apologetic note to
the flyleaf of his first copy of Shelley:

> This book was given to me—probably as soon as published by
> my cousin J. S.: the foolish markings and still more foolish
> scribblings show the impression made on a boy by this first
> specimen of Shelley's poetry. Robert Browning, June 2, 1878
> "O World O Life O Time."[14]

For five or six years, Browning continued the autobiography
of his intellectual development on the fly-leaves of books—
a process both self-conscious and self-critical. Browning's actions upon his library were also self-effacing, since he scribbled
over, scratched out, or cut out his effusive marginalia sur-

[13] See letters to Forman in 1876 and 1877 in *Letters of Robert Browning,*
coll. by *Thomas J. Wise,* ed. Thurman L. Hood (New Haven, 1933), pp. 174,
176, 177, 179.
[14] *Sale Catalogues of Libraries of Eminent Persons,* 6, ed. John Woolford
(London, 1972), p. 158.

rounding Shelley's poems. However, he did allow the comment, "splendid" to remain near Shelley's "Hymn of Apollo."
   Spoken by the god himself, the Hymn claims great power for
the artistic imagination, even for Shelley:

> I am the eye with which the Universe
> Beholds itself and knows itself divine.

   In the eipgraph to "Apollo and the Fates," Browning cites
the Homeric "Hymn to Mercury," a poem which Shelley had
translated. As opposed to the solipsistic narcissim of Shelley's
hymn, the Homeric poem portrays a human, fallible Apollo. In
addition to recounting the youthful god's challenge to the
Fates, this poem contains a myth of poetic succession: Hermes
bestows the lyre upon Apollo.[15]
   In reappraising his feelings for Shelley, Browning was providing himself with material for his autobiography. From this
perspective, "Apollo and the Fates" indirectly parleys with
Shelley. The opening line, "Flame at my footfall, Parnassus!"
echoes Shelley's "My footsteps pave the clouds with fire."
(l. 10). Although Browning's Apollo conveys the appeal of
Shelley's sun-treader, the Victorian poet hedges this light with
a dimmed aura. The Fates supply a corrective to this naive
youth as they oppose the radiant sun with a dark orb. This
darker awareness has been too little acknowledged as part of
Browning's life view. Although good can be disguised as evil,
he knows that the opposite is also likely:

> So, even so! From without,—at due distance
>   If viewed,—set a-sparkle, reflecting thy rays,—
> Life mimics the sun: but withdraw such assistance,
>   The counterfeit goes, the reality stays—
> An ice ball disguised as a fire-orb.
>
>   (ll. 86-90)

Although he chose to minimize them, a profound understanding of the counterfeit in men and an uneasy knowledge of the
unrealiability of reality itself lie at the center of Browning's

---

[15]*Shelley's Poetical Works*, 5, ed. H. Buxton Forman (London, 1883), p. 29.

art. Like the device of the sunflower in "Rudel to the Lady of Tripoli," life mimics the sun. But what if life is an ice-ball disguised as a fire-orb? This question, only touched upon here, recurs throughout the entire work. What men call reality constantly threatens to collapse. Then men are seen as dangling helplessly, clouds instead of ground beneath their feet with Atropos threatening coldly to snip the thread:

ATROPOS

— Which I make an end of: the smooth as the tangled
  My shears cut asunder: each snap shrieks 'One more
Mortal makes sport for us Moirai who dangled
  The puppet grotesquely till earth's solid floor
Proved film he fell through, lost in Nought as before.'

Apollo himself is a false god who depends upon inebriation to persuade men of goodness. Browning again portrays the Sun-Treader as an inadequate though appealing light as the Prologue ends with the mocking laughter of the Fates, silenced only by the last word of the section: "Darkness."

IV

"Fust and His Friends" balances and completes "Apollo and the Fates" and lays to rest many of the ghosts of *Pauline*. The Prologue raised serious reservations about man's goodness; the Epilogue suggests a way out of the dilemma without denying the presence of evil. As in the Prologue, the difficulty of distinguishing between semblance and reality remains as epistemological problem, here suggested by the terms of the dramatic episode as well as by linguistic doublings: puns, plays upon names, grotesque rhymes. Browning also unveils a final emblem of man's art, a printing press, and prophesies the coming of a true prophet who will use common language to spread the true Gospel.

The setting is Mayence where, in 1457, John Fust, a banker,

has supposedly sold his soul to the devil.[16] The scene opens as seven of his clerical friends climb up to his shop in hopes of saving him:

> Up, up, up—next step of the staircase
> Lands us, lo, at the chamber of dread!
> (ll. 1-2)

The verbal echo of "dread" from the Prologue indicates that this chamber and that hollow are equivalent; the lights have changed, but this is a sacred place. In addition these seven— one for each parleying—are analogous in function to the troop of shadows from *Pauline*. One disclaims a diabolic intent: "No foul hell-brood flock we!" Another reveals their divine mission of hearing Fust's confession and of absolving him: "And soul, wakened, unloads / Much sin by confession: no mere palinodes!" In terms of a literary work, however, this is both a confession and a palinode, since the confession requires a revision of the work. Fust's first confession in fact echoes the first confession of the *Pauline* poet: "I sucked / —Got drunk at the nipple of sense." Since this whole work is about poetry, the pun on "sense" refers both to the senses and to meaning, Fust, too, became intoxicated by learning. And he too has nursed energies which prey upon him.

Fust also admits to excesses; he knows about pride, concupiscence, and the false magic of drunkeness. A long passage denounces the wisdom produced by wine, the "potable madness." Wine brings about false vision through "optics drink-dimmed." This diatribe answers the celebration of wine in the Prologue. Seeing plain was essential to Browning, who described his objective in *Men and Women:* "to get people to hear and see."

[16]Browning combined elements of the Faust legend with the biography of Johann Fust, a banker who lent money to Gutenberg for his press and then, when Gutenberg did not repay him, took possession of it and printed books himself. Browning makes Fust, whose father was a goldsmith, the inventor of printing, possibly so he could combine the trades of goldsmith and printer to serve as a metaphor for the poet. See DeVane, *Handbook,* p. 523, and *Browning's Parleyings,* pp. 292-295.

Having heard from Fust's assistant that his master hides an invention which can spread speech so that all men can hear it in the "same magic moment," the clerics believe Fust has the Devil's cooperation. Even men of the church cannot distinguish good from evil. As a last resort, they prepare to exorcise the evil spirit, but they cannot remember the prayer, evidence of his invention, validation that he is a good man.

He then unveils his printing press and indicates that he believes that in creating it, he was performing God's work. The printing press will vanquish falsehood by publishing truth. These claims resemble Browning's assertions about his poetry. If truth is printed, it can be rescued—as Browning rescued the truth of the Roman murder story. And if truth can be "broadcast over Europe," it can be possessed by all men, not only by churchmen.

In terms of the dramatic fiction, Browning explains his own aesthetic. Furthermore, he reveals the secret source of his art. Fust, a goldsmith by trade, learned his art from a "Tuscan artificer" who engraved on gold. Having stolen the secret, Fust applied it to another metal:

> 'The goldsmith,' I said
> 'Graves limning on gold: why not letters on lead?'
> So, Tuscan artificer, grudge not thy pardon
>   To me who played false, made a furtive descent,
>   Found the sly secret workshop, —thy genius kept guard on
>   Too slackly for once—and surprised thee low-bent
> O'er thy labor—.
>
> (ll. 329-35)

This Tuscan artificer is Dante, and the moment alluded to is a transformation from Browning's favorite passage of the *Vita Nuova*. Dante's work, like the *Parleyings,* is a discussion and a demonstration of the poet's art; the passage above transforms the Dante passage alluded to in "One Word More," the Epilogue to *Men and Women,* where Browning dedicates the volume to Elizabeth and his life to poetry.

In Chapter XXXIV of the *Vita Nuova,* Dante tells of drawing an angel on the first anniversary of Beatrice's death. So enrapt was he in his drawing that he did not notice standing beside him certain people of importance. The men tell him that they have been watching him for some time. After they leave, Dante resumes his drawing but is soon inspired to write some anniversary verses and to dedicate them to these men.

In "One Word More," the watchers destroy Dante's inspiration, and Browning portrays them as evil souls from the *Inferno*. In the Epilogue to the *Parleyings*, however, it is Fust, as speaker for Browning, who intrudes to steal the secret of the Tuscan's art while the artist is too engrossed in his work to notice. Since Browning had compared his own poetic art with that of the goldsmith in *The Ring and the Book*, the reader is prepared for this trope. Browning honors a source of his own art, but he also confesses to his sin. He has stolen a secret of dramatic art from Dante and has adapted it to a new use. As he strongly suggests here, he used more than the monologue form; he also learned from Dante how to apply typology to literary uses. Since the infernal speeches, with their ironic self-deceptions, could be Browningesque dramatic monologues, Browning could view himself as "chopping" them free from their context, translating them to a new language, and calling them his own creations

> High, O Printing, and holy
> Thy mission! These types, see, I chop and I change
> Till the words, every letter a pageful, not slowly
> Yet surely lies fixed.
>
> (ll. 356-59)

For Browning to use Dante, the Catholic orientation must be changed as well as chopped. Fust's despondency comes from his recognition that types can be used in the service of false doctrine. He dedicates his invention to help men to descry new truth:

> Give chase, soul! Be sure each new capture consigned
> To my Types will go forth to the world, like God's bread
> Miraculous food not for body but mind,
> Truth's manna!
>
> (ll. 434-39)

Fust calls for someone who will counteract the "gross fables" of false prophets, here "Beghards, Waldenses, / Jeronimites,

Jussites." The final line foretells the coming of a man who will restore types to a heavenly purpose as truth's manna. Although he is not named, the man is Martin Luther, the reformer, founder of evangelical Protestantism, translator of the Bible into a common language.

Luther appears in the last line of Browning's autobiographical work as one who has not yet arrived. "I forsee such a man." The nineteenth century viewed Luther as a liberal who interpreted the truth of the Bible into the idiom of the people. Like Browning, he was occasionally coarse. For Luther, the New Testament was a Pauline book; his theology heightened, intensified, and clarified the teachings of Paul. Furthermore, Luther claimed that a passage from Paul's Epistle to the Romans became for him the gateway to heaven.[17]

Luther is thus an appropriate figure for Browning's final vision of himself. Browning, too, is a Pauline reformer. As a type of priest, the poet gave a Pauline reading to Romanticism and sent out his types to all men and women with his deliberately earthy language and with concrete images replacing abstractions.

In the Prologue his figure for his Romantic self is a Shelleyan Apollo, a youthfully optimistic upholder of the imagination at the expense of other realities. In the Epilogue his figure for his mature Victorian self is Luther (as well as Fust), the "shadowy third" prophesied by Paracelsus, who will combine knowing and loving and will thereby read correctly and convey convincingly the fancy made of fact, the imaginative reality of truth. The final claim of the *Parleyings* returns to the last line of *Pauline*. By reconciling Apollo to Christ, by seeing in him a type, Browning asserts that he has become a priest and a lover as of old—like Dante, like Paul, like Luther. Browning frequently echoed Luther's famous and revolutionary challenge: Here I stand.

The eclecticism of Victorian aesthetices raises particular difficulties for tracing any part of it. The Victorians seemed content to borrow wholesale from contradictory styles, ideas,

[17]Roland Bainton, *Here I Stand: A Life of Martin Luther* (Nashville, Tennessee: Abington Press, 1950), pp. 60-68; Richard Friedenthal, *Luther* (London: Weidenfeld and Nicolson, 1967), pp. 102, 120.

and modes without feeling the necessity either of making a coherent whole or of hiding their sources. Browning's use of types illustrates this creative mix. He adapted Quarles, Dante, St. Paul, Luther, to cite only a few examples, without trying to resolve apparently contradictory traditions. Any attempt to reconcile these contradictions for the sake of argument inevitably ends in a distortion of Browning, To adumbrate Browning's types is to suggest a general outline of his poetic notion of a troop of shadowy presences, figures of great poets. As he tells us in *Pauline,* it is through these that Browning learned to view and name reality. It is in them as he conjured them fourth in the *Parleyings* that Browning saw dim outlines of his own life as an artist.

November, 1889

by Richard Howard

FOR HAROLD BLOOM

Well met, children! yet *I* am not well.
In their corruption, dear Fanny, all things are
possible, none without. I thought so
today, riding on the water here to you,
    ill as I am, but not
    so ill as not to think,
and with my burden besides —
as blessings are a burden.
Has your man brought in
a bolted box, safe
    from the gondola? The burden
    I must give into your hands...
    Do I express myself,
    or but exploit myself?
Astonishing, Pen, what you have done,
and managed yet to leave undone! Ruin at bay,
procrastinated, nay proannuated!
Ca' Rezzonico and its eternal glooms,
    but not eternal now.
    We use the word amiss,
    as if it meant no more than
    "everlasting". Well! each bird
Sings to itself, so
then shall I, and make
    no more of your palace than

that you have not made it less:
here is a pile at last
enabled to assume
the full aspect of the past, which is
in Venice the period taken, or given,
for crystallization. I had thought
these walls beyond repair, like all such
castles of misconduct,
victims of villainous
improvements else, reduced
or even enlarged to being
one further orifice
in the peep-show here,
lurid, livid, but always
burnt out. It is easier,
Venice and I have learnt,
to endure than to change—
hardest of all to endure what you
have not changed into. The bolted box is... but
I shall explain. I am not very well.
Last week at Mrs Bronson's, it was no more
than a migraine, or so
the doctor in Asolo
pronounced it—splendid fellow,
what I liked most in him was,
he did not leave me
verses of his own.
Curious symptoms withal
for migraine: patterns moving
over surfaces, faint
most often, fine designs
that would come as a kind of cobweb
cast iridescent upon others, a net
intervening between me and them.
Lord! the things one sees when a fever-lit mind
grants no middle distance.
Prolixity of the real!
And just when we are grateful
for the dark, when night resumes us,
comes prolixity
of what is unreal,

the melting waxworks of our sleep
called dreams. I am against dreams,
   not being one to trust
   memory to itself.
In my delirium, then, I had
conviction of divided identity,
   never ceasing to be two persons who
ever thwarted and opposed one another.
   Then wakened to the faint
   smell of drugs and nostrums
   from the bedside — like a new-made
mummy. And as if in answer,
the post at Padua
   (last month's, to be sure)
   announcing Collins is gone.
   Collins, Pen — Wilkie Collins,
      the *Moonstone* man, although
      fits and starts are the best
of what he left us: perhaps their length
is his measure. Well, we are all stewing-pans,
   and can cook only what we can hold.
Some more than others. Collins had, poor fellow,
      finicking manners but
      a luxurious gut,
   and he took his way sadly,
   certain he had fallen among
grocers. A kind of
indispensable
      liability to life,
      that man's power of suspense;
      and his tenacity!
      One only does not call
a labor like *The Woman in White*
Herculean because Hercules could not
   have done it! Whereas your father runs
after interruptions, leading or led by
   the intransitive life
   of a fool who foments
   his poems whilst he dines out
   and disappoints. Consider:
the torment of starch

in my new shirts, Fan,
　　has made me physically
　　irritable, morally
　　　impotent, and *for days!*
　　　Who could write, with a sense
　of chalky grit rubbed into each pore,
clogging all perspiration, chafing every
　inch of cuticle, desiccating
the blood itself! I share Gautier's opinion
　　　that Christianity
　　　and laundry cannot sort
　　together. Perhaps it was
　　Christianity and sculpture.
In either case, for
laundry *and* sculpture,
　　we should have one leg firm on
　　the Acropolis, and one
　　　in Florence, For God's sake!
　　　what organ have we then,
　　my boy, in Venice? If Asolo
be my *pied-à-terre,* here you keep, I suppose,
　your *ventre-à-l'eau.* Monstrous levity,
to mask a lack. Shelley calls the great god Pan
　　　a want, you know, and all
　　　this Italian earth seems
　　　now to me the sense of what
　　　can never be. It burgeons
without us, and lives
the lewd life of things
　　that look for no existence
　　but in themselves. The canal
　　　I came by—leave it and
　　　it comprehends you not.
　　Worse, the admiration of mountains,
　surely a Calvinist plot: strange confusion,
　　among minds defiant of meaning,
　between the mere lofty and the beautiful.
　　　If mountains turn a tree
　　　into a fir, fancy
　　what they can do with a man!
　　Italy lets us know it:

the life of April
sunlight has to die;
   it is now quite dead, and I
   have another kind of life.
      Beauties there, of course, but
      coming only in bursts.
  coming to a mind long crumpled (till
the creases stay), coming only in escapes
   from the thing itself! Take Asolo,
that long Virgilian country round about—
      half mystery and half
      morality, but then!
   then the scramble of rural
   royalty, with royal thoughts!
"It is, at bottom,
would you not say, sir,
      a criticism of life?" I:
      "Rather take it at the top,
      burning ever upward
      to its blank point of bliss."
   Sumptuous, of course, the dinner,
views from the villa entrancing, as you know:
   the valley full of mist and looking
like a sea of absinthe, distant hills rising
      from it, forming the shore
      of Purgatory, past
   Acheron. And the Russian
   Duchess looked on indifferent,
staring as she ate,
watching the Brenta
      as if she were but watching
      the Grand Duke's body pass by:
      "What is there, that you make
      so much of, in water?"—
leaving off the lobster—"I am quite
tired of it. There it goes: flow flow flow, always
   the same." She demands to see me here,
a Princess by birth, a Nihilist by trade!
      offers a rendex-vous,
      my dears, at her hotel,
   that I may explain stanzas
   she found *obscure.* I suppose

it is dangerous,
if you have not had
    the advantage of dying,
    to attempt a description
        of death, and afterwards
        there are, unfortunately,
    obstacles in the way...though Ba came
not to believe in those either. It is all
    rigmarole and rhodomontade, even
at the hands of a Grand Duchess practicing
        mesmerism and miracles
        on all sides. I sink to
    precious trifling, yet better
    than the fate of a fallen
rocket that likely
will be mine as well.
        I neither hope nor deserve
        to be loved by anybody,
            nor much, nor at all, yet
            I am very grateful
    when someone is at pains to do it.
A great many such ladies of the first rank
    were present at that dinner, and if
honeyed words from pretty lips could surfeit,
        I had enough—though one
        can swallow quantities
    of whipped cream and do no harm
    to an old stomach. They seem
to care so deeply
for what they call *art:*
    I suppose it is like one
    of those indelicate subjects
        which always sound better
        in a foreign language.
    I am not interested in art.
I am interested in the obstacles
to art. One creature with queenly airs
and a snake, I vow, tattooed on her ankle,
        clung to me like ivy:
        whatever should she do
    in order to become, say,
    a poet? *In order!* Never

have I pretended
to afford anyone
   such literature as might
   substitute for a cigar,
     but so much I told her:
     "Don't twitter, though sparrows
all do; things happen, and then we get
a lark or a nightingale or even an owl,
   which last is by no means to be scorned."
Kay Bronson cannot abide, you know, the rule
   of an equal number
   in men and women guests.
She says she invites her friends
for conversation, not mating.
Even so, there are
surprises. Walking
   in the woods with my snake-lady,

   I said: "Let us sit here"; then,
   after regarding me
   steadily a moment,
   her pale eyes glowing like grapes,
she said: "You may make love to me, if you like."
   The old have death, and the young have love,
but death comes once—love over and over.
   Or is it to the old
   that death comes back and back.
   and love no longer at all?
   I told her, it was for poetry
I ate and drank and
dressed and had my being,
   but she would not let me go.
   To be quit of her and them
   is a godsend to me,
   for all the graying wreck
of nature here, where if not divine
it is diabolic. I said I was not well,
   yet well or ill, up at the villa
I am a man smothered with society
   of women, like a duck
   with onions. I will not
   be Victorian in their way:
   I would be...Albertian!

In the one year, Ba
died, then Albert died.
   Ours were the Great Marriages,
   I cannot help but think, for
     I know ours to be, still,
     the Great Bereavements,
   the weeds worn so long neither the Queen
nor I remembers quite the flowers, I daresay,
   sprouted by now to something emblematic,
something gone out of the garden altogether.
   Wife to husband, widow
   to widower, ah, Pen,
   we remember the flowers,
   in thirty years forget the weeds!
I want nothing left
out, and nothing back,
   no, nothing ever again.
   Don't expurgate: exorcise
     your losses! In Venice
     we learn about losses:
   they affect us only till we have
lost altogether. Then comes a poisonous
   impalpability that simulates
a form beneath the flow of time's gray garment,
     and through the place we see
     is signified a place
   we never saw. Life is all
   salutation. No reply.
Drifting through Venice
after twenty years'
   such drifting, and year by year
   seeing only the bruises
     in the marble blacker,
     the patience of ruin
   deeper, every stone an image of
accumulated sea-change, it was all one—
   one of my numerous visions which so
numerously leave me. As I came, my box
     beside me and my eyes
     too old for disbelief,
   clouds soon covered up the sun,
   as if too good to be seen,
granting a dead glare,

visions from the verge
   shadowless in the steel air,
   unaccountable, violent
      against an ultimate
      horizon. At that hour
   the ends of the earth were closing in,
and I thought: my boy, my Pen, cold walls hold him
   among shades and silences, mostly
darkness there, under a grim incessant sky
      grayer with each moment
      since Asolo. It was
   a pale departure into
   this perfect decrepitude,
suffering this dim
disgrace of daylight
      as the noiseless town neared us.
      Neared *us!* We could not even
         creep to it, but Venice
         rose up out of the sea
      to meet us, a momentary shape
made magnificent by perennial touching.
      Ah, Fanny, there are times I can guess
what you good young Americans must feel, times—
         I feel them too—when we
         are nothing but the heirs
         or an humiliating
         splendor. As you have taught me,
   it takes a great deal
   to make one successful
         American, but to make
         one happy Venetian takes
            a mere handful of life
            among old stones. Indeed,
      if there be disagreeable things
   in Venice, nothing is so disagreeable
      as the visitors, jostling for boats
   around one. Lady Gordon warned I should find
         a *bateau-mouche* plying
         the Grand Canal! I had
         no distaste for it, myself,
         but the gondoliers, finding
   their custom lessened,

had all struck, and we
  could barely get a *barca*
  for love as *well as* money!
    Poor fellows, they shall learn,
    as others have, that steam
  is stronger than they. We left behind
those foreigners fuming round the Redentore,
  and I knew: what is dead or dying
is more readily apprehended by us
    than what is part of life.
    Nothing in writing is
    easier than to raise the dead.
    Do not let me wander, Pen —
I am not enough
myself now to be
    spontaneous. I must *scheme.*
    Last year, Eliot Norton
      (I have learnt to admire
      if not to endure him)
  showed me the letters to Jane Carlyle
and those from her to Thomas, before and since
  their marriage, both. He will not print them,
even to correct Froude's falsifications,
    will not violate *anew*
    the prostrate confidence
of husband and wife, will not
  be known as the one to do it,
at any rate. Pen,
such must not be my fate.
    I dread but one thing: biography.
    The truth which is in this box,
    once unlatched, once published
    to the world, is worth all
  the tragedy of errors after:
time finds a withered leaf in every laurel,
  age makes egoism more eager,
less enjoying. It shall be her words, my words,
    no more than that, no less.
    There are enough of them,
    five-hundred letters, by my count —
    long ago. What our words are,
I am not certain.

It is done. Old love
    is slow in going, but goes.
    Some twenty years since I looked
    at what is in the box.
    Cowardice, call it that;
    I do not know the name. Sufficient
for me, knowing they are there. Without opening,
    I can say the words, some of the words:
"My power lives in me like the fire in those mad
        Mediterranean
        phares I have watched at sea,
        wherein the light is ever
        turning in a dark gallery,
still bright and alive.
    and only after
        a wary interval leaps out,
        for a moment, from the one
            mean chink, and then goes on
            with between it and you
    the blind wall." Perhaps because I can
recite that much, I do not care for the rest.
    You keep them now, Pen, and once I am
gone, give them to Smith. It should be two volumes...
        Nothing but ourselves then,
        though that be too much now
    for me. Put the box away,
    high and dry. I am still here.

Now this is splendid,
what you have done with
        the stairs, Fanny, this is warm!
    it shows what *can* be done. If,
        as I have always said,
        these people are ever
    refined, it will be by fire. A few
coals do it: the life in us abolishes
    the death in things. I recall, last time,
how drear it all looked, and how I dreaded
        to feel the pale hush
        of the irreparable
        on all these blighted rooms,
        the relics of how many

Doges littering
your inhuman walls?
   A pressure of sanctity
   almost profane, disorder
      in the very daylight...
      All gone, now, and well gone
  behind us, or ahead — like the letters:
too far behind me to be endured, too far
  ahead to be dared. Let them rest here.
Ah, Venice! Pen, your Venice now, how it rocks
      all ambitions to sleep,
      floats a man to his doom,
   even when the secular truth
   is a stroll on the sandbars.
Again the delusion!
We are all under
   a net that covers the world!
   Or is it but the canal,
      lapping in light on your
      ceilings? It is nothing,
  then, no cause for alarm, dear children,
it has passed, as all spells do, however cast.
  The preponderance of some dissolving
force, mine or water's, need not be contended with,
      merely endured, merely
      survived. Strange, though, how close
   the meshes were, everywhere
   entrapping, overtaking...
If I am to go
out to the Lido
   at all, I must go before
   I am too sick to go, and
      above all, before I mind
      being sicker. Let me have
  my cloak again, Fanny, and your man
to row me beyond these wicked walls. I want
  to see the grass, if it be but gray
wires curling on the beach. I need to walk now,
      without these palaces
      pressing in upon me;
   they make, for all their marble
   pride, a valley of darkness —

at its end I see
vast uncertainty.
    I want room now, not solace,
    I must have the roar and release
        of some open water,
        even if it be black.
  Then here, returning, then the firelight,
then, in the winter half of the world, to sleep...

Chronology of Important Dates

1812	May 7; born in Camberwell near London, son of Robert Browning and Sarah Anna Wiedemann Browning.
1824	*Incondita* submitted by parents to publishers without success.
1826	Discovers Shelley's poetry.
1828-29	Briefly attends newly established London University.
1833	*Pauline.*
1834	Journey to St. Petersburg.
1835	*Paracelsus.*
1836	Meets Landor, Wordsworth; Macready invites him to write a play.
1840	*Sordello.*
1841-46	*Bells and Pomegranates,* a series of eight pamphlets; *Pippa Passes* (1841); *King Victor and King Charles* (1842); *Dramatic Lyrics* (1842); *The Return of the Druses* (1843); *A Blot in the 'Scutcheon* (1843) performed and failed at the Drury Lane Theatre; *Colombe's Birthday* (1844); *Dramatic Romances and Lyrics* (1845); *Luria* and *A Soul's Tragedy* (1846).
1845	January 10, First letter to Elizabeth Barrett; May 20, first call to Wimpole Street.
1846	September 12, secret marriage to Elizabeth Barrett; Brownings move to Pisa.
1847	Brownings move to Casa Guidi in Florence.
1849	Robert Wiedemann Barrett Browning (Pen) born; poet's mother dies.
1850	*Christmas-Eve and Easter Day.*
1855	*Men and Women.*

1861   Death of Elizabeth; Browning leaves Italy and lives at Warwick Crescent in London.

1864   *Dramatis Personae.*

1867   Honorary M.A. at Oxford; Honorary Fellow at Balliol.

1868-69   *The Ring and the Book.*

1871   *Balaustion's Adventure; Prince Hohenstiel Schwangau, Saviour of Society.*

1872   *Fifine at the Fair.*

1875   *Red Cotton Night-Cap Country* or *Turf and Towers; The Inn Album.*

1876   *"Pacchiarotto and How He Worked in Distemper" with Other Poems.*

1877   *The Agamemnon of Aeschylus.*

1878   *La Saisiaz, The Two Poets of Croisic.*

1879   *Dramatic Idyls: First Series.*

1880   *Dramatic Idyls: Second Series.*

1881   Browning Society founded by Furnival.

1883   *Jocoseria.*

1884   *Ferishtah's Fancies.*

1887   *Parleyings with Certain People of Importance in their Day.*

1888-89   *The Poetical Works* (sixteen volumes).

1889   *Asolando: Fancies and Facts;* December 12, died at son's palazzo in Venice; December 31, burial in Westminster Abbey.

Notes on the Editors and Contributors

HAROLD BLOOM, professor of humanities at Yale, has published twelve books of criticism, including *The Anxiety of Influence, A Map of Misreading,* and *Wallace Stevens: The Poems of Our Climate.* His most recent work is a prose romance, *The Flight to Lucifer: A Gnostic Fantasy.*

ADRIENNE MUNICH, a fellow at the Center for Independent Study, New Haven, Connecticut, is a director of the Browning Institute and a lecturer at Yale.

LESLIE BRISMAN is an associate professor of English at Yale. He is the author of *Milton's Poetry of Choice and Its Romantic Heirs* and *Romantic Origins.*

JOHN HOLLANDER is a poet and critic who teaches at Yale. His most recent books are *Spectral Emanations: New and Selected Poems* and *Vision and Resonance.*

RICHARD HOWARD is a poet, critic and translator. His best-known volumes of poetry are *Untitled Subjects* and *Findings;* his principal critical work is *Alone With America.*

JOHN KILLHAM is a reader in English language and literature at the University of Keele. He is author of *Tennyson and the Princess: Reflections of an Age.*

ROBERT LANGBAUM is James Branch Cabell Professor of English at the University of Virginia. His critical works include *The Poetry of Experience, The Modern Spirit,* and *The Mysteries of Identity.*

LOY D. MARTIN teaches at Stanford and is completing a book on the dramatic monologue.

GEORGE M. RIDENOUR is professor of English at the City University of New York Graduate School. He has written *The Style of "Don Juan"* and many essays on nineteenth-century poetry.

ANN WORDSWORTH teaches English at St. Hughs College, Oxford University, where she helps to edit the *Oxford Literary Review.* She has published articles on Lacan, Derrida, and critical theory.

Selected Bibliography

Editions

The Complete Works of Robert Browning. Edited by Charlotte Porter and Helen A. Clarke. 12 vols. New York, 1898. (The Florentine Edition.) Interesting notes.

The Works of Robert Browning. Edited by F. G. Kenyon. 10 vols. London; Smith, Elder, 1912. (The Centenary Edition.)

The Complete Works of Robert Browning. Edited by Roma A. King, Jr. 4 vols. of 13 published. Athens, Ohio: University of Ohio Press, 1969-.

The Complete Poetical Works of Robert Browning. Edited by Horace E. Scudder. Boston: Houghton Mifflin, 1895. (The Cambridge Edition.) A one-volume edition with a complete and standard text, but with antiquated notes, introduction, and appendix.

Letters

The Letters of Robert Browning and Elizabeth Barrett Browning: 1845-1846. Edited by Elvan Kinter. Cambridge; Harvard University Press, 1969.

Letters of Robert Browning, Collected by T. J. Wise. Edited by Thurman Hood. New Haven: Yale University Press, 1933.

New Letters of Robert Browning. Edited by W. C. DeVane and K. L. Knickerbocker. New Haven: Yale University Press, 1950.

Robert Browning and Julia Wedgewood: A Broken Friendship as Revealed by their Letters. Edited by Richard Curle. New York: Frederick A. Stokes, 1937. A particularly interesting exchange during the composition of *The Ring and the Book.*

Robert Browning and Alfred Domett. Edited by F. G. Kenyon. London: Smith Elder, 1906.

Dearest Isa: Robert Browning's Letters to Isabella Blagden. Edited by Edward C. McAleer. Austin: University of Texas Press, 1951.

Learned Lady: Letters from Robert Browning to Mrs. Thomas Fitzgerald, 1876-1889. Edited by Edward C. McAleer. Cambridge: Harvard University Press, 1966.

Biographies

Griffin, W. H., and Minchen, H. C. *The Life of Robert Browning.* Rev. ed. London: Macmillan, 1938.

Irvine, William, and Honan, Park. *The Book, the Ring, and the Poet.* New York: McGraw-Hill, 1974.

Maynard, John. *Young Robert Browning.* Cambridge: Harvard University Press, 1977.

Miller, Betty. *Robert Browning: A Portrait.* London: John Murray, 1952.

Reference

Broughton, Leslie N., and Stetler. *A Concordance to the Poems of Robert Browning.* 2 vols. New York, 1924-1925.

Broughton, Leslie N.; Northup, C. S.; and Pearsall, R. *Robert Browning: A Bibliography; 1830-1950.* Ithaca, N.Y.: Cornell University Press, 1953.

Cook, A. K. *A Commentary upon Browning's "The Ring and the Book."* Reprinted. Hamden, Conn.: Archon Books, 1966. (Originally published 1920.)

DeVane, William Clyde. *A Browning Handbook.* 2nd ed. New York: Appleton-Century-Crofts, 1955. Indispensable.

Orr, Mrs. Sutherland. *Handbook to Browning's Works.* London: G. Bell and Sons, 1886 and succeeding years. Intelligent readings by Mrs. Orr, who was supervised in the earliest editions by Browning himself.

Peterson, William S. *Robert and Elizabeth Browning: An Annotated Bibliography, 1951-1970.* New York: Browning Institute, 1974. A continuation of this bibliography appears annually in *Browning*

Institute Studies. Other bibliographies appear in *Victorian Studies,* *MLA* bibliography, and *Studies in Browning and his Circle.*

General Studies

Altick, Richard, and Loucks, James. *Browning's Roman Murder Story: A Reading of "The Ring and the Book."* Chicago: University of Chicago Press, 1968.

Armstrong, Isobel, ed. *Robert Browning: Writers and Their Background.* Londin, G. Bell, 1974.

Harrold, William E. *The Variance and the Unity: A Commentary on the Complimentary Poems of Robert Browning.* Athens, Ohio: Ohio University Press, 1973.

Honan, Park. *Browning's Characters.* New Haven: Yale University Press, 1961.

Jack, Ian. *Browning's Major Poetry.* London: Oxford University Press, 1973.

Johnson, E. D. H. *The Alien Vision of Victorian Poetry.* Princeton: Princeton University Press, 1952 "Browning," pp. 71-143.

Kaplan, Fred. *Miracles of Rare Device: The Poet's Sense of Self in Nineteenth-Century Poetry.* Detroit: Wayne State University Press, 1972. Two chapters: "Browning's Painter in Wasteland," pp. 94-108, and "Le Byron de Nos Jours," pp. 109-23.

King, Roma A. *The Bow and the Lyre: The Art of Robert Browning.* Ann Arbor: University of Michigan Press, 1964.

———. *The Focusing Artifice: The Poetry of Robert Browning.* Athens, Ohio: Ohio University Press, 1968.

Langbaum, Robert. *The Poetry of Experience: The Dramatic Monologue in Modern Literary Tradition.* New York: Random House, 1957.

Melchiori, Barbara. *Browning's Poetry of Reticence.* New York: Barnes and Noble, 1968.

Miller, J. Hillis. *The Disappearance of God.* Cambridge: Harvard University Press, 1963. Paperback Ed.: New York: Schoeken, 1965. "Robert Browning," pp. 81-156.

Poston, Lawrence, III. *Loss and Gain: An Essay on Browning's Dramatis Personae.* Lincoln: University of Nebraska Press, 1974.

Raymond, R. O. *The Infinite Moment and Other Essays on Robert Browning.* Enlarged ed. Toronto: University of Toronto Press, 1965.

Ryals, Clyde de L. *Browning's Later Poetry, 1871-1889.* Ithaca, N.Y.: Cornell University Press, 1925.

Sullivan, Mary Rose. *Browning's Voices in "The Ring and the Book."* Toronto: University of Toronto Press, 1969.